THE VANISHING

ARJAY LEWIS

MIND
BENDER
PRESS

Cover Design: Marianne Nowicki; www.PremadeEbookCoverShop.com
Editing: Libby Broadbent

ISBN 13: 978-1734229134
ISBN 10: 1734229136

Published by:
Mindbender Press
474 South Main Street
Phillipsburg NJ 08865
www.mindbenderpress.com

Dedication:

To Libby Broadbent
Author, editor, and a lady
who knows her stuff

"Nature is forever arriving and forever departing, forever approaching, forever vanishing; but in her vanishings there seems to be ever the waving of a hand, in all her partings a promise of meetings farther along the road."

—Richard Le Gallienne

"The modern world is devoted to vanishing species, vanishing weather, and vanishing capacity for wonder."

—Douglas Coupland

PART I:
FURNACE RUN

ONE

A Sound In The Dark

D rake Harper drove his Ford Escape through the dark roads of the Pinelands. He still had three beers left in his six-pack, within easy reach on the dashboard.

He was beginning to calm down. As soon as he'd arrived home, Bonnie had started with her nagging. She always came home from her shift at the Shop-Rite in a bad mood. He wished she'd get pregnant, but they both knew that wasn't going to happen. They didn't have the money for the expensive in-vitro treatments.

He knew in her heart she blamed him. It wasn't his fault that he had a low sperm count, or that she had fibroids. It's just the way things were.

In the past, their arguments had morphed into brawls that damn near wrecked the little house they lived in off the highway.

One time he'd hit her.

The violence had shocked both of them, him more profoundly than her. That he could lose control like that scared him so much that he immediately left the small house and went for a drive, his father's words—*You don't never hit a girl*—running through his mind.

He'd be damned if he let it go that far these days. His work with his brother's construction company was good. He showed up most days, and he and Bonnie had even put away a little money. The last thing they needed was to break the furniture throwing things at each other.

He would never lift his hand to her again.

If Bonnie would just shut up, none of this would happen.

He turned onto a one-lane sandy backroad through the State Park. Even going slow, he'd save twenty minutes this way and be on Route 206 in no time. By now Bonnie would have calmed down and might even be feeling in the mood.

He shouldn't have driven so far, but this time he'd needed some beer. He'd had three of them looking over the cranberry bogs near the Ocean Spray factory. It was a first-quarter moon and the light reflecting on the placid waters of the bogs always calmed him.

Since he was only going fifteen miles an hour, he reached up and grabbed another beer from the ring, and with one hand, pulled the tab. The road here was nothing but sugar sand, so fine that it moved and slid as you drove over it. The last thing he needed was to hit an axle-breaking pothole or slide into a ditch.

The only light was the car's headlights. It was easy to stay on the one-lane path as the whiteness of the sand was framed by the dark undergrowth of woods on either side of the road.

He took a sip of beer, just as the car hit an unseen pothole and bounced. It wasn't a bad bounce, but the beer spilled out of the can and onto Drake.

Great! Now he would smell like a brewery, and that would start Bonnie going off again. He hoped that she'd become contrite since he stormed out and be more interested in sex than squabbling.

That was what they did after an argument, like fighting was foreplay. She'd nag, he'd storm out to get a couple of beers to calm down, and then she'd be crying and begging him not to leave her, and they'd do it.

Something hung diagonally across the road ahead, and Drake was roused from his thoughts of getting Bonnie naked.

He pressed on the brake carefully, not wanting to skid in the sand, and the car came gently to a stop.

A thick branch had fallen from one of the pitch pines. It wasn't all that big, and Drake figured he could push it aside by just driving into it, but he didn't want to scratch the car. It was almost twenty years old, yet the thing still ran like a champ.

He opened his door, beer in hand, and stepped out to look at the branch. It wasn't too big for him to lift.

He went to the back and sifted through his toolbox until he found his hatchet. This would take care of the problem, and he'd be on his way in no time.

He put his half-empty beer on the roof of the vehicle, moved into the beam of the headlights, and froze as a piercing scream rang through the woods.

He spun around in alarm, holding the small hatchet like a weapon. It sounded like a cow being slaughtered, only louder, and much closer than he would prefer.

His breathing was ragged in his ears as he scanned the darkness for movement.

There was none.

He proceeded slowly in the blinding light of his headlights and wished he'd turned down the high beams. He looked up at the tree and saw there were three scars down the front and the wood behind it was pale and white, as if these deep scratches were fresh.

He frowned. Someone had done this. These grooves had to be made with an axe, they were too deep to be made by an animal, even a bear. Besides, there weren't a lot of bears in the Pine Barrens. You had to watch out for encroaching coyotes, but they didn't slash trees.

That meant a human did it. But who and *why*? The branch had been cut recently as well. Were some teenagers hiding in the darkness, cutting down branches to screw with motorists?

He shook his head and began to chop at the pale wood. The branch was more attached than he'd assumed and he began to sweat from the effort.

There was another shriek, closer this time.

Drake stopped and listened.

He looked around again, not sure what that damn noise had been. The headlights kept him from seeing anything around his car. It would be damn stupid if the kids that cut down the branch got in his car and drove away after he'd cleared the path.

"Anyone there?" he yelled, the hatchet held high in his hand.

Silence.

The Pinelands were creepy in March. During the summer, there'd be insects, birds, bats, and all kinds of creatures buzzing about in a reassuring way, but tonight, the silence was eerie.

And after that bizarre scream…

He went back to work and after a few more hits with the hatchet, the branch fell away. He put the tool on the hood of the car, grabbed the branch, and began to pull.

It was heavy, and it took a moment for him to get traction in the sugar sand and slide the chunk of wood to the side of the road. It left a track where it dragged through the sand.

He stepped into the underbrush and his foot sank into something wet.

"Dammit all to Hell," he muttered. He had stepped right into one of the hundreds of boggy streams that coursed through the Barrens. He took a step back and carefully pulled his boot out. It was lucky that he was still in his work boots that laced up past his ankle. If he'd been in sneakers, it would have been pulled right off his foot. The soft sand made a perfect quicksand in these bogs, and there were numerous stories of hikers getting stuck.

And of people who just vanished.

He returned to the road, shaking his foot to kick off some of the mud. He'd have to leave his work boots outside when he got home, because if he tracked mud on the floor, Bonnie would go off on him again.

He cursed as he retrieved the axe, headed for the driver's door, and reached to the roof for his beer.

It wasn't there.

He peered around in the darkness. He looked to see if the can had fallen and wished he'd grabbed his flashlight.

He looked into the woods again to see if, just perhaps, a teenager had indeed cut down the branch, and then stolen his beer. He opened the car door and peered in as the light inside came on.

His two remaining cans sat on the dashboard.

He pulled one free, shut the door, popped the tab with a hiss, and took a swallow.

There was a sound above him like the wings of a large owl. He looked up, hoping the first-quarter moon would give him enough light to see whatever might be flying by.

Remembered tales of the famed Jersey Devil ran through his mind, unbidden. As a young man, like many others, he'd sat around a campfire on a dark night telling and retelling the legends of the cursed creature with a head like a horse and wings like a bat. And claws. The creature had claws that could rip a man apart, and a long tail that could knock you off your feet.

Drake chuckled.

That's what this was. Some teenagers had carved the tree and knocked over that branch to frighten some 'Piney' out of his wits and have him run off with tales about a near-encounter with the monster of legend.

He yelled out. "All right, you brats. You had your fun, good job, had me going. I'm getting out of here and going home."

He turned around and froze.

A massive seven-foot-tall silhouette stood near the front of the car.

Drake's mind whirled, his first thought was that it had to be a bear, up on its back legs and ready to attack, but there were horns on the shadowy head, like a buck's rack. He fumbled for the hatchet. He put the can on the roof of the car and held up the axe in front of himself with shaking hands.

A three-fingered claw came forward but did not reach for him. Instead, it moved to the beer as Drake trembled.

The clawed fingers wrapped around the can, lifting it to the oversized head. It was *massive*. Shaped like a horse or a large goat, the mouth opened and the thing poured the beer into its gaping maw. In the reflection of the headlights he saw a gleaming row of sharp teeth.

Drake was rooted to the spot, shaking uncontrollably as he stared up at the monster. He needed to take a piss *now*. He attempted to speak, but his voice quavered.

"Y-you like beer?" he asked as his heart beat double time in his chest. "I g-got another, in th-the car."

The creature had finished its drink and peered at the empty can, the red color of its eyes seeming to glow from within.

The creature threw the can into the woods.

Holding the hatchet in front of him, Drake moved to the door. If he could get out the last beer and distract this thing, he'd be able to get back into the car and get the hell out of there.

He gently pulled the door open. The car light reflected on the face of the creature as it growled and moved closer to Drake. Drake groped for the final can of beer, trying to keep the hatchet between him and the beast.

"Easy, easy," he soothed. The light from the car only gave Drake a better view of what stood before him. It had a long neck like a horse, and the two arms that bent backwards, moving like knees instead of elbows. The three-fingered hands resembled the talons of a huge bird. Shaggy brown fur covered the thing's body, and a large tail waved behind it in the darkness.

It growled again, drooling from the equine snout, as Drake fumbled for the can without taking his eyes off the monstrosity that stood before him.

He slowly extracted the plastic holder with one beer can hanging off it. He left the car door ajar. The monster's flaming eyes moved from Drake to the can.

This calmed Drake a bit. "You want this, d-don't you?"

The creature turned to him and growled again.

"It's okay...it's for you," he said as gently as he could. He pulled the can from the ring and popped the tab. It hissed as it opened, and the creature shied back from the noise.

Drake put the can on top of his car.

If I get out of this, I will have the greatest story ever.

Drake held the hatchet with both hands as he carefully took a step back from the monster, whose attention was now riveted on the can on top of the car.

It stepped forward and leaned against the driver's door, shutting it with a 'click' and blocking it with its massive frame. With its talon, the creature grabbed the can, gave a fiery glare at Drake, and brought the cylinder to its mouth.

As the driver's door was now blocked, Drake decided he only had one chance: the passenger door. He could get in there and shut himself safely in the car. When the creature's head leaned back to drink the foamy liquid, he ducked, dashed behind the tailgate, and rushed to the door on the far side of the car. He yanked it open and the light came on inside the car as he dove in.

A sharp pain tore through his left leg as he lunged into the vehicle, and Drake cried out. The monster, with shocking speed, had come around the car and grabbed his leg with one of those clawed hands.

The creature gave another screech, louder than the last one, which echoed through the woods. Drake kicked out with his right leg to get free and felt he may have actually struck the creature in the chest, but that didn't even slow it down as it yanked Drake bodily from the car.

Drake fell to the ground, sand and debris blowing into his eyes. The creature pulled him up into the air like a rag doll. His hands flopped uselessly, and the axe fell from his fingers.

Drake looked down to see his car below him, the headlights still on and the passenger door wide open. Above him, the huge bat wings flapped and hauled the pair of them into the dark sky.

The car grew smaller and Drake lost control of his bladder, the warm pee traveling up his chest as he screamed in terror.

TWO

Home

S he was so small, just five, but she wanted to help Grandma Natalia as she prepared things in the kitchen. Grandma's house appeared so big, but everything seemed large to her. The strange sticks that the old woman burned all day made it smell funny.

She walked up to her grandma, so much taller than she was, as she stirred a pot on the stove while humming an ancient tune.

There was a banging on the outer door of the house. It was a wooden door with nine small windows in the middle, only a foot or two from the stove.

"*Mami?*" Lil said, fear in her small voice. "What was that?"

Her grandmother faced her, looking kindly at her granddaughter. She spoke with her thick accent. "The bad things, I am afraid," she told her.

Again, something huge and powerful slammed against the outside door of the small kitchen.

"Make it stop," Lil whined, clutching her grandmother's leg.

"I cannot, my precious one. I have done what I can, but they are coming through and I cannot stop them."

With a crash, an arm smashed through one of the small windows, and sparkling glass fell to the floor. At the end of the arm was not a hand, but a three-finger claw that only a predator could possess. It waved in the empty air, and a long hairy arm was exposed. It reached downward, grasping for Lil, who screamed as the claw brushed her hair.

Lil jumped up in bed, her eyes open and her heart beating fast in her chest. It took her a moment to calm herself. She wasn't a child, she was a grown woman.

It was the same dream again. Her dear sweet Grandma Natalia, warning her in the dreams, and *something* trying to get into the house, get at *her*. Lil never saw what made the noise, she always awoke once the claw came through the glass. But she knew it was huge, hairy, and terrifying.

She shook her head and got out of bed. Since it was a mattress on the floor, it was a struggle to get to her feet. She wore her long flannel nightgown to keep away the chill of early March.

With a glance around the simple room, she pulled on slippers and a robe and turned the thermostat up.

She straightened the pair of wooden chairs with padded cushions in the corner, then bent to pull the bed sheets and blanket up to neaten them, a habit she'd practiced since early childhood.

Walking on the white tile floor, she made her way down the one step and turned to enter the kitchen of the cottage. She measured water with a coffee mug and put two cups in the bottom of the old percolator. Filling the metal basket in the top, the familiar sadness crept over her. Tears began to fall before she had assembled the coffee pot and plugged it in.

It wasn't real, just a dream...

She was surprised to feel the wetness on her face and reached up to touch her cheek as a tear rolled down. Pulling a paper towel from the holder on the wall, she dabbed at her eyes and wished she could have one morning where she had coffee *before* she started to cry.

Moving to the tiny bathroom, Lil found the container of the antidepressant, *Paxil,* and downed a pill with a glass of water from the sink. Bad enough she had scary dreams, the predictable tears were an additional annoyance. Lately, she would just start crying without even thinking of Chad.

Underneath everything else was grief. That didn't go away.

That *never* went away.

She didn't like the tears, but it beat the panic attacks she'd experienced in New York. The quieter lifestyle in New Jersey had helped alleviate those.

Why was her grandmother visiting her in her sleep? Wasn't her life tortured enough at this point? She considered that perhaps she should stop taking her evening dosage of *Paxil.* Her therapist had warned her that a possible side effect could be nightmares.

She returned to the kitchen as the coffeemaker chugged and hissed. She stared out the kitchen window toward her parent's house a scant hundred yards from her tiny cottage.

Home.

She had been an up-and-coming detective with the NYPD, engaged to someone who was a good cop and a good man.

And now, she was living at home with her parents—a failure. At least the old farm had this separate cottage for a hired workman. If she'd had to move back into her old room, it would have overwhelmed her.

If it weren't for her parents, she'd have had nowhere to go.

"Gypsy families stick together," her father always told her, though using that term was considered derogatory. When she'd announced to her parents that Chad had proposed, her father was upset because he wasn't Romani, but of Anglo-Saxon descent. Over time, Chad had won her parents over with his quick wit and great love for her.

She remembered living in New York, their shared apartment. She'd wake up and marvel at his pale skin and fine features and wonder why such a light-skinned man fell in love with a brown woman like her. He explained that it was part of the reason he loved her.

"You're dark and mysterious," he joked, pulling her into his arms and caressing her. "You used your gypsy voodoo on me, I couldn't resist it."

She kissed him and told him, "Romani don't do voodoo."

As he began to undress her, he said, "Your magic is far more powerful."

She sighed at the memory. He had made love to her then, before the pair of them dressed and strapped on their weapon harnesses.

It was simple then. It all made sense.

What didn't make sense was what she was living through now.

It had been a simple bust. She and her partner and Chad with his, went to arrest a drug dealer named Paulo for the murder of one of his competitors. The New York drug trade was a rough business and Paulo had worked his way up the chain. They finally had evidence that proved he was involved in the midnight shooting of Guardio, his main competition.

But the bust went wrong. Chad and his partner were dead, and she had discharged her firearm in a "reckless and dangerous manner," according to Internal Affairs. What she had done was kill the bastards that shot the love of her life, and then she got herself and her partner out of there, alive.

Julius, her African-American partner, was a decorated detective, twenty years on the job, and had been trapped behind a trash dumpster by the gunfire. But IA had been correct, she had been the reckless one. Seeing Chad fall, bleeding, had done something to her. Ultimately they were right, she had not followed protocol, she had endangered herself and anyone else in that housing unit not involved with Paulo's gang.

She had gone before the IA board and was stripped of her shield and her weapon, and put on desk duty, but the recurring dreams made it impossible to sleep, and she soon left the job under a psychiatrist's care for PTSD, and gave up the beloved Manhattan apartment.

With most of her things in storage, she moved back to her parent's house. They were kind enough to offer the cottage for her to live in, but always asked her to come for dinner. She often joined them out of duty, but not every night.

Seeing her mother and father's happiness with each other only made her feel her loss more profoundly. To add to her stress, the dreams of Chad dying had been replaced with images of her Grandma Natalia. Each one twisted into a frightening vision that ended with an attack by an unknown inhuman assailant.

She had traded one set of nightmares for another.

She poured coffee into her mug and added some cream. With the warm cup in hand, she went to her bedroom to sit in one of the wooden chairs and look out the back window at the fenced area well behind her parent's house.

Her father was outside, feeding the alpacas their morning hay, and getting them out of their stable. The animals were tall with long necks and a quiet demeanor when they weren't annoyed and spitting. They were covered in thick fur, as they had come through the long winter, and their valuable coat would not be shorn until late spring.

She watched her father, his sturdy body moving with ease, his brown face filled with kindness as he spoke to the animals, which he did every morning.

Vano Slavik was almost sixty, yet he worked as tirelessly as he always had. The alpacas were added to the farm a few short years ago. When she was growing up they only cultivated blueberries, which did well in the sandy soil on their twenty-acre farm in the middle of the Pine Barrens of New Jersey.

She sat back in the wooden chair and wanted to cry again, but the *Paxil* had taken effect and it always stopped the more powerful emotions from peeking out. It was a blessing and a curse. She wanted to grieve and get over it, but the losses were just too overwhelming.

In annoyance, she yanked off her nightgown, and pulled on a bra and panties. She added a flannel shirt, denim pants, and work boots as well as the heavy denim coat with the faux-fur collar. She grabbed her phone and keys and went outside.

The cool spring air struck her lungs and chilled her but helped her to wake up more than the coffee. She headed to where her father stood with the animals, calling out, "*Sastipe!*"

This was a casual Romani greeting she had learned as a child when large family get-togethers would take place. As grandparents passed away and younger people became more Americanized, such large gatherings had ceased. The *Roma* either joined established communities or were isolated, like her family.

"*Lachi tiri divés*," her father yelled to her, which meant "Good morning to you." He always used a formal greeting, as if she were royalty and he was nothing but a serf. He walked away from the camel-like creatures and joined her at the fence.

"How can I help, Poppa?" she asked.

He frowned, which made his broad face wrinkle and his big mustache move up. "I'm fine, Liliana. You should rest."

She shook her head. "I'm tired of resting, Poppa. Give me something to do."

He nodded, as if he understood. He was a man who needed to work, to do things. "If you could gather the eggs for your momma, and then we could go check the blueberries in the afternoon. It's time to lay down the fertilizer."

She nodded, familiar with both tasks having performed them many times in her childhood. She could remember going with her father to lay down the smelly homemade fertilizer. It was a combination of fish meal to provide nitrogen, coffee grounds that added acidity, bone meal and powdered seaweed for the potassium and phosphorus. Her father would blend this pungent mix in a large metal trash can. They would drive between the rows and rows of bushes in the battered used golf cart her father had bought from a country club.

Using a scoop, she would place the fertilizer around each bush as her father instructed her. "That's right, Liliana, around the drip line of the plant. Not too close, you want to make the ground around it full of nutrients, but too much on the plant, not good."

"I'll get the eggs," she said, heading to the coop. This was what she needed, to do work, use her body and not think.

The coop was a small building that smelled of hay and chicken droppings. Lil grabbed the basket which hung on a nail just inside the door and put on a large pair of rubber gloves.

She spoke gentle words to the hens on their nests, keeping them calm as she collected their eggs. Lil knew to move slowly and easily. Getting pecked by an aggressive hen was not something she enjoyed.

With the eggs collected, she headed toward her parent's farmhouse as her mobile phone rang. She pulled off one glove and answered it.

"Hello?"

"Lil?" The voice was familiar, but she couldn't place it.

"Yeah, who's this?"

A chuckle came over the phone. "Leave it to you to have the same cell phone number after ten years. It's Dennis."

She stopped walking, trying to get her head around the voice in her ear. Dennis Decatur had been her high school boyfriend, what her mother referred to at the time as her "Sweetheart."

"Oh…hi," was all Lil could say.

He chuckled again. "You don't sound happy to hear from me."

She cleared her throat. "It's…been a long time."

"I know," Dennis replied.

She stood there in the open field, fifty feet from her parent's house and her world seemed to shift. "Now is not a good time, Dennis."

He sighed. "I heard you were back."

"Do you know why?" she spat, not happy that she sounded so angry.

"Yeah, I do," he stated flatly. "I thought you'd like to meet for lunch, maybe talk a bit."

She hadn't spoken to Dennis since high school, a lifetime ago.

"I have to help at the farm…"

"It won't take long, we can meet at the Dine Rite," he offered. "Come on, you've got to eat."

She thought of the therapist in New York who told her that she needed to reconnect with people, reconnect with her life. The Dine Rite was only about ten miles away.

"I guess," she replied finally.

"Come by in an hour," he said. "I'll see you then."

He ended the call before she could argue. With a sigh, she walked into the house and moved to the sink to wash the eggs.

As she heated the water, her mother came into the kitchen. "Good morning, C*haj*. You didn't have to do that, I was just about to—"

"It's all right, *Daj*," Lil interrupted. "I can pull my weight around here, just like anyone else."

She placed the eggs in the sink and plugged the drain so that the tub began to fill.

She could feel her mother's stare. Selina Slavik had a stare that could burn through steel. Lil finally looked back at the older woman. "What?"

"I worry about you, and you yell at me," her mother complained.

Lil held her tongue, as another wave of anger washed over her. Like all other strong emotions, the *Paxil* made it fade in mere moments.

"I'm sorry, D*aj*," she said respectfully. "Poppa asked me to help fertilize the plants."

"Ah," Selina said. "That would be nice. But now is too early in the day. You should do that in the afternoon."

Lil gently scrubbed each of the eggs with a soft brush that served only that function. She put the eggs into a wire basket over the sink to cool and dry. "I thought I would go to the diner for… um…breakfast."

"I can make you breakfast," Selina offered. "With our own eggs, nice and fresh."

Lil hung her head. "Dennis invited me."

There was silence as Lil continued to clean the eggs and move them to the basket.

"You are going to meet that *Gorger,*" her mother chided, using the Romani term for a non-gypsy. In this case, Selina made it sound as if Dennis was lower than a worm.

"Yes, I am," Lil answered defiantly.

"That bastard?" her mother exclaimed, then spat on the floor. "He is no better than a dog."

"I'm going to see him, Momma," Lil insisted as she drained the sink.

"He'll only break your heart," her mother whined. "Haven't you had enough pain?"

"It's *brunch*, Momma," Lil said. "Not a date. My therapist said to talk to old friends."

"He is not your friend, he was a man who used you!"

"I have to get ready," Lil said, as she grabbed the basket with the gloves and headed for the door. "Tell Poppa I'll help this afternoon."

She went outside before Selina could argue with her. She knew her mother meant well, but unlike her father she couldn't accept that Lil was a grown woman who could make her own decisions.

Then again, those decisions lately had been disastrous.

As she made her way back to the chicken coop to return the basket and the gloves, she wondered what it would be like to see her former boyfriend after ten years.

THREE

Missing Persons

L il drove toward the center of town, but the scenery did not get better. Single houses, deposited near the highway in various states of disrepair, many in need of paint. Several were working farms like her parents', but no greenery showed in early March. Here in the middle of the Pine Barrens, the opportunities were limited.

When casinos opened in Atlantic City, everyone thought the entire area would boom, but it only helped the towns that resided near the shoreline. Out in the middle of the Barrens, towns had been abandoned and disappeared over the years, and only a few businesses remained, mostly the blueberry and cranberry farmers. The sandy soil had been given the name "Barrens" because, with the exception of those two crops, little could flourish.

Lil had been desperate to leave, to get someplace where she could grow beyond the stilted trees and scrub brush.

But here she was, back where she had started…

Her hair was still wet and hanging loose from her quick shower. Her natural curl meant she merely had to wash it and it would puff up by itself. Sometimes it turned into a kinky mess, but either way, Chad had loved it.

Chad had loved every inch of her.

She was driving the little car her parents had presented to her when she returned. It was a white car, but the hood was brown, probably from an accident that ruined the front end. The important thing was that it ran well, and since she hadn't paid for it, she was grateful to have it at all.

The Dine Rite was a throwback to another age when Jersey diners resembled train cars. It was stainless-steel and shiny, with vintage swivel stools, booths and menus that hadn't changed in years. At night, it would be resplendent with colorful neon tubes that made the eatery visible as far away as the Atlantic City Expressway.

Lil pulled into the diner right on time. Inside, the curved metal ceiling and tiny tiles on the floor were spotless. She looked around for her tall former boyfriend. A waitress with gray hair in a bun and too much makeup told her, "Sit anywhere, hon."

She found an empty booth and grabbed the menu and thought about Dennis.

They had both been so young when they started dating as freshmen in high school. Dennis had been her first lover, and they had waited years to become intimate. She could recall the night they'd first made love, parked in the big station wagon Dennis had bought working the harvest the previous fall.

It had been a spring night in May, and they had parked on a sugar sand road in the middle of the vast Pine Barrens, near an old stone building abandoned long ago. For a pair of Pineys, it was the perfect place to affirm their love.

There had been some pain for her, and she was not thrilled by the encounter, but after several weeks of repeated attempts, she began to enjoy the experience, and even revel in it.

Toward the end of their senior year, they both chose to pursue a criminal justice degree. She had been accepted by the prestigious Rider University, near Trenton. But Dennis had only managed to get into Stockton Community College. Still, they were both in New Jersey, and there were the weekends to continue the relationship, with a plan to get married down the line.

One afternoon, he came to her sheepishly and explained that he'd been unfaithful. At first Lil didn't believe it, she was so shocked. But he confessed that one night during harvest, when everyone on her parent's farm worked late into the evening, Dennis had visited Carrie Randolph, one of Lil's friends. They both had been drinking and one thing led to another—or so he told her.

The betrayal had so shocked Lil that she vowed to never speak to him again. She had also vowed to leave this place and never return.

Looking back now, and with the emotional suppression of the *Paxil*, Lil had to admit that the breakup had pushed her into her studies with a vengeance. She burned through the two-year program and went right to the police academy in New York. She didn't allow another man to get near her. Her mother had been right and *Gorger* men were all pigs, not worthy of her time.

Until Chad.

Good, sweet Chad, who was a kick-ass cop and yet so loving. When they met, he looked at her as if she was the embodiment of every fantasy he'd ever dreamed.

And it turned out that she was. And he had been her fantasies come to life, as well. He won her over slowly, sometimes frustratingly so. Finally, she had to take charge and press the physical side of the relationship, only to discover that their chemistry was remarkable.

She sighed at this much more pleasant memory as a police car pulled up outside and a uniformed officer stepped out.

Lil gazed casually out the window waiting for Dennis, thinking nothing of the police car. After all, the Dine Rite was the best place in town to get a good cup of coffee.

As the tall officer turned to pull his baton, take off his hat, and place both on the driver's seat, she immediately recognized him. His strong chin with that exquisite dimple in the middle of it. His short brown hair and his clear blue eyes. He locked the car and strode into the diner, a man obviously comfortable in his own skin.

His upper body was more developed than she recalled, and he was lean and strong. He obviously was not the clichéd donut-chewing cop with a gut. No, he had filled out nicely and looked to be in great physical condition.

As he entered the diner, he glanced about the room, all cop. She knew the look, as it was something both she and Chad always did when they entered a location while on duty. Looking to see if something didn't fit, for anything out of place. When he saw Lil, his face relaxed and a big smile appeared.

He walked over to the table and Lil stood, not nearly as tall as his six-foot-two frame. He gave her an unexpected hug, and Lil was a bit surprised. But it was nice to feel a man's body against her own after the months of solitude.

He pulled back. "Thanks for coming to meet me, Lil."

She sat down, a bit flustered. "I…needed to get out of the house."

He still had that big grin on his face, and he adjusted the belt with his gun to allow him to sit.

The gray-haired waitress came right over with her coffee pot, like a choreographed dance. "Hey Dennis," she all but sang as she poured coffee for him. "The usual?" she asked as she filled Lil's cup.

Dennis nodded. "Yep, Sally. Egg white omelette with broccoli and low-fat cheese. Hash browns, no toast."

Sally turned to Lil, "And what'll you have?"

Lil had not even looked at the menu, and paused for a moment before she said, "I'll have the same."

Sally sauntered off, and Dennis grabbed some creamers off of a nearby plate.

"How're your folks?" Dennis asked casually, as he opened the little plastic container and added its contents to his coffee.

"Fine, fine. Still working the farm. I'm going to help my father fertilize the bushes after we eat."

Dennis nodded. "Oh yeah. I still help my parents at their blueberry farm on the weekends. Of course, they have full time people and it's a lot bigger than your place."

"Poppa got alpacas," Lil said.

Dennis lifted an eyebrow. "Really? Well, their wool is a hot item these days."

"So, you're a cop," Lil said, looking at her coffee cup and stirring the contents.

"Is that so much of a surprise?" Dennis smiled. "It's what we talked about, what we planned."

"Well, one of us didn't stick to the plan," Lil said, her eyes on her coffee.

"Lil," Dennis sighed.

Lil's head shot up. "So, seeing anyone? Carrie maybe?"

"Carrie was a long time ago, Lil."

"So your taste has improved." Lil kept her eyes on the cup. "At the time, I wanted to cut your head off."

This got a small smile. "Which one?"

"Both of them."

This made Dennis chuckle. "As it turns out, Carrie moved up north. Millburn, I think."

"It's good to know I won't run into her," Lil affirmed.

"So, you made detective."

Lil looked back at her coffee cup. "Yeah, homicide."

"And in New York City, no less."

"I stuck to the plan, Dennis," she told him. "But, I'd rather not talk about that right now."

"Sorry," Dennis grunted.

The silence hung heavily over the pair of them as they sipped their coffee.

Finally Lil asked,   "Any interesting local cases?"

He shook his head. "Nothing that would excite a homicide cop."

"Try me," Lil pushed.

Dennis sighed. "The most interesting case is a missing person."

Lil looked disappointed. "You're right, that isn't much."

"I know, but it's *how* he went missing." Dennis sat back in the booth.

"What do you mean?"

"We found his SUV left in the middle of one of those tiny roads in the Barrens. Guy named Drake Harper. The battery was dead, the passenger door was open, and it had been abandoned, just left there."

"Odd place to leave your car. Maybe the car died and he went to get help. I mean if it was in the Barrens, his cell phone wouldn't work."

Dennis nodded. "I love the way your mind works. Pure detective."

Lil flushed at the compliment.

"That's what we thought, but Jamarr Bowman—he's a car guy—said he thought the vehicle was still running when it was left."

Lil considered what he'd said. "Wait. Jamarr? From high school? The basketball player?"

Dennis smiled, pleased that she recalled. "That's right. He got a scholarship, did pretty well for his college team. He tried to go pro, but couldn't cut it. He's on the force, now."

"Jamarr is a cop?" Lil hooted. "Wasn't he the one who was always breaking the rules? Smoking cigarettes, as well as other things?"

Dennis nodded. "Believe it or not, he's a real straight shooter now. One of the best on the force."

Lil shook her head, but her mind went back to the abandoned vehicle. "So what's the theory about the car?"

"We're floating the idea that he stopped to take a whizz and stepped into some quicksand. The area we found the car was surrounded by bogs. You know how treacherous it can be out there."

Lil considered this and sipped her coffee. "That wouldn't explain why the passenger door was open."

"We found the ring from a six pack near the car and a couple of empty cans in the woods. So, if he was drunk, he could have stumbled and fallen into a bog."

"Did the police who searched the scene find any quicksand?"

Dennis smiled. "No, and I was one of them. Got my boots muddy as hell. But it was during the day, and we didn't go very far into the woods."

Lil considered this as Sally came around and put two large oval plates of piping hot, beautifully folded egg creations surrounded with browned potatoes.

Before Lil could speak Dennis turned to the waitress, "Could we get mustard, please?"

"Mustard?" Sally asked. "Since when do you eat your omelette with mustard?"

"I don't," Dennis answered and pointed his index finger at Lil. "But she does."

Sally shrugged and went to fetch the condiment from the kitchen.

Dennis smiled. "I mean, you used to."

"Still do," Lil said and looked at her food. It was nice that Dennis remembered.

Yeah, then he went out and banged a friend of mine.

The sudden flash of anger made her flush, but it passed as quickly as it had come.

"So, let me get this straight," Lil said as Sally placed the plastic squeeze bottle of brown mustard in front of her. "Some drunken guy goes to take a whizz. Walks into a bog and gets swallowed up? That's your theory?"

"Jamarr has one that's a little more up your alley."

Lil squeezed mustard on her omelette. "Do tell?"

"He reminded me that we were always getting complaints from the neighbors about Drake and his old lady arguing loudly, and there was a domestic abuse charge that the wife dropped."

"What does Jamarr think?" Lil said and cut into the omelette.

Dennis shrugged as he began to eat as well. "He thinks they got into a fight, old lady took him out, and then drove out to leave the body in one of the deep pools of water. Hell, she could've buried him. Then she abandoned the car a ways from where the body was left. By next spring, all that's left of ol' Drake is a skeleton."

Lil took a bite of the home fries. They were cooked perfectly and had a little onion mixed in. "You can see all the holes in that premise, right?"

"Sure. She would have to have an accomplice to move the body and give her a ride home. Plus, we questioned the neighbors and they admitted the Harper's had a fight, but that Drake drove off by himself."

"So much for the homicide theory," Lil sighed as she took another bite.

Dennis took the nearby squeeze bottle of ketchup and sprayed his home fries with it. "Plus, I interviewed the wife, Bonnie Harper. She was really broken up about it, and she'd have to be a hell of an actress to pull off her reaction."

Lil shook her head. "They fought like that, and then she breaks down when she thinks he's gone? I don't get some women."

"Every relationship has ups and downs."

"Well, you're the expert on that," Lil muttered.

Dennis stopped eating and stared at her. "It seems you're still mad about me and Carrie."

"Yeah, I guess I still am," she snapped and leaned back in the chair to push the plate away, her appetite gone. She took a deep breath and released it slowly. "That was uncalled for, Dennis. I'm dealing with a lot right now, and my first instinct is to lash out at everyone. Sorry."

"You've got a right to still be mad. You and I had plans, and I got stupid and ruined them."

Lil nodded and sipped her coffee, desperately wanting to change the subject. "What will you do about this Harper guy?"

"Do? Not much we *can* do. Chalk it up to another person vanishing in the Barrens."

Lil's head came up. "Wait, *another*? You have more than one?"

Dennis exhaled. "Lil, you lived here through high school. You know that people get lost in the Barrens all the time: hikers, explorers, hunters. And look, my job is to protect Furnace Run. The Barrens are thousands of acres and there are dozens of towns in the area."

"But Furnace Run is in the center of the Barrens," Lil said. "We're surrounded by the forest on all sides. Hammonton, May's Landing, they're all on the outskirts—"

"Even so, do you know how many people go missing in the Barrens every year? I got enough to do without tracking down everybody who is stupid enough to get lost out there."

Lil nodded. "I guess." She looked down, annoyed that she needed to ask her next question. "So, any openings in the department? I…uh…kind of need a job."

Dennis sighed and focused on his food. "Lil…"

"Just be honest with me, Dennis," Lil asserted, her back straightening.

"The department is small, the tax base isn't growing," Dennis confessed. "We thought the new Assisted Living housing would be a real boon, but we've had to just get by with what we have."

"I saw the new sewage treatment plant. That's a lot bigger."

Dennis nodded. "Yeah, and it was a real budget buster as well. Also, I gotta tell you the truth, Lil—"

Her arms were braced on the table as if to fend off a blow. "Please do."

He took another mouthful, unable to meet her eyes. "The story about you hit all the newspapers, all about the takedown and the subsequent investigation."

Her mouth was a tight line. "The papers were pretty one-sided. The side against me, anyway."

"Look, there isn't a cop who would condemn you," Dennis consoled her. "But no one wants that kind of publicity and New York is not that far away."

Lil glowered at her old boyfriend. "So you're saying if I want to be a cop, I should move to the Midwest?"

Dennis considered this. "If I was in your shoes, it's what I would do." He reached out and touched her hand. "But, I'm glad you're here."

Lil slid her hand away. "Thanks, Dennis. I have to go."

She rose, grabbed her purse, and went for her wallet.

"I got this," Dennis said, also standing. "Look, if you need someone to talk to, give me a call, okay?"

"So you can tell me that I can't be a cop?" she snapped.

"I'm just being honest with you, Lil."

She wanted to yell at him, tell him what a pig he was to have broken her heart all those years ago, tell him to save his sympathetic bullshit for the next broad he wanted to screw.

"Yeah, I know," she muttered and moved quickly to the door.

She glanced at him through the window as he sat down to his food. Lil got into her two-toned vehicle and drove away.

FOUR

Nowhere To Be Found

The afternoon passed quickly.

Lil rode with her father, wearing elbow-length rubber gloves and using the oversized hand scoop to carefully put the fertilizer around each plant. Her father knew the older from the newer plants and explained how much every bush needed.

They were more than just plants to him. Every one was his baby, and he knew each one's habits as he would a beloved child.

For Lil, it was tough work. In the months since the "incident" as she tried to think of it, she hadn't hit the gym. It felt good to stretch and lift and do the physically demanding work.

As the sun began to set, her father said, "We've done enough for one day."

Lil was sweaty and dirty, and longed for a shower. She also could no longer feel the influence of the *Paxil*. She had been too busy to think about her grief. She wondered if avoiding the evening dose would prevent the recurring vivid nightmares.

He pulled the electric vehicle into the barn and inserted the plug from the charging station, as Lil removed the metal trash can and put the lid back in place to protect the fertilizer.

"We did good." He praised her. "Much less to do tomorrow. Tell you what, you get cleaned up and come for dinner."

"I'd rather be alone tonight, Poppa," Lil stated. It had been a good afternoon, but she had interacted with more people today than she had in months.

"Are you sure? She is making *Sarmi*."

Lil paused. His father was referring to a traditional Romani dish of cabbage stuffed with meat, rice and spices. Her mother's version of this recipe was a mouthwatering treat that Lil could never get the hang of making.

Not that she was much of a cook anyway.

"No, I just want to be alone," she explained.

Her father looked worried, knowing how much Lil enjoyed her mother's specialty. As a child, she requested it almost every night.

He forced a smile. "Well, I'll bring you the leftovers tomorrow."

Lil nodded, and headed for her cottage where she stripped off her clothes and took a shower, the water as hot as she could bear. She stepped out of the tub, her dusky skin reddened by the heat, and looked in the full-length mirror on the door as she dried herself. She'd lost weight and a bit of muscle mass, though today she'd pushed those muscles. Her breasts had gotten a bit smaller, which she knew from the fact she had to tighten the straps on her bra.

"Why do you always look at yourself after a shower?" Chad's voice said in memory.

"I have to be aware of any changes in my body," Lil explained. "It's important to notice any lumps in my breasts."

Chad had walked into the bathroom, moved behind her, and brought both hands to her chest, "Let me check."

He caressed the roundness of her bosom and Lil chuckled. "I think this is more for your benefit than mine."

"Oh yeah," he said as he kissed her shoulder.

Lil was alone in her small bathroom as her hand moved to her breast. She shook her head to clear it, finished drying, and threw on clean clothes as she tried to dismiss the memory. She grabbed a frozen dinner from her small refrigerator and placed it in the oven to heat.

The large table stood in the room that served as both dining room and living room and currently held her laptop. As she sat, she thought that it was fortunate her parents had equipped the cottage with high-speed wifi. Lil had lost interest in going on social media or looking at her email in recent months. She had pulled her Facebook page soon after the "incident", as the media onslaught which plastered her name and the words "Killer Cop" in the same sentence had attracted death threats and worse.

However, her discussion with Dennis at the Dine Rite had piqued her curiosity. She felt an odd urge to do a search for missing persons in New Jersey. She wasn't sure why, but it felt important.

She ran the national numbers from a news site that listed people missing by the hundreds of thousands each year. As she stumbled through different search criteria, a New Jersey missing persons list appeared, which broke it down by county.

She checked out the neighboring counties of Ocean and Atlantic, where the numbers were a few dozen.

When she pulled up Burlington County, where Furnace Run was located, the numbers became staggering. Over three hundred people had gone missing in the previous twelve months. This was far above the numbers of all the other counties combined.

Lil frowned at this. Was there some kind of cover-up involved? Three hundred people should be the amount for the entire state, not the sum of a single county. Why weren't people up in arms about it?

She went over the individual records and studied the information. Again and again there were the phrases, "In the New Jersey State Park" and "Traveling through the Pinelands" as well as mentions of 'hiking' and 'nature trails'.

She sat back in her chair. There were numerous people vanishing from the Pinelands forests around Furnace Run. Dennis had seemed so blasé about it, as if it was not a big deal at all.

But Lil felt this *was* a big deal, a very big deal, and she couldn't fight the feeling that it was important to look into.

The timer went off and she quickly rose to pull the tray out of the oven. She placed the melted blob that was supposed to be Eggplant Parmesan on the table near her computer and pulled the bottle of wine from the refrigerator.

She knew damn well that drinking wine while taking *Paxil* was a dumb idea, and the doctor had warned her that the combination could cause everything from sleeplessness to suicidal thoughts. But her last *Paxil* had been in the morning and she needed a drink right then and there. What she really craved was to sleep free of the nightmares.

She filled a jelly jar with the white wine and read more about missing persons, as she attempted to eat the soggy mess on the cardboard tray.

She'd passed on her mother's cabbage rolls for *this*?

She sipped the wine and continued to search numbers for other states and localities that reflected the upsurge in Burlington County.

The FBI figures were just as disheartening. She brought up page after page of statistics. She learned that since 1997, the number of missing person cases had gone down which again made the spike in Burlington County even more unusual.

She took a break and retrieved her phone from her dresser.

The last call she'd received had been from Dennis, so she pulled the number up and hit the button to dial it.

"Hello?" Dennis answered. "Is that you, Lil?"

"Yes."

"I didn't expect to hear from you so soon. In fact, after this morning, not at all."

"Calm down, this is business," she chided.

This got a chuckle from Dennis. "Forgive me, but I'm out of uniform at this point."

"Good, because this is off the record," Lil insisted as she sat down in front of the laptop again. "Were you going to tell me about the spike in missing person cases?"

"With all due respect, Lil, why would I?"

"Because I'm a cop and it's happening near my town."

She heard Dennis exhale loudly in exasperation. "Okay, off the record. As in, you don't mention it to anyone…ever."

"Dennis, it's me!"

"I mean it, Lil."

"All right, I pinky-swear and spit shake. Will that do?"

She heard him repeat the loud exhalation.

"I know you're there, Dennis, I can hear you sighing."

"Okay, but the cases have mostly been given to the State Police and the FBI."

"FBI?"

"Those numbers were mostly out-of-towners, people visiting the state and national forests. In fact there were only a few from Furnace Run—"

"So that makes it okay, to hide these numbers?"

"It wasn't hidden," Dennis interrupted, annoyed. "I mean, you obviously found them. We just let the cases be the state or the federal government's problem as opposed to ours. I told you Lil, we have a small force, and we can't go tracking people on state or federal land."

"How long has this been going on?"

"Mostly this last year. We get notices from the state, and we've increased patrols on the outskirts of the parks trying to keep people from going into them at night. But with all those sugar sand roads crisscrossing through the Barrens, we can't possibly cover them all."

"Any idea of the cause? Is it a gang in there stopping cars and abducting people?"

"Lil, for all I know it's the Jersey Devil."

Lil shook her head. "Come on, I'm serious."

"Lil, you and I are Pineys, you know the stories."

Of course Lil knew the stories. Anyone who grew up in South Jersey knew the tale.

According to legend, Mother Leeds of Leeds Point had twelve children with her husband, who was the town drunk. She found out she was pregnant with her thirteenth, and shouted, "I hope it's a devil." She got her wish. The child was born with horns, a tail, and a horse-like head. She sheltered him in the house so the curious couldn't see him.

On a stormy night, the child flapped its arms, which turned into wings, and escaped out the chimney and was never seen by the family again. This began a reign of terror with the monster consuming local livestock and terrorizing citizens over the next two hundred and fifty years. The creature was assumed to live in the Barrens, getting sighted every few decades or so, sometimes tracked, but always disappearing back into the vast forests.

The legend was a running joke in the Pinelands, and parents would scare their children into coming home at nightfall with the admonition, "The Jersey Devil will get you if you're out after dark."

"Can I look into this?" Lil pressed.

"What? Look into this Harper guy?" Dennis replied, taken aback.

"And the other missing persons. Can I look over the files?"

"Shit, Lil," Dennis muttered. "All those cases are the State Police's problem. I can't let you come in here and look over police files—"

"Then tell me what you can. Give me a starting point, and I'll do the work."

"If you're looking for a job," Dennis suggested. "This isn't a good way to do it."

Lil exhaled heavily. "It's not about the job. It's…something to do. I'm a detective, I like mysteries—"

"Have you considered reading a book?" Dennis complained. "There are a lot of good murder mysteries out there."

"Come on, just get me some info," Lil begged. "Where Harper's car was found, and any other locals who disappeared. Just give me what you can."

"All right," Dennis acquiesced. "I'll get you something…what I can…tomorrow. Are you staying with your parents in your old room?"

"No, I'm in the foreman's cottage," Lil corrected. "You don't even have to talk to my parents."

"Good thing," Dennis confirmed. "Your mother never liked me."

"Well, she hates your guts at this point," Lil chuckled. "I wouldn't be around her unless you want to be the next person who goes missing."

This got a laugh from Dennis. "I guess. See you tomorrow, Lil."

She ended the call and went to the refrigerator to refill her glass. With the white wine, she returned to her laptop and stared at it.

"Lil, for all I know it's the Jersey Devil."

She had an odd feeling, a sense of impending doom. She felt that if she turned over this rock, she would be forced to look at the black, slick bugs, strange worms, and ugly multi-legged myriapods that would be uncovered, and that thought made her shiver.

But she also thought of the odd dream where *something* was just outside the door of her grandmother's house.

Something big, terrifying, and…from another time.

She set her jaw, and with a hand that shook only once, she opened her browser, and began a search for "Jersey Devil."

The screen filled with multiple articles, everything from Wikipedia to Weird NJ, a famed magazine about supernatural happenings in the state.

She went through the articles and was surprised to read mythology of which she was unaware.

It turned out there were multiple legends, Mother Leeds merely being the most famous. One of the oft-repeated tales spoke of a young woman who encountered a passing gypsy begging for food. When the girl refused, the gypsy cursed her.

Years later, when she gave birth to her first child, he became a devil and fled into the woods.

"Great," Lil muttered to herself. "They always blame my people for this stuff."

As she continued to read, she saw famed tales of sightings of the creature by legitimate sources that included naval captains and even Napoleon Bonaparte's brother.

But there were also fanciful tales, such as Captain Kidd beheading a crewman so his spirit would guard a treasure. According to some, the ghost of the dead sailor and the Jersey Devil took moonlight strolls along the beaches of the Jersey shore.

A former governor, Walter Edge, had even made the Jersey Devil the official state demon in 1939.

However, there were also records from the year 1909, when the famed creature went on a ten-day rampage throughout south Jersey and as far as Philadelphia. During that time, literally thousands of people saw the beast. Some described it as a huge demonic creature, some recounted that it was only three feet tall, and its rampage seemed more like a lost creature in search of food than an attack by hellish hordes out for destruction.

Finally she stumbled across a site that reported the "real" story from a skeptical point of view. This brought up facts about Daniel Leeds, who was a pamphleteer in the time before the Revolutionary War. Leeds was a Quaker but had broken away from his church to publish views that were unpopular with the elders.

His son, Titan, took over the 'Almanac' upon his death and added the Leeds family crest to the paper. This crest had a dragon-like creature with a fearsome face, clawed feet, and bat-like wings, known as a *Wyvern*. The description was suspiciously similar to that of the Jersey Devil.

Titan Leeds was loyal to the British crown, and died in 1738, though the seeds of the revolution were already planted. It seemed logical that he would be compared with the devil in future years. The Almanac's printed pages furnished enemies with an idea for the creature's appearance.

She finally shut down the browser, too tired to continue. Her wine glass was empty and it was almost midnight.

As she put on her nightgown and slid into bed, her mind wandered. As she drifted off to sleep, one last thought occurred to her:

These legends had to come from somewhere.

FIVE

The Trail

She was in the kitchen, the great big kitchen where everything was so high up and she was so small.

Grandma Natalia was burning the incense again, sage was what she called it. It smelled bad.

Lil approached the table carefully. She was too small to see the tabletop, but could see her grandma sitting in a chair, her sturdy legs underneath.

She climbed into a chair and knelt on the seat to see her grandma dealing out cards in a row. The cards were long and thin and had funny pictures on them.

The old woman looked up at Lil and spoke in a soft sing-song voice. "Precious one, how do you do?"

"Wha'cha doing, *Mami?*" she asked with her high, little girl voice.

"I am laying out the tarot cards," Natalia told her. "To see what the future holds."

"Can you tell me mine?" Lil asked.

"I can try, but there are too many possibilities with one so young as you."

"Please, *Mami?*"

Natalia looked up and gave a big smile. "I cannot resist giving you anything you ask for." She picked up all the cards and handed them to Lil. "Here, mix these up."

The cards were well used, and very big in her small hands but Lil did her best to shuffle them.

"That is fine, child, very fine." She quickly put out five cards, one in the center and four around it, forming a makeshift cross.

Natalia looked at them. "First are the gifts you have." She turned it over to reveal a woman all in red with a tall crown on her head and a staff with three crosses on it.

"Is that me? Am I a princess?" Lil asked hopefully.

"This is the Hierophant, and it means you have great magical powers."

"Like a princess," Lil said with excitement.

Natalia laughed. "Yes, like a princess. Now this second card is what is blocking you."

She turned the card over, and there was a man with horns on his head and black bat wings on his back.

"The devil," Natalia fretted.

Lil looked up at her grandmother but her face had become a skull, with empty eye sockets and her jaw hanging loose. As Lil screamed, the figure on the card jumped off it to the floor and began to grow, getting bigger and bigger—

Lil cried out as she sat up in bed, the sheets pulled close to her and balled so tightly in her fists that it made her hands hurt.

She panted for a moment, then raced into the bathroom and threw up in the toilet.

She rinsed out her mouth, drank several cups of water, and dressed in jeans and a long sleeve pullover. It was past eight thirty, so at least the bad dream had let her sleep through the night.

She couldn't understand why the nightmares were still happening. She purposely neglected to take her evening dose of *Paxil* to stop them, but that hadn't worked at all.

She made coffee as she tried to understand the dream. Her grandmother had read her cards many times when she was a child, in fact she'd taught Lil how to read the cards, their meaning and their interpretations.

But there was never a time when the devil jumped off the card.

I'm just thinking about the Jersey Devil too much.

The coffee didn't sit well in her empty stomach, and she felt she should pass on her *Paxil* today. Maybe if she didn't take it, the dreams would stop. But she couldn't help the upsetting feeling that the dream was trying to tell her something, trying to warn her.

But, enough was enough and she needed to focus on the real world. She would help her mother by collecting the eggs this morning and finish the fertilizing of the blueberry bushes that afternoon with her father.

It was after she had brought the eggs to the house and washed them, and was on her way back to her cottage that she realized she hadn't thought of Chad all morning. It was like a stab of guilt instead of grief. How could she go about her day without a thought of him?

Back in the cottage, she started another pot of coffee as she considered what action to take. She wanted to get on the computer and make a list of the people who had gone missing from the State Police database. If she did, she could create a spreadsheet to track where they were last seen, perhaps cross check it with others who had disappeared and their locations.

She quickly set to work and began to go through the database to organize the names with the limited amount of information she had. She was annoyed that the national numbers indicated that four hundred and fifty people had gone missing in New Jersey the previous year. Despite that, the listings on the New Jersey State Police site only showed about fifty, and most were outdated, from the late 1990s and early 2000s.

Was it because the reports were only posted when family members insisted?

She felt herself getting frustrated, just as a car pulled into the gravel driveway for the cottage.

She peeked out the window to see Dennis approaching in full uniform. She had to admit, he wore it well, and his sleek hard body was much more impressive than when he'd been a skinny teenager.

She opened the door before Dennis could knock.

He smiled to see her. He wore his sidearm and carried a scuffed leather portfolio bag. "Morning, Lil."

"Can I offer you some coffee, Dennis?"

"Sure, I could use a cup."

As he stepped through the doorway, Lil saw her mother peek out her kitchen curtains across the space between their houses. Selina made a look of disgust and shook her head.

None of your business, Mother. If I want to invite Dennis in, I can. I can even screw him if I want to.

She blushed as she closed the door. Where had that thought come from? Since Chad's death, sex was nonexistent, as well as any desires.

Lil remembered that the doctor in New York had said that *Paxil* could affect sexual desire. She hadn't taken the pill last night or this morning. Was her body experiencing a reawakening of some sort?

She took a deep breath, surprised that her mind had turned to sex at all. Instead, she focused on pouring a cup of coffee for Dennis.

Meanwhile, he put the leather bag on the table where Lil was set up with her computer and looked around the neat cottage. "I've never been in here. This is a pretty nice place."

Lil handed him the cup. "Look around, you'll like the other rooms."

She returned to her seat behind the computer, mortified. She had almost said, "You'll like the bedroom." Fortunately, the connotation had struck her before the words came out of her mouth.

Dennis went through the small house, and quickly returned to the table. "Pretty small place."

"My New York apartment was smaller," Lil said. "And there were two people…"

Grief struck her again and she stumbled into silence.

Dennis put his hand on top of Lil's. "I'm sorry about Chad."

She yanked her hand away, suddenly angry. "You looked up his name? You'll make detective in no time."

Dennis looked at the floor. "I meant no disrespect, Lil. I just figure he had to be quite a guy to win your love after…"

He stopped talking.

Lil stood up, fuming, looking up at him as he was a good six inches taller. "After *you*? You egotistical bastard, is that what you thought? That I was so broken up over *you* that I needed a 'really special guy'?"

She faced him, fighting the desire to grab her cup of coffee and throw it in his face.

Dennis met her eyes. "I didn't mean it that way."

She slowly returned to her seat, aware that she wasn't used to powerful emotions anymore; the rush of sexual desire, the fire of her anger. She had become used to the drug-induced calm that had steadied her broken life. The highs and lows had been removed, and she could see why. She was still on edge. She had to remember to take her *Paxil* once Dennis left, to return to that state of calm, where nothing bothered her because nothing ran too deep.

"It's okay," she sighed. "I'm just a little sensitive right now."

"I noticed," Dennis said. He held the leather bag and watched her. Finally he sat, adjusting his belt as he did. "I want to ask you a really important question."

She glanced at him, concerned. "That sounds ominous."

He gave that shy smile, the one that always made her want him, back in the day.

"Sorry, I didn't mean it to be," he attempted. "I want to know why you want to do this."

Lil was confused. She had been thinking about so many things the last few moments. "I don't quite—"

"Searching for these people?" Dennis blurted. "Trying to find them, or find out what happened to them? I want to know why you want to do this."

"I told you, I'm a detective, I have free time—"

"Anyone else would buy that, Lil. But not me."

She looked at him for a long moment, considering his words, and wondered herself. Why had she been drawn to find these lost people, or at least find out what happened to them? It had gone from a spark of interest to an obsession in one short night.

She looked at her coffee cup as if it might hold the answer, her mind racing.

"I—I'm not sure, to be honest."

"What do you *think* is your reason?"

"If I can help these lost people…maybe it will make up….for what I did," Lil admitted.

"You're doing it to make amends?"

"Something like that," she confirmed. "It's just I'm feeling kind of lost, myself. And if I have the skills that could save other lost people—"

"Then maybe *you* won't feel so lost?" Dennis offered.

Lil clamped her lips together tightly and nodded, suddenly fighting back tears. This confession had been tough.

Dennis picked up the leather bag and put it on his lap. He took a thick collection of pages and put them on the table. "These are copies of the reports you wanted."

Her eyes grew wide. "All of them?"

"Pretty much," Dennis replied. "I went in early and made copies. But Lil, if anyone sees these, I could lose my job."

And it's no less than you deserve.

Lil shook her head at the odd thought. She was certainly all over the place this morning. From thoughts of sex to vengeance all in a heartbeat. She didn't want Dennis to lose his job. She'd lost hers and it had been crushing. No matter what had happened in their past, there was no victory in hurting him.

"I will be careful and share them with no one," Lil finally said. "But I can use them to build my database."

Dennis rose. "Let me see what you've got." He stood behind her and leaned on the back of her chair to peer over her shoulder.

Lil could feel his warm breath on the back of her neck and it made her shiver.

"It's…um…a spreadsheet to coordinate each person's vital statistics, age, race, and all that, and the place they were last seen," she explained, feeling another sudden rush of desire. "I'm hoping

I can see any similarities in each disappearance, come up with common denominators."

Dennis chuckled. "I can see why you were a good detective, Lil."

She turned to see that his face was mere inches from her own.

Close enough to kiss.

She rose up from her seat which made Dennis stand up as well. "This is good, I'd better get to work on it," she said picking up the pile of papers to keep her hands from shaking. "I'll want to see what you came up with."

She stepped back into the kitchen, feeling an overwhelming need to create distance. "I…um…guess you need to be back on patrol."

Dennis gulped the rest of his coffee and handed Lil the cup. "Yes, and I don't want your mom to get the wrong idea."

"She already has that."

Dennis smirked. "Should I adjust my clothes as I go out the door?"

Lil gave a quick, explosive laugh. "No, please, I'll never hear the end of it."

But she kept laughing, the whole idea tickled her so much. The idea that Dennis came by for a morning quickie was silly. Or was it?

"Okay, then, I won't," Dennis replied, smiling as she laughed. "But you stay in touch and no crazy stuff."

Lil finally got her giggles under control. "What do you mean, crazy stuff?"

"No going off on your own," Dennis chided, which got an annoyed look from her. "Lil, I know you. You get on something and you're like a dog with a bone."

"I can handle myself."

"I know you can, but whatever is causing people to go missing, it's not anything either of us have been trained for."

She nodded. He could be right.

He moved close and planted a chaste kiss on the top of her head that made Lil blush.

God, I want him, right here, right now, and my mother be damned.

She kept her arms rigidly at her sides, to prevent herself from pulling him into her arms and acting on her desires.

"Stay in touch," Dennis told her as he stepped out the door.

Lil was holding herself tightly and all she could do was nod.

He went out and she relaxed and returned to the computer as she heard his car pull out of the drive and back onto the highway.

She began to go through the papers, inputting the data, marking each incident on its own row, and was pleased that each bit of information was in a separate column, so she'd be able to do a trace by location or any other pertinent data.

As she typed, her mind began to wander back to that first night so long ago in the Barrens. Dennis had just become old enough to drive, and they were on a side road near the stone foundation of one of the old iron works which used to be plentiful in the area around Furnace Run.

That's how the town had received its name, from the many smelting facilities that were all in one location. The Pine Barrens was the center of Revolutionary War iron-making. There was ore-rich water from bogs which provided the raw material. Add to that, vast forests for charcoal-making to be used as fuel and piles of clam and oyster shells from nearby shore areas which contained the lime necessary in the traditional process.

But that night, the smelting facility was an empty stone foundation. There was a full moon, she and Dennis were in the old 1996 Chevrolet Caprice station wagon he'd bought. Dennis had put foam rubber padding in the back and a blanket and they lay there, both half-dressed.

"I wish I could've taken you some place nice, Lil," Dennis told her between kisses and panted breaths.

She took his head in her hands. "No, Dennis, this is perfect. We're Pineys, and what better place to celebrate life than here in the Barrens?"

She kissed him and his hands were all over her, touching her breasts, and then sliding lower.

Lil jumped up from the table as if she'd been shocked. She didn't want to fantasize about sex, but her mind had wandered from the repetitive work of inputting data. She needed to get out of the house and put this pent-up energy into something physical.

Looking at the blank wall above her computer, an idea struck her. She thought that a map would be helpful to turn the dull information into a visual representation.

She knew there were programs to create digital maps, but she wanted to do it old school. She could go to the large office supply store in town and get a county map, as well as supplies to trace out the disappearances.

As she grabbed her purse and jacket and stepped outside, she saw her mother rapidly approaching the cottage. She did not look happy.

"What was he doing here?" her mother demanded as she drew near.

"He brought me some information." Lil really did not want to get into this with her mother.

Damn, maybe I should have taken that Paxil.

"So just like that, he shows up and you take him into your house?"

Lil's hands went to her hips in defiance. "Yes, Mother, and we made mad, passionate love on top of the refrigerator."

"Don't talk like a whore," Selina chided as she drew close.

Lil sighed. "*Daj*, he brought me some papers. I have no interest in that stuff."

Except this morning.

"I don't like him here," Selina snapped. "After what he did to you, you invite him into my house?"

Lil's jaw set. "I thought it was *my* house."

"It belongs to your father and me! You just live in it!"

This made Lil's temper burn. "Then I guess I need to make plans to leave."

Selina backed down at this. "Lilliana, I didn't mean…"

"Mother, I have been running my own life for years." Lil put her hand to her head. "Please, *Daj*, I don't want to fight."

"You all right?" her mother asked.

"I keep having dreams, nightmares, so I'm not sleeping well," Lil explained.

"Dreams? Are they telling you things?"

"No, they just scare me," Lil said and headed towards her car.

"You should see what they are trying to tell you. Dreams are one way to see the future," her mother insisted, following her. "You have the blood of a gifted family. Your grandmother had visions, she could see things—"

"I know!" Lil shot back as she unlocked the driver's door, annoyed again. "It's all I ever heard growing up. My grandmother, the sainted Natalia, who could read the future in a tea cup or from the turn of one card."

"You have the same ability. You read the cards when you were younger, and you were good at it!"

"That was a long time ago, *Daj*," Lil said, fighting to not scream at her mother in frustration.

"It is passed from mother to daughter. And you waste it pursuing the *Gorojo* men!"

This was it, Lil's temper was hot, and she felt if she didn't release it she would explode. She shouted at her mother, "I don't have to buy into this superstitious nonsense, I live my own life. If you don't want me here, I'll just fucking leave!"

She got into the car and slammed the door as her mother stood there in shock. She backed out of the driveway and drove away.

She was furious, and a part of her reveled in it. After months of perceiving things through a peaceful veil, the emotions that went through her were so strong. Anger at her mother, the big laugh at Dennis' joke, the sudden rush of sexual longing.

She had been so intent to quash the pain and the loneliness that all of her emotions had been suppressed.

It was time to change that.

Furnace Run itself was a town from another time, with hundred-year-old brick and stone buildings lining the street. There were diagonal parking spaces on both sides of Main Street making the two-lane road very wide and impressive. On the corner was the old firehouse, which had been converted into a local bar and restaurant. On the other side of the street were single story shops most of which were closed, with paper in the windows. The liquor store up the block was open and still doing a thriving business, but it was the only open business besides the bar and a check-cashing establishment up the street.

They could tear this whole town down and no one would care.

She made a right turn and passed the more modern businesses, the Dine Rite and fast-food restaurants with familiar signage and arches.

She pulled into the lot of the large office supply store, and noticed that there were several other cars there. She went in and quickly approached a young bespectacled woman wearing a red shirt and a name tag. "Excuse me, do you have a map of Burlington County?"

The young woman studied Lil. "I'm not sure. Come with me."

She led Lil down an aisle, where there was an assortment of wall hangings and posters.

"Just Burlington?" she asked.

"Yes, something large please," Lil admitted. She was looking around the store. The place had several customers meandering through the aisles and two people lined up at the registers.

Suddenly it alarmed her, and she didn't know why.

"The only map of Burlington County we have is a historical map from 1859." The woman held up a map about three feet by two feet mounted on cardboard and wrapped in plastic. It was attractive, but more of an artifact than a map listing current roads and towns. However, it was in full color with each township highlighted in a different hue.

"Yes, that should work," Lil said. She was sweating and glanced around as fear gripped her heart. She felt so exposed, so vulnerable. Was it getting hot in here?

She sucked in several deep breaths, and the salesgirl asked, "Are you all right?"

Lil nodded a bit frantically. "Yes, I just need to use the ladies' room."

The young woman pointed to the rear of the store, looking unnerved by the way Lil was acting. "It's right back there. Do you need help?"

"That's fine. I'll get the poster on my way back," Lil assured her, and without another word headed for the back of the store. The thoughts were accelerating inside her head.

Something bad coming…

One gunman could wipe out this whole place…

No way out…

She wanted the sudden fears running through her mind to slow down so she could get more air, but they didn't. Her breaths came in gasps as she moved into the hallway leading to the washroom, with a small water fountain mounted to the wall.

Paxil…

She always carried a small supply in her purse, she needed it the first few weeks, when panic attacks like this had washed over her and left her helpless.

She gasped for air as she went to her knees in front of the water fountain feeling like she was going to black out. Her heart hammered in her chest as she tore through her purse looking for the prescription bottle.

"Where is it?" she muttered angrily.

The room was beginning to spin when she touched the bottle and pulled it out with a sense of victory, but a desire to vomit washed over her. She tried to open the child-proof lid, but her hands didn't seem to work.

A woman came out of the nearby ladies' room, the sound of a flushing toilet behind her. She stopped and looked down at Lil. "Do you need help?"

Lil glanced up at the woman standing over her. She was middle aged, with well-coiffed hair, a nice dress, and a compassionate expression on her face.

Lil wanted to scream at her, tell her to leave her alone.

Instead Lil held up the prescription bottle and murmured, "Could you open this, please. I'm having a little trouble."

The woman took the bottle and simply opened it and handed Lil one pill.

"Thank you," Lil gasped and snatched the pill away like a tiger attacking prey. She thrust it into her mouth, pulled herself to her feet and started the stream of the water fountain. She sucked the water greedily as the woman returned the lid to the bottle.

"Dearie, I think I should call a doctor, don't you?"

Lil fought the urge to snap at the woman, but instead raised her head and spoke quietly. "It's a medical thing. I'll be fine in a couple of minutes."

The woman handed Lil the bottle and warily walked away. Lil still felt sick. She almost wanted the woman to call an ambulance, but then her parents would insist she spend time with doctors.

They wouldn't understand that she had a mission and needed to get back to work. Lil pushed herself off the wall and went into the ladies' room. She moved into the first stall clutching her purse, which she hung on the hook on the back of the door. She sat on the toilet, trying to calm her breathing.

She thought maybe she should call someone, but didn't know who. Chad was gone...he'd never seen her like this. Thank God for that. She couldn't have endured him seeing her so weak.

She couldn't call her parents or Dennis, as they would want her to go to the hospital or see a therapist or something.

She just focused on slowing her breath. The confined space of the stall was actually quite comforting. She grabbed her knees and worked to talk herself out of it, the way her therapist had instructed her.

She needed to recognize that this was a panic attack, that's all. She just needed to breathe slowly and wait for the *Paxil* to take effect.

She was angry at herself. She'd enjoyed the emotions that had blossomed in her this morning, the naughty ache of sexual longing had made her feel more alive than she had in months. The problem was that she'd forgotten why she'd been prescribed the *Paxil*. She thought she could give it up, just go cold turkey, get on with life.

But it was all too much.

She closed her eyes and tried to calm down as she sat in the cubicle, shivering, waiting for the drug to take effect.

SIX

Mapping the Sites

Half an hour later, Lil collected the map and two boxes of multi-colored push-pins. She grabbed some colored markers and held them tightly with the other items as she went up to the register to pay.

When the pill had finally taken effect, she washed her face in the sink and ran a brush through her black, kinky hair to look presentable.

Even so, she was aware that people looked askance at her as she moved through the aisles to locate her items. She could see them whisper to each other and look at her.

It didn't matter. She was back to being dead inside.

After paying for her items, Lil was back in her car and headed towards her parents' farm.

It had been a rough morning, but she had work to do.

Back home, she mounted the map on the wall, then organized the pins to start marking locations of disappearances.

Since it was a historic map and missing many of the modern roads, Lil pulled up a current map on her laptop, and used the markers to add the roadways. If she tried to mark every small sandy road that went through the Barrens, she would have made it a criss-crossed mess. Besides, those tiny roads were not listed on any map anywhere.

With the major roads in place, she started with the spreadsheet she'd already cobbled together to find each location. Carefully, she began to apply pins to the appropriate locations, knowing that they might not be perfect, but it would give her a rough idea of the areas where most of the victims were last seen.

It was slow and painstaking work, and at noon there was a knock on her door. She pulled herself away and opened it to find her father holding a plate of her mother's cabbage rolls.

"I thought you might be hungry," he said as he stepped into the room.

Lil was touched, but the emotion immediately quieted under the effects of her antidepressant.

"Thank you, Poppa," Lil said as he put the plate on her table. He gazed up at her map.

"What are you working on?"

"Just something I got interested in," she replied dully. She moved to the table. Her father probably wanted to watch her eat. She should be hungry, all she'd had that morning was coffee.

Vano Slavik looked at the wall, observing it as Lil got a knife and fork from a drawer.

"You know, you're going to have to apologize to your mother."

"I know," Lil sighed. "Tell her I forgot to take my *Paxil* this morning."

"Did you take it now?"

"Yes," Lil assured him. She had no intention of telling her father about the panic attack in the office supply store.

"Your mother is upset that boy came to see you."

Lil wanted to laugh. It was hard to imagine Dennis as anything but a man at this point. But, once again the *Paxil* shut down any strong emotions. "I know."

"I don't like it either, to be honest. But you are a grown woman, you must make your own decisions."

"Thank you, Poppa."

"But apologize to your mother. She gets upset when you fight, and then she takes it out on me."

This got a smile from Lil. "Sorry for that."

He shrugged. "We have been married for thirty-five years. I know when it is best to sit and talk to her. I also know when it is best to go check the blueberries or the alpacas."

"You are most wise, Poppa."

"So, eat. Can you help me with the plants this afternoon?"

"In an hour?" Lil requested. "That way I can eat, grovel to Momma, and get ready."

He nodded. "Make it a good grovel, please."

"I'll give it my all."

He smiled. "That's my girl."

He bent to give her a hug as she sat, then stood and looked at the map one last time. "You know, it's amazing that there are all these towns on this map that don't exist anymore."

Lil was cutting into the cabbage roll, the smell of the spices making her mouth water. "What?"

"These towns, you see?" He pointed at the map. "Three Bridges? It's gone. Penn Point, also gone. Not to mention famous ghost towns like Harrisville, Martha, or Pines Edge."

"Seems like a lot doesn't it?" Lil frowned.

"It was the way they were abandoned that people wonder about. I mean, when iron-making moved to Pennsylvania, that was one thing—killed the jobs of the small towns in the Barrens

—but Pines Edge was different. According to the legend, everyone just disappeared."

Lil bolted upright. "Disappeared?"

"Yes, one winter a man left his family and went north for work. When he returned in January or February, everyone was gone, his family as well. Horses, chickens, livestock too, all gone. The odd thing was, even though the houses were abandoned, all of the possessions were left behind."

Lil leaned closer to the map. "Where was this place?"

Vano pointed with a stubby finger to a spot on the map. "Here, see?"

Lil could see the crossroads indicated on the map and the words "Pines Edge" printed in small letters.

It was just a short distance south of Furnace Run.

The afternoon was spent in a flurry of activity for Lil as she rode with her father in the old golf cart, scooping the smelly fertilizer around the base of the plants.

She had done as her father asked when she returned the empty plate to her parent's kitchen. Selina stood with crossed arms, not speaking.

"I need to apologize for how I acted earlier," Lil said sheepishly. "I should not speak in such a disrespectful way, *Daj.*"

Her mother's stern expression faded and she opened her arms to take her daughter into a hug.

"I just worry about my baby," her mother wailed.

Lil was surprised to see her mother was crying. "Thank you…I guess…"

"I don't want you hurt again," her mother lamented. "All this pain for so young a woman, it is not good."

"I know, *Daj*," Lil muttered.

Her mother pulled back and wiped her eyes with the back of her hand. "I know you are a good girl. You just like the *Gorojo* men too much."

"Only some of them, Momma."

Her mother became excited. "You know your second cousin has a friend, Bo. He is looking to find a wife. Maybe an arranged marriage would be good for you, yes?"

Lil was alarmed but felt it would be best not to start another fight. "We can...look into that, *Daj*. But now, I have to help Poppa."

Lil headed out the door before her mother could say another word and rushed to the barn. An arranged marriage? Was her mother insane? Lil knew it was a Romani custom, and that her parents had been part of such an agreement, but that was for previous generations. To have a modern woman even suggest it surprised the hell out of her.

The hours of mindless physical labor soon relaxed her, and her mind moved back to her map and the towns that had gone empty over the last century.

And most of all to Pines Edge.

She was interested in the legends, and as she and her father moved slowly from each skeletal plant to the next she asked him questions.

"What did they do in Pines Edge?" Lil asked as she got another scoopful of fertilizer.

"There was a big paper mill. Very, very big." Her father released the steering wheel to gesture with his hands, as if claiming the size of a fish that got away.

"So it wasn't the failure of the iron industry that got them?"

Vano shook his head. "No, they had business other than iron. The founder of the town, Jacob Pines, he made paper using salt marsh hay, pine trees, and rags for the raw materials. After the town went empty, relatives came and took the possessions away. The buildings eventually burned down, even the paper mill."

"There's nothing left?" Lil asked.

"I guess not. Why do you want to know?"

"I'm just curious."

"Well, don't get too curious, I don't want you to disappear as well."

By late afternoon they were finished and Lil removed the supplies from the back of the cart as her father plugged in the charging cable.

"Tonight you come for dinner, eh?" her father said. "After you clean up."

"I'm a little nervous, Poppa. *Daj* said she wanted to talk to someone about making me an arranged marriage."

Her father shrugged. "Might not be a bad idea, you could meet a good Romani man."

Lil's mouth fell open. "You would support this, *Dati*?"

His mouth curled into a smile. "Your mother and I were an arranged marriage."

"I know, but that was a different time—"

"I take it you do not want this?"

Lil controlled herself. It wouldn't help to have an outburst with her father. "No, I want to pick the man I marry. I am not something to be traded for two donkeys and a chicken!"

There was a twinkle in her father's eyes. "I don't think so either."

"Good!"

"Most I could get for you is two goats."

Her mouth fell open again. "What?"

Vano chuckled. "You are too headstrong, like your mother. Now, if you were a good gypsy woman, I *might* be able to get two donkeys."

She grinned. "Should I get better at my tarot cards?"

"You were always good with those. Your palm-reading could use a brush-up, I think."

"Any more gypsy stereotypes you want to run by me, Poppa?"

"I think I'm done. And relax, your mother will forget this idea in a few days."

"Are you sure?" Lil worried.

"Probably. If not, then in a few days I will speak to her."

"Can't you talk to her tonight?"

"Why?" Vano shrugged. "She will no longer be mad at me, and I don't want to ruin her mood. I am feeling romantic tonight."

"Poppa!"

He waved and headed towards the house.

Lil shook her head and went back to her cottage where her map waited. She worried that more dreams might come this night.

And what would they foretell?

SEVEN

A Circle of Events

She was back in the kitchen with Grandma Natalia, looking around. The room didn't seem quite as big, so she was older, maybe eight or nine.

"Ah, my precious one," Natalia said, as she walked into the kitchen.

Lil turned to her grandmother, afraid she might be a skull as in her previous dream, but she was as Lil remembered her, a matronly woman with long dark hair and an easy smile. Her hands were behind her back, as if hiding something.

"What have you got, *Mami*?" Lil asked. "A cookie?"

"This is something you will need, but not for many years, precious one."

Lil frowned. "I don't understand."

"I know, child, in many ways, neither do I," Natalia said, and held out a small, thick black cloth.

Lil took the cloth carefully. She could feel an object within it that was hard and smooth. She opened it and in the middle was a dark black gem stone. It had traces of brown on its surface and was shaped like a large egg and polished until it gleamed. "What is it?"

"It is the key," Natalia told her.

"The key?" Lil repeated looking at the stone. "It doesn't look like any kind of key I've ever seen."

"No, but who knows the door it can open? I found it in the woods, and I know you will need it, but I do not see *when* it will be needed."

Lil stared at the shiny stone in her small hands. "It's sparkly."

Natalia smiled. "Yes, it is. And you must be sure that you know where it is."

There was a bang at the door.

They both looked over and Lil felt fear rise up inside her.

Natalia sighed and walked toward the door cautiously.

"Grandma, don't," Lil begged, as terror gripped her heart.

"I must, precious one," Natalia told her quietly. "If I do not, they will come after you."

"I'll stop them, Grandma," Lil said. "I'll stop them when I become a policeman."

There was another bang at the door louder than the first.

"You will do more than be a policeman," Natalia affirmed. "You will save many lives."

She stood next to the door when it crashed open. A powerful wind, like a hurricane or tornado, whipped through the room, pulling at Natalia's long hair. Outside the door was something large and dark, but Lil couldn't quite see it from the dust blowing in her eyes.

A pair of arms appeared, covered in dark fur. At the end of them were claws much larger than a human hand. The claws grabbed Natalia by the shoulders with talons that pierced her skin and made her cry out.

"Grandma!" Lil yelled over the roar of the wind. She rushed forward, fighting the gale as her grandmother was pulled out the door.

Lil sat up in bed, drenched in sweat and panting. Sunlight peeked through her drapes, and she looked at her digital clock which read: 7:00 AM.

Lil got out of bed, every muscle heavy. Her back and arms were sore, and her legs seemed to have weights on them.

She changed into sweats as coffee brewed and she pondered the dream, in an attempt to make sense of it. The first part was based on reality. Years ago, her grandmother had given her a small cloth, and within it was a piece of obsidian stone that contained multiple shades of brown and black. The stone had an oval shape and had been highly polished so it was smooth and shiny.

The second half of the dream had not happened, but monsters seemed to appear in all her dreams recently.

Lil had kept her grandmother's gift as a good luck symbol and a connection to her. But she hadn't thought about it in years, and wasn't sure where she'd last seen it. It could be in storage with her other things, but then it occurred to her that it might still be in her old bedroom in her parent's house.

She would have to ask her mother.

Over coffee, she decided to go for a run and went to the bathroom to take her Paxil. The last thing she needed was a panic attack to overtake her while she was out on the trail. Her concerns about the stone could wait until later.

Lil went outside and stretched, waving to her father who was already up and feeding the alpacas. She started on the roadway into the blueberry field, but her goal was beyond it.

Like many farms in the Barrens, their acreage was attached to the vast forests that surrounded them. Soon she was past the rows of plants and down a trail into the woods.

She followed this trail that had been there her entire life, a wide path of white sandy soil with untouched trees and underbrush on both sides.

The Barrens hosted several types of pine tree that enjoyed the iron-laden sand-filled dirt. She passed jack pine, red pine, pitch pine, all of them looking boney and worn, though they still bore their green boughs, unlike the blackjack oak she passed that was nothing but empty branches shoved out in all directions.

Spring had not yet come, and the trees had yet to recover from their long winter's sleep.

She slowed down as she passed a clearing with a small earthen hill in one corner. This had been a shooting range where her father trained her on the use of firearms as a young woman. When she was a teenager and knew that she wanted to go into law enforcement, she and Dennis had spent afternoons out on this range shooting handguns and rifles.

Until she broke up with him.

After that incident, she'd come out here and literally shot the place up, destroying the wooden platforms that held the targets. All that was left was the dirt hill that acted as a backstop.

Lil was breathing hard, but she pressed on to the end of the path. The track led directly into one of the sugar sand thoroughfares that zigzagged throughout the Barrens and few people drove on. If she were to follow it in either direction, it would eventually lead to one of several major roads. She could head down that route, but instead, walked over it and into a copse of trees beyond.

She slowed down as it was much darker in here than on the trail. The tall evergreens above her were so thick they created a canopy. These branches blocked the light of the sun so effectively, it made the area around her like twilight.

She came to a stop and looked around, leaning forward to put her hands on her knees and catch her breath.

There was not a sound except for her breathing.

This was unusual. It was still too early in the year for the buzzing of insects or the mating song of spring peepers, those tiny tree frogs that heralded the season of growth, but there should be the sounds of birds. Many birds were returning north, and there were several species that remained all winter.

The silence and the darkness seemed to press in on her. And yet she heard something…a dull hum that seemed to vibrate in the soil around her.

The quiet was broken by a shrill screech that rang throughout the forest.

It was so loud and inhuman that Lil jumped in fright and raised her hands to cover her ears as a chill ran up her spine.

Whatever it had been, it sounded far too close. Lil was overwhelmed with the idea that there was something there, watching her. Instead of running back to the trail, Lil turned and moved very quietly in the direction of the noise. She walked slowly, alert to anything that might be there. She tried not to make any sudden noises and attract the attention of whatever it was she'd just heard.

There was a sound overhead, the loud flapping of wings.

Lil crouched and with the reflexes of a cop, she moved quickly to a nearby tree and slipped under its boughs. Her hand went to the trunk to steady herself and she gazed up to track the noise.

"Help me," a voice croaked.

Lil spun, her hands up in a defensive pose. A few feet from her a man was hidden under the boughs of the same tree. He lay on the ground and there was a wound on his head that was bleeding. His clothes were tattered and damaged, his hair wild, and he had stubble upon his chin. She guessed he was about forty and his damaged clothing looked like he was a hunter.

Lil glanced around and knelt close to him. "Are you hurt?"

"Where am I?" the man asked, slipping in and out of consciousness.

"You're in the Pine Barrens," she informed him. Looking him over she saw several other large spots on his clothing discolored by blood. This guy was in bad shape.

"No, I was in another place," he admitted, struggling with each word. "It was terrible, all red...filled with monsters...hidden..."

He made a dry cough.

"Sir, I have to get you an ambulance."

"No time, no time. It's following me!"

"What is?"

He reached out with a dry hand, the fingernails dirty with red clay under them. "The Jersey Devil." He fell into another coughing fit, as Lil retrieved her cell phone only to see she wasn't getting a signal.

"What's your name?"

"Brian Kent," the man looked up at the sky. "You have to help me, it's trying to find me."

There was the sound of the huge wings again, and Lil searched the dark canopy above for a sign of any movement.

"Look...Mister Kent...I have to get a signal, call for backup," she told him. "I'll just walk over there and call. I'll be back in a few minutes."

"Please, don't leave me," he whined weakly.

"I'll be back soon," Lil said. With one last look to the sky she ducked and moved to the path, watching the screen of her phone. A bar finally appeared and Lil immediately hit the number for Dennis.

"Hello?"

Lil glanced over to see the man, and then stood near a tree and turned her back to him to talk. "Dennis, it's Lil. I found a man in the woods. He appears to be in bad shape. I need an ambulance."

"Are you at your parent's farm?"

"No, one of the sugar sand roads off Route 206," Lil said and closed her eyes. "I think the entrance to it is near the Emilio Carranza Monument."

"I know where that is, that's not far. Okay, I'm on my way."

Lil hung up the phone, just as a piercing screech from behind her made her freeze. She whipped around, and it seemed that the copse of trees was darker than it had been. She grabbed a fallen branch as a weapon and moved back to where she had seen the wounded man.

He was gone.

She ran to the dark thicket and then scanned the sky, her breath ragged, though it was no longer from running.

What was that shriek? It wasn't the sound of a turkey vulture.

And where did the man go?

She began to search the area.

There was a trail of blood and drag marks in the sand that led to the tree where they had sought refuge. She followed it back to a clearing about a dozen feet away. From the look of the shrubs and ground vegetation, Lil imagined the man had dragged himself to the trees, pulling himself through the sandy soil.

Oddly, the blood trail started from a thin line of burnt sand in the center of the clearing. Lil had never seen anything like it.

Campers would often build campfires if they stayed in the Barrens, but a perfectly straight line, three feet long? It could be from fireworks or something, but she could find no remnants of such.

And why did the blood trail *start* here? Had the man been setting off fireworks and blown himself up? She doubted it, the wounds were on his chest and legs, not his hands.

Where did he go from there? He couldn't have just flown away. She recalled the sound of heavy flapping wings and a chill went up her spine.

Dennis arrived fifteen minutes after the phone call. Instead of the police cruiser, he was driving a black pick-up truck, with large tires that jacked it up. When he stepped out of the vehicle he was in jeans, cowboy boots, and a shirt that was tight against his muscular chest.

"Hey, Lil. You look like you've seen a ghost."

"Maybe I did," she sighed. "I'm sorry, I didn't know you were off-duty."

"Yeah, a Sunday off. Doesn't happen very often," Dennis said as he pulled a bag from behind his seat. "I have my first aid kit. Where's the wounded man?"

"He's…um…gone."

Dennis frowned "Where'd he go?"

"I don't know."

Dennis sighed. "Then, I'd better call off the ambulance." He got back in the truck and activated a police radio that was mounted under the dashboard. He soon spoke to the dispatcher, and then, still with the first-aid bag, joined Lil on the ground as they both explored where the man had been.

"Lil, I'm going to ask a question you're not going to like," Dennis announced.

"Go ahead."

"Are you sure that you saw him?"

"Yes," Lil said adamantly. "Of course I did."

"Lil, certain antidepressants have been known to cause hallucinations that seem very real—"

"I am aware of that, but let me show you what I found." She led Dennis to the blood trail and showed him the drag marks. Dennis pulled on a nitrile glove from his kit and touched the blood.

"Is it fresh?" Lil asked.

"It's wet. It appears to be," Dennis said looking at the red smear on his finger.

"What about these marks on the ground?" Lil pointed. "I didn't imagine them."

"I agree, but the blood could be from an animal, even a bird. As far as the drag marks, those could have been here for years."

Lil crossed her arms. "You think I'm crazy?"

Dennis put up his hands in a calming gesture. "No, I'm suggesting that you saw the blood and the drag marks and your mind created a story that fit the clues. I mean, if this guy was wounded as badly as you think, he couldn't just disappear."

"Dennis, you have to admit, it's weird that the blood trail started at that burnt line."

"I agree, and I don't have an explanation. Do you want to look around a little further?"

She put her hands on her hips. "To humor me?"

"No, in case there *is* a wounded guy out here."

This appeased Lil. "Maybe for a few more minutes, if you don't mind."

"Sure, then let me drive you home."

"Agreed. His name is Brian Kent."

Dennis stopped and stared at her. "Where did you get that name?"

"He told it to me."

Dennis stood there not moving.

"Now, you look like the one who saw a ghost, Dennis."

"Let me show you a photo," Dennis finally said and pulled out his smart phone to bring a picture up on the screen and show it to Lil.

"That's him," Lil said.

Dennis looked at the photo himself. "We got a report of another missing man, Brian Kent, yesterday afternoon. He went camping with his buddies and disappeared when they were setting up their tents near nightfall."

"I guess I found him—"

"That's what's strange. They were in the woods near Batsto Village, at least twenty miles from here."

"Dennis, this man's legs were injured, you saw the drag marks. He couldn't walk twenty feet, let alone twenty miles."

Dennis nodded, a stern look in his eyes. "Let's just see if we can find him."

They separated, circling out calling the man's name. Lil couldn't help but notice that the dark area in the trees seemed lighter now. Was it a trick of the light or had something dark left?

After about twenty minutes Lil returned to the truck, getting there just as Dennis returned.

"You had no luck I take it," Dennis said.

"None. I don't think we can find him."

"I agree. We may as well get out of here."

Dennis unlocked the truck, and Lil climbed into the passenger side. Dennis did a very careful K turn to head back out to the highway.

"Is there anything else you can tell me about this guy? Anything at all?"

Lil nodded. "The man said he'd escaped from a place that looked like hell. He said it was hidden."

"That doesn't help much," Dennis replied.

"Because he wasn't real?"

"No, because from what you've told me about his injuries, he was probably delirious."

"He said he was being hunted," Lil added. "By the Jersey Devil."

Dennis' jaw tightened. "That again? You sure do have the Jersey Devil on your mind."

Lil thought she should be offended by Dennis' tone, but the odd circumstances forced her to agree. "I know."

They drove on in silence, getting off the sugar sand road and back onto the two lane highway. It took almost longer to drive Lil home than it took for her to jog.

"I have an idea," Dennis suggested. "How about a day away from all this?"

Lil considered this and asked. "Do you want to take a ride with me up to Batsto Village?"

Dennis frowned. "Do you want to talk to Brian Kent's friends? I think they left."

"No, I just want to take a look around."

Dennis lips stuck out in thought. "If I agree, you have to go on a detour along the way."

"What's that?"

"I want to stop by my shooting club."

Lil froze, her breath caught in her throat. "I haven't touched my weapon in months."

"Why not?"

"No reason," Lil blurted, avoiding the question. "Look, can you drop me off down the road, so we don't upset my mother?"

"Okay," Dennis said and pulled over to the side of the road. He stopped the car and faced her. "Come with me. We used to go shooting together all the time."

"I have to get cleaned up. How about I meet you there?"

"Sure, I'll text you the address."

"Give me about an hour?"

"It's a date," Dennis said as Lil stepped out. Before she could respond, the tall man drove off.

"A date?" she repeated out loud.

After a shower, Lil felt calmer, still trying to get her head around the man in the woods. She was almost willing to believe he really was a hallucination. An injured man didn't just up and disappear.

Dennis had his photo on his phone...and there was the sound of those wings and that screech...

She mixed herself a protein shake, just as she remembered her dream, and Grandma Natalia giving her that shiny stone and telling her it was the key.

The key to what? And for what?

Before she knew what she was doing, she picked up her phone and called her mother.

Selina answered the phone. "Yes, *Chaj*."

She sounded very happy, and Lil concluded that her father had indeed been 'romantic' with his wife the previous night.

"*Daj*, do you remember a strange stone *Mami* gave me?"

"Hm? Oh, the dark one that was all shiny and polished?"

"Yes, *Daj*."

"It is in your old room, right where you left it when you moved to New York."

"Really?" Lil couldn't quite recall. "Once I'm dressed, can I come get it?"

"No need, I'll bring it to you!" her mother gushed and ended the call.

"No, Momma—" Lil attempted but it was too late. She wondered if she should throw on clothes as she wore only a ratty robe and had a towel wrapped around her hair.

She sipped the shake and studied the map on the wall with all the pins she'd added. It was close to one hundred.

She had chosen pin colors based on the month of the disappearances and made a simple legend using colored pencils to match the pins. Patterns were beginning to emerge, certain locations where the numbers of disappearances spiked.

And they were all in the Pine Barrens.

Burlington County extended across the state, on the west side was the Delaware River just north of Philadelphia. The east section of the county touched the Jersey shore all the way to Mystic Island.

Yet the vast majority of the pins, based on the last known locations of the victims, were all in the Pine Barrens. The pins formed tiny circles with many in the townships of Tabernacle and Washington, near to where Furnace Run was located. In fact, the majority were just outside the borders of her town.

A grouping of the disappearances had also occurred near Batsto Village. This was a long-abandoned town that had been purchased by the state and restored into a historic site illustrating life in the Revolutionary period.

There was a knock at her back door, the one in the bedroom. She pocketed the phone, wrapped the robe tighter, and went into the bedroom to open it, making sure she had arranged her bed that morning. The last thing she wanted was her mother complaining about her housekeeping skills.

She opened the door to see Selina with a big grin on her face. The older woman pushed past her and into the cottage.

"You're keeping the place nice," she gushed and looked down at the mattress on the floor. "Oh, we have to get you a bed frame."

"It's fine, Momma."

Selina looked over at her daughter. "Look how skinny you are, *Chaj*. You need to eat."

"I've got a protein shake right here, *Daj*," Lil said and held up the half-full glass to demonstrate.

She felt her mother wanted to disapprove, but Selina seemed in too good a mood to chide her daughter.

"You look happy today."

"Why shouldn't I be happy?" her mother asked. She reached into a pocket of the apron she wore, pulled out the small cloth, and handed it to Lil. "Here, is this what you were looking for?"

Lil took the cloth and let the stone slide into her hand. It was an oval a little larger than a hen's egg and shiny. The stone itself was black with numerous shades of brown throughout it in small clumps.

"Thank you, yes," Lil said. "Do you know where Grandma Natalia got this?"

"She found it," Selina explained with a shrug. "The day your father and I bought this farm, she walked into the woods and came back with it. It was bigger then, and really just a ragged black rock."

"How did it end up polished like this?"

"Grandma had a cousin who made jewelry. He cut it and polished it. It was funny, because the man couldn't believe she found such an item here in the Barrens."

"Why not?"

"He said it was obsidian, fused with sand, and that it was impossible. You need a volcano to make obsidian."

Lil nodded. "And there are no volcanoes in the Barrens."

"Exactly," Selina agreed. "Why do you need this now?"

Lil shrugged. "I'm not sure. Natalia came to me in a dream."

"See, I told you! What did she say?"

"It's pretty confusing, and there were monsters in the dream."

"Oh? That is not a good sign."

"But she told me I needed the stone. Now, *Daj*, I want to get dressed."

"You can't get dressed in front of your mother?"

"No, because I don't need comments on how I'm too skinny."

Her mother made a dismissive gesture and headed to the bedroom door. "Come for dinner. You need to eat."

Lil looked at the stone gleaming in the light, then returned it to its cloth holder. She placed it on her bed and got dressed.

Once clothed, she grabbed the covered stone and slipped it into the front pocket of her jeans. The jeans were a loose cut and the small stone didn't show.

Then she pulled out a large purse to carry her things, and extracted a waist pack with a quick release pocket from her dresser, and slipped it into her purse. She could use it to carry her gun if she needed to.

She then stared at the lockbox that contained her revolver.

She had a legal carry permit for New Jersey that had taken months for the paperwork to be approved.

Since the move, she had not opened the box, never cleaned it, in fact had not touched it for the last few months. The memory of the one night in New York when she was desperate made her scared of it.

Summoning her courage, she picked up the box and put it on her bureau top. Then she took the key and opened the box to look at her weapon. It was a Smith & Wesson 642 Airweight Double-Action Revolver that fired a thirty-eight caliber slug. She understood how it worked, and just how much damage it could do.

Just looking at it made her blood run cold.

EIGHT

Into The Woods

L il pulled into a small dirt road a half-hour later and parked in the lot of a one-story concrete building. It boasted a new roof and was constructed with a huge chimney in its center. Several other cars were parked in the lot, some newer, but several were older vehicles, not well maintained, what she'd always referred to as 'clunkers.' However, one of them was the big, black pick-up truck that Dennis had used to meet her in the woods.

She heard gunfire in the distance as she got out of the car with her lockbox and headed towards the truck.

"Hey, there," Dennis said as she walked over. He had two rifle cases, one on each shoulder. "I see you found the place okay."

"This looks like a cheap bar for Pineys." Lil inclined her head to the building.

"It's not a cheap bar, it's an inexpensive club...for Pineys," Dennis smirked. "It's the Tall Eagle Hunting Club. I'm a member."

"Tall Eagle?" Lil repeated with one lifted eyebrow.

"Hey, I didn't name it," Dennis admitted, a bit defensively. "Come on, let me show you the range."

They walked up a well-worn path into the woods, and a huge clearing opened up. It consisted of a wooden target range that faced large tables made from heavy boards. These were in a picnic table style and were designed to lay out weapons.

Lil looked around to see several people with a variety of firearms, mostly rifles.

Dennis chose the bench and table for slot number six and laid out his bags to unzip them. He set out a pair of rifles on the table. One was a semi-automatic with a walnut stock and a large scope. He set it up on a stand atop a green shooting bag and placed a small shooter mat under it.

The other weapon was a boxy short rifle painted green with a short barrel, an exaggerated stock, and a large suppressor on the front.

Dennis inclined his head towards her lockbox. "Is that all you brought?"

"It'll do," Lil replied.

He was focused on the large gun, checking it thoroughly.

"How long have you been a member?" Lil asked.

"A few years. It is a good place to see people, relax a bit."

"And go shooting."

Dennis nodded. "Agreed. I missed the shooting range out back of your parent's house. I guess that's long gone."

"Oh, yes. After you broke up with me, I put about a thousand bullets into the targets we built and then tore down the whole place."

He nodded and didn't look up. "Sorry about that."

Lil shrugged. "Better that I put the bullets in the target instead of where I wanted to put them. What are you shooting?"

He held it out to her. "Savage 64 FXP, semi-automatic with a twenty-inch barrel, and a four by fifteen millimeter scope."

Lil kept her hands to herself. "How many rounds can it hold?"

"Ten plus one. You want to try it?"

She shook her head. "I'll watch you."

Dennis unrolled a target and signaled to the other shooters as he went to the backstop and attached it. Then he strolled back, sat at the table, and faced the range.

Dennis prepared the weapon and rested it on the shooting bag.

"What is that, fifty yards?" Lil wondered.

"That's right. I would have picked the kiddie lane if I'd known you were bringing the pop gun."

Lil looked over at the next table. There, a big man with a wild beard was instructing a young man no more than thirteen on the use of his weapon.

Lil returned her attention to Dennis, who was putting on his eyewear and hearing protection, which resembled large headphones. Lil opened her lockbox that held the pistol, her ammunition, and her own hearing protectors and lenses. She put these on quickly and nodded to Dennis.

He pulled the trigger, and as the loud report sounded, she saw a mark appear on the paper target Dennis had attached to the wooden holder in the distance.

"Missed the bullseye," she acknowledged as she moved the hearing suppressor off her head. She looked down at her open lockbox and picked up the weapon to open the cylinder. Her hand was shaking.

"Do you think you could do better?" he challenged.

"No, I'll just watch," Lil said as she clumsily attempted to load her pistol, but dropped several bullets.

Dennis did not miss how uneasy she was. "Lil, what's wrong?"

"Nothing," she snapped and attempted to load another bullet that missed the hole in the cylinder and fell to the ground.

Dennis did not seem fooled. "You used to love to go shooting, it was one of the things we did together all the time."

She recovered the dropped round and shoved it home, anger stilling the shake of her hands. "Times have changed, Dennis."

He glanced at the other lanes where people were shooting and lowered his voice. "Lil, I'm serious."

She closed the cylinder of the pistol and stared at the weapon in her hand.

"Are you scared, Lil? I mean, after what happened?"

She glared at him and put her hearing and eye protection in place. She stared at the target, and in a blazing fast move, lifted the handgun and fired.

Dennis peered through the scope of his rifle. "Lil, you're as good as you ever were. You hit the bullseye right in the middle."

He looked up at her, but she was pale, and her eyes brimmed with tears.

"Lil?"

She put the handgun into the lockbox followed by her protective gear and slammed the box closed. "They got a bar in this place?"

"Um…yes, inside."

"Good," Lil ordered. "Watch my lockbox."

She stormed away down the path toward the concrete building, as Dennis stood there dumbfounded.

It was dark inside the shabby bar decorated with wood panelling on the walls, card tables and folding chairs that could be cleared in a hurry. There was a built in bar and Lil ordered a glass of white wine and sat at one of the tables trying to control the shakes that had returned.

The wine was terrible with a bitter aftertaste.

She could feel the calming effect of the *Paxil*, especially reinforced with the alcohol, which her therapist told her never to mix with the drug.

Lil didn't care, it was too much. Holding her gun again had felt like she was looking at the instrument of her own destruction. Yet, what frightened her more was the ease and skill she still possessed, and how easy it had been to hit the bullseye from 50 yards.

The gun flowed with her and for her, just like the night Chad was shot. But that dark night, she went on a killing spree. She could recall the smell of the gunpowder as she worked her way through that apartment, killing everyone in it. It was so easy, so effortless because she and the gun were one, it was half alive and she was half machine, interacting in a perfect union of death.

She came here thinking she could handle a shooting range, she'd spent most of her teenage years in the one in back of her house, shooting with Dennis, just like now. But now the gun felt like a foreign thing, a horrible creature that had used her to bring destruction to her own life.

Dennis came in just as she finished her glass of wine and signaled to the bartender for another.

Dennis sat quietly and ordered a club soda, watching her.

"Don't stare at me like that."

"Sorry, I'm worried about you."

"I…just haven't used my gun since I've been back home. I'm a little gun shy, okay?"

"I'm just surprised. You handled that gun like it was second nature. If you didn't want to come here, why did you accept my invitation?"

"I…thought it would be…different…"

"Lil, I've known you since grade school. And I read reports of what happened that night that Chad died. I just don't understand this, okay?"

The wine and club soda arrived and Lil took a sip. They were not close to any other table, and only three other people were in the bar.

Lil took a deep breath. "It was a night after the 'incident' when I was alone in the Manhattan apartment that Chad and I shared."

"You two had been living together?"

"Yeah. It was tough. Chad was dead, his parents and brother had come to take away his belongings, I was under investigation with IA and I knew they were going to take my badge away."

"What happened?"

"At some point I had my lockbox out, because I didn't want one of Chad's family to think it was his and take it. After they left, I opened the box, you know, just checking on it."

"Sure, normal thing to do," Dennis said quietly.

"I looked at my weapon and thought how one quick pull on the trigger would make my pain all go away. I...I loaded it and held it, overwhelmed by my loss and the loneliness of life without Chad."

"Oh God, Lil!"

"I was close, Dennis, so fucking close. I sat there with it in my hands for over an hour, and I held it so tight that my fingers ached. Finally, I forced myself to empty the revolver and lock it away. I sat shivering in bed, awake for the rest of that night. The next day I contacted the union and asked to go into therapy."

Dennis reached over and took Lil's hand. For this one time, she didn't resist but returned the grip, needing the reassuring touch of another person's hand.

They rode in Dennis' truck, both of them having left their drinks unfinished.

They travelled in silence. Lil wasn't sure she should have revealed so much to Dennis. It was a level of intimacy she had not planned to share, and now she was uncomfortable. She pulled out her cell phone and went over the Batsto information she had downloaded and focused on where she wanted to visit.

"Why are we going to Batsto?" Dennis finally asked.

"I started marking the disappearances on my map with colored pins. Batsto was one of the hot spots. Weren't you aware of it?"

"Lil, that's not in my jurisdiction. Occasionally we get alerts, like with that Kent guy, but that's the exception. Are people vanishing from Batsto?"

"Not in the village, from the woods surrounding it," Lil explained. "It's a popular camping area."

Dennis frowned. "I'm not following."

"Most of the disappearances are happening in the woods around two major places: Batsto Village and Furnace Run. Furnace Run much more than Batsto. It's like both towns are protected but something is prowling around the edges."

"The Jersey Devil?" Dennis said, rolling his eyes.

Lil didn't say anything as they drove on.

After about a minute, Dennis finally declared, "Oh come on, you don't think that, do you?"

"My only thought is that there are people missing," Lil explained. "And I told you what Brian Kent said, that he was being pursued by the Jersey Devil."

"Lil, that's nuts."

"I agree. I want to see if we can find evidence that precludes that notion."

Dennis considered this. "Okay, I'll go along with that, just as a baseline. But if you think I'm going to start believing in the Jersey Devil—"

"Have you read any of the history?"

"You mean beside Mother Leeds, or the tale of the visitations from the monster? No, that's all garbage. People saw a crane at night and scared themselves."

Lil nodded. "And then again, there was Brian Kent this morning."

Dennis sighed.

"You still don't think he was really there?" she pressed him.

"Lil, I certainly don't think the Jersey Devil came and took the man away. You would have seen it."

They rode on in an uncomfortable silence again. Brown wooden signs with bright yellow lettering carved into the wood announced that they were approaching the site.

"Do we want to go to the hiking trails or the Visitor's Center?" Dennis asked.

"Visitor Center first, then the trails. It's the trails where the disappearances occurred."

"How will we find the locations?"

"I mapped them out and put the longitude and latitude into my phone for each victim."

"What? All of them?"

"Just the first fifty so far."

"*Fifty?*" Dennis started and glanced over at Lil. "That must have taken hours."

"I have a lot of time on my hands. Even my parents, they want me to rest all the freaking time. I finally got my father to let me help fertilize the plants this week, and that was like pulling teeth."

"We all want you to get better, Lil," Dennis confided.

Lil lifted her hands to end the conversation. "Look, I took my *Paxil* this morning so I'm not going to flip out, okay?"

They pulled up the dirt and gravel road and turned into the parking lot which was very full for a Sunday in March.

Dennis drove around looking for an empty space and asked gently, "Have you been flipping out?"

Yes, and I ended up shivering in a stall at the office supply store.

She wanted to be honest with Dennis, but how could she tell him the truth? If she did, he'd fuss over her like her parents, and she was tired of that, tired of the whole damn thing. She just wanted to get back to work, to do something.

"I'm fine," she assured, her jaw set.

Dennis pulled the big truck into a space recently vacated. "By the way, that one shot today was impressive."

Lil shrugged, not wanting to talk about guns. "My firearms trainer at the academy taught me some tricks. He wanted me to become a SWAT sharpshooter."

"Why didn't you?"

"My goal was always to become a detective, remember?"

Dennis nodded as they got out of the truck. They headed toward the simple one story building where people were milling about. Outside the building were a series of small white tents, each with an open front. People were selling things at tables and each tent offered different products.

As they drew near the center, a large sign announced:

Indigenous People's Day
Here at Batsto Village
Come see some wonderful
Native American Creations

Lil glanced over to see that each of the tents had products, from hand-woven blankets to beadwork and turquoise jewelry.

"Shall we take a look?" Lil smiled, as they moved to the tents to inspect the wares.

They went to a tent that had jewelry and Lil stopped. "Look Dennis," she pointed.

On a velvet board was a decorative pin that featured a creature. The thing had antlers like a deer on its head, a gaping mouth of sharp teeth. It bore bat wings and a long tail, but its body was covered in green scales.

Lil turned to the proprietor, a man about her height with a round face and features like an apple doll.

"Is this the Jersey Devil?" she asked.

He looked at the pin and chuckled. "No, that is the *Piasa* bird."

"Looks like a dragon," Dennis proposed. "Except for the antlers."

"This is a reproduction of a carving in stone they found on a limestone bluff overlooking the Mississippi," the man explained. "It was very big. The legends say that this creature existed long before the Europeans arrived. They claimed it was a bird 'that devours men'."

"Can I buy it please?" Lil said and pulled her wallet from her purse.

"A bit unusual for you, isn't it, Lil?" Dennis suggested.

"I'm drawn to it," Lil explained as she offered a credit card to the man.

"It's not surprising," the proprietor told Lil as he ran her credit card through his phone. "This land we are on, the Pine Barrens? In the old days it was known as *Popussing*."

"Popussing?" Dennis repeated with a frown.

"What does *that* mean?" Lil asked.

"It means the place of the dragon," he explained. "Even the early Swedish settlers called the rivers Drake Kill."

"You know Swedish as well?" Lil questioned.

The older man shrugged as he returned Lil her card. "Not much, but I know that Drake Kill means 'dragon river'."

On a whim, Lil pressed on. "Is there anyone who might know of the legends?"

"Like a history guy?" the man asked with a frown.

"Someone familiar with the Lenni-Lenape legends."

This made the brown-skinned man smile. "At least, you know that our people here were called the Lenni-Lenape. I thought you were going to just say 'Indian legends'."

"I grew up in the Barrens."

He nodded thoughtfully. "I know a guy, but he doesn't talk to just anyone."

"Can you tell me how we could get in touch?" Lil insisted.

The man considered this, his eyes narrowed. "He teaches at a university. I think you can track him down there."

"Which university?"

"Not sure. Maybe someplace in north Jersey," the man explained.

"Garden State University?" Dennis wondered. "That's up north."

"What's this man's name?" Lil queried.

"Max."

Dennis frowned. "Doesn't sound like a Native American name."

The old man chuckled. "No, it doesn't. His surname is Ag-well or something. But trust me, this man is definitely an Indian."

Lil looked at the pin as they headed into the Visitor Center as the words repeated through her mind: *the place of the dragon.*

They soon pulled into the parking lot near the trails, and Lil put aside the copy of *The Jersey Devil* she had purchased at the gift shop. She knew it annoyed Dennis that she read it as they walked back to the truck and drove over.

Dennis got out and pulled on a prepared backpack from his truck and armed himself with one of his rifles on his shoulder.

"Is that really necessary?" Lil asked.

"Yes, and I want you to bring your handgun."

"*What?*"

"Lil, you said that we are investigating places where people disappeared. We both should be armed. I saw that you had a waist pack in your purse."

Lil pulled the waist pack out and stared at it. Dennis was right, this was used to carry her weapon, and she couldn't figure out why she'd even brought it. She had just thrown it in her bag.

Like you knew you'd need it.

She prepared the pack, placing her wallet and phone in the appropriate pockets, as well as a bottle of water in a harness on the fabric belt.

She then picked up her lockbox and opened it, pleased that her hands didn't shake this time.

With her teeth pressed together so tight it made her jaw ache, she took out the Smith & Wesson. She hadn't unloaded it, so there were still five bullets in the cylinder. She carefully shoved it into the waist pack where it was held by Velcro in a quick release position.

"You ready?" Dennis demanded impatiently.

"Just give me a minute," Lil insisted as she closed the lockbox and stowed it under the passenger seat. She was not pleased that

Dennis wanted to be armed, but she could understand why he thought it was necessary.

They began their walk, with Lil's attention now on her smart phone, seeking the locations she had programmed into the device.

Dennis dutifully followed her, his rifle slung on his shoulder with the barrel pointing up. The pair spoke little as they approached the first spot, and Lil circled around in a clearing.

"Okay, this was a location where Simon Jacobs vanished about three weeks ago."

"Not much to see," Dennis claimed, giving the forest a cursory glance.

"Look harder," Lil suggested.

"What are you talking about?"

"How about those two trees in the center?"

"The branches are broken, so what?"

"Come on," Lil chided. "You're better than that. All the branches near the ground are broken off, as if there was a struggle."

"Lil, that could have been campers making a place to hang their tent," Dennis said in frustration. "This could have been done either by man or animal. This area is trodden by people all the time."

"But a man *disappeared* after he came in here," Lil said, putting her hands on her hips.

"I just don't want to jump to conclusions," he stated calmly. "You buying that book about the Jersey Devil in the gift shop was not a great idea. You're filling your head with…with…"

"What?" she demanded.

"Myths!" his voice was much louder than it needed to be. He paused for a moment and took a deep breath. "Those are nothing but kid's stories and the stuff of bad 'B' movies. You can't take them seriously."

"Okay," Lil said, and headed back to the path. "Let's see the next location."

They walked on in a heavy silence again for another twenty minutes until Lil reached another clearing and began to walk around this one as well.

"So, what's your solution?" Lil insisted.

"What?"

"To the people vanishing. You must have some theories."

"My solution is to make it the state's problem," he grumbled.

"Christ, I expected more from you," Lil spat.

"What?" he replied, turning to face her.

"We both wanted to be cops, that's what we talked about since we were kids. Detectives, solving cases like those guys on TV."

"After working with NYPD, you have to know what bullshit those shows were," Dennis explained.

"Okay, I admit it. A lot of times we didn't catch the bad guy and a lot of times when we did, he was back on the street ten minutes later," Lil confessed.

"Yes, and in a small town, I don't have to deal with any of that."

"You shove it off to the state," Lil said, and then did a bad imitation of Dennis. "Not my problem!" She stepped away and turned from him. "Dammit, sometimes you have to make hard choices, and sometimes people die."

Dennis looked over and saw tears on Lil's face.

"Lil, I—" was all he could manage, immediately contrite.

She turned her back to him. "I'll be fine. Just give me a minute."

She pulled a tissue from her waist pack, wiped her face and blew her nose.

"I'm sorry," he finally said.

"I'm all right, the *Paxil* evens out all my emotions."

"Evens out?"

"Suppresses them, if you want the truth. My therapist liked the term 'evens out,' but all it does is kill all my feelings. I want to stop taking it."

"Then why don't you?"

She turned back to him, putting the used tissue in an outer pocket of the waist pack. She couldn't meet his eyes. "Because I can't take life without it, yet."

"What do you mean?"

"I had a frigging panic attack in the office supply store," she yelled, shocked that she admitted it.

"Lil, I'm—"

"If you say you're sorry one more time, I will seriously kick your ass," she interrupted.

"I'm just sorry to see you like this."

"Yeah, well so am I. I am one sorry-ass lady at this point," she muttered. "Guess you're not upset that we didn't get married now, are you?"

"Lil—"

"Let's keep walking," she grunted, and headed up the path. "I have one more spot I want to see, and then we can walk back to your truck and you can drive me to my car."

Dennis quickly caught up to her, and gently took her arm to turn her to face him. She looked down at the ground.

"What?" Lil demanded.

"I've thought about what happened and how I hurt you for years."

"I got over it."

"Yes, and when I heard that you were engaged, I was glad for you. Glad you had someone who cared for you and that you loved."

"Well, that didn't last," she lamented.

"When I heard what happened to your guy, and to you, I was devastated. I thought that you'd finally made it, the big time, the NYPD."

"It all fell apart pretty quick," Lil admitted. "And so did I."

"Which is why…I'm afraid for you."

"For me?"

"Yes, taking on this obsession…I'm just worried."

She looked up at him, and saw the soft expression on his face. It was unmistakable, he had an appearance of concern coupled with a puppy dog look of devotion.

Just like the night they made love all those years ago.

She pulled his face to her and kissed him, hard.

Dennis' back stiffened, but then he fell into the kiss, pulling her into his arms.

She was the one who pulled back, broke the kiss, stunned by her own brazen actions.

"Lil…I…" Dennis replied, amazed.

She stepped back and put a sardonic tone to her voice. "Relax, it was just a kiss. Let's go."

They walked on, Lil confused by her own actions. Did she want Dennis? Hell, she had just thrown herself at him, and he seemed quite willing to be carried away in the moment. A part of her wanted to lose herself in an act of intimacy, but once again, the *Paxil* took away the desire soon after she felt it. She could remember how much she wanted him the other day, before the panic attack, and remembered how good it felt to experience that level of emotion and desire.

The panic attack had scared her, and she couldn't risk it.

However, that had been a great kiss.

Lil was focused on her phone as they entered an area with a thick covering of branches overhead, blocking the sunlight. She pulled her coat tighter, as it was much cooler in this dark part of the forest. She looked back to see Dennis pulling his own leather coat closer around himself as well.

"Are you getting a signal out here?" he asked.

"No, I loaded all of the locations onto the map app while we were at the truck. I'm not getting any bars at all."

"That could be why people get lost out here," he suggested. "People's phones stop working and they don't know where to go without them."

"Come on, there are walking trails. All you have to do is head back to your—"

A screech filled the air. Dennis and Lil froze, looking all around.

"What the hell was that?" Dennis muttered.

They both moved to a nearby tree off the pathway, their eyes scanning the treetops.

Dennis slid the rifle off his shoulder and took it in both hands.

"Did you see something?" Lil asked.

"Not a thing, but it doesn't hurt to be armed."

"Could it have been a screech owl?"

Dennis shook his head. "The only owls out here are swamp owls."

"Barred owls," she corrected.

"What?"

"A swamp owl is a barred owl. And they're an endangered species, so please don't shoot one."

He nodded and pointed the rifle at the ground.

Lil checked her phone again. "This was the last place Charles Blake was seen by his friends."

"Right here?"

"That's right. They headed back up the trail and Charles told them he would join them in a few minutes."

"And he never did?"

"They were parked in a lot about ten minutes, that way." She pointed in a direction different from the one they had come.

"How did they get to it? I don't see a path."

"I think there is one up ahead."

"Okay, then let's head for it, and maybe walk on the road to get back to the truck."

"Who's scared now?" Lil jibed, as she returned the phone to her waist pack.

Another screech rang through the woods and Lil and Dennis froze again. He had both of his hands on the rifle, his finger just outside the trigger guard.

"Still think it's an owl?" Lil said, breathing hard from the adrenalin rush.

"I could be wrong," he confessed.

"What's that?" Lil asked, looking away from him at the path ahead of them.

"What?" he said, and pulled himself around the tree to look past her.

He took a step away from the tree and his boot sunk into the damp ground.

"Dammit," he hissed. "This is a bog! Now, my boot's all muddy—"

"Dennis, what is that?" Lil interrupted, and pointed at a clearing about twenty feet away

A strange light had appeared, with no source.

Dennis quickly scanned the canopy, but there was no break in the covering where sunlight could pour through.

Lil stared at the light, but couldn't conflate the two situations. There obviously was an illuminated area ahead of them on the path, and there was no logical place where it could have originated.

"I have no idea," Dennis said, as the light grew brighter.

Lil also could hear a noise, like a tingling in the air, or the hum of an electric circuit. It put her teeth on edge to hear it.

"I don't—" Lil began.

Lil jumped, and frantically yanked at her pocket, and pulled it inside out. An object wrapped in cloth fell heavily to the ground. The cloth fell away, and in the center was a dark obsidian stone that glowed with an unsteady light.

"What's that?" Dennis asked.

"A rock…a keepsake. But it got hot, it felt like it was burning."

"Hot?" Dennis repeated and leaned closer to look at the polished stone as it glowed.

Another loud screech shook the forest and Lil and Dennis pushed themselves against the trunk of the tree. Dennis held tight to his rifle, while Lil raised her hands to cover her ears.

The scream faded, but another sound filled the air.

Flapping wings.

"Move to the other side," Lil ordered and indicated the far side of the tree. Dennis, without question, did as he was told.

The noise of flapping wings sounded again, much closer and much louder than any bird, even a large one.

The light in the clearing grew brighter, and so did the tinkling sound. There was the loud flapping of wings, as something dropped out of the tree branches and landed on the path not fifteen feet from Dennis and Lil.

The bright light silhouetted the large creature, which stood at least seven feet tall on two legs. A large pair of bat wings lowered and neatly folded against its back, pulling in close to the body. The silhouetted shape had a pair of antlers on its head, and the shadow was uneven, as if it was covered with heavy fur.

It stood on a pair of powerful legs that came down to a pair of large hoofed feet. It walked upright with an ungainly step, toward the light. The ball of light had expanded into an oval shape that hung in the air just an inch off the ground. The creature took only two steps, then stopped and lifted its head in the air.

Lil peeked from around the tree at what stood in front of the circle. The light behind the monster had grown brighter and it was hard to see its features.

It had a long neck that rose up to a head similar to a horse. A heavy, thick tail swung behind the body, coiling and shifting like a separate entity.

It lifted its long snout and the large nostrils sniffed the air. Its ears folding back in a similar way to certain breeds of dogs.

It turned to face Lil as drool came out of its mouth, which opened to show pointed teeth like a predator. A pair of twin fire-red eyes bore into her.

The creature gave another shriek, deafening at this close range, and leapt towards both of them.

Lil found that her weapon was in her hands, as if she conjured it like a magic trick and before the creature could pounce, she had it in a two-handed grip and fired off a pair of shots.

The impact of the rounds knocked the creature off its trajectory and it fell sideways into a thin pine tree that broke in two under its weight. Lil stepped out, her gun focused on their would-be attacker, but the creature gave another strange cry, this one filled with shock, pain, and anger.

It pushed itself to its feet and leapt for Lil, but Dennis put himself in front of her and lunged forward to strike the creature in the chest with the barrel of his rifle.

The huge monstrosity fell back, rolled, and scrambled to its feet, moving with astounding speed toward the glowing oval.

It leaped at the oval and went through it, and Dennis ran forward, lifted his rifle, and discharged the weapon into the light, which made the creature cry out again. But this time, the cry sounded far away.

Dennis stepped back as the circle of light began to grow smaller.

Lil moved to Dennis, breathing hard. "You okay?"

"Fine, you?" he panted.

They both stared at the oval as it shrank into a small ball that just vanished right in front of their startled eyes. Dennis was left standing on the sandy trail in the dark woods with Lil a few feet behind him.

A wisp of smoke rose from the ground, and they approached carefully and looked down. A small straight line, a burn mark about three feet long, was on the ground where the oval had been hovering. It smoldered as if the ground had been burning in that one place.

Lil looked at the weapon in her hand as if she had stuck her hands into a corpse and now wriggling maggots covered her fingers. The weapon fell to the ground, Lil took two steps away, fell to her knees and vomited.

Dennis went to her as she retched, and knelt beside her, holding her.

"What the...Hell...was that?" he gasped. "And where did it go?"

"Why didn't you shoot it?" Lil moaned.

"I...don't know. You were in danger. Hitting it was the only thing I could think of," Dennis quavered.

Lil pulled her water bottle and took a long swallow. Then she rolled over and sat on the ground.

"Still think it couldn't be the Jersey Devil?" she stated simply.

Dennis stared at the spot the thing had vanished and shook his head.

PART II:
THE HIDDEN LAND

NINE

A Man and His Dog

E rnest Fowler had been walking in the Pine Barrens his
entire life. Now at seventy-eight and recovering from a
hip replacement, he moved slower than he used to.

He had driven out with Hammer, his boxer, and parked on the
side of the road near the northern entrance of the Wharton State
Park. He headed into the trees with his six-foot-tall walking stick
and Hammer walking excitedly beside him.

To the naked eye, there was nothing to differentiate this spot
from the rest of the trees, but Ernest could recall the days he'd run
around these woods as a child. He didn't know why he'd driven
out to walk here. He lived in Furnace Run, and almost everyone
in town had land that backed into one forest or another, but
instead, he'd driven to this location, the site of his family home,
before it was made part of the huge park in 1954. He was eleven
at the time, and he hated the state for stealing his family's land
using eminent domain. Growing up, they didn't have much, but
their home was theirs, and he still felt the loss.

It was the threats he remembered most. Either his father sold
the land to the state willingly, or they would go through the
condemnation process and take it anyway. The price they offered

was low, but his father, a day laborer, could not afford an attorney to help, or even review the paperwork, so he accepted it.

That was when Ernest and his four siblings all moved out of the little house that had been their home, and into a series of rentals over the next few years.

By seventeen, Ernest had moved out and taken his first job. Through hard work and strong study habits he paid his way through college and landed a good job. Now, all these years later, he could grudgingly forgive the state for taking the land, because he could walk on this trail that only he knew about.

He found it odd that at this twilight time in his life, when he often forgot simple things, how strong and powerful the memories of his childhood had become. You would think it would be the other way around, that the oldest memories would fade, and the newer ones would be bright and sharp.

He strolled up the property line of the old house near the highway for a few minutes and the dog did his business.

Well, no need to clean up after him out here.

He headed back up the almost invisible trail. It really took a trained eye to see it, and the one thing that had not faded was his eyesight. He needed reading glasses now, but his eyes were still reliable.

Besides, he could walk these woods blindfolded and know the way. He remembered the pain and loss when his brother, Tommy, had disappeared in the woods near his home all those years ago. The boy, who was the oldest and sixteen at the time, had snuck out of the house one night, never to be seen again.

The police came by, even searched the woods with dogs, but no trace of Tommy was ever found. Some said he got lost in the woods, fell in a bog, and the quicksand buried him.

Billy, his younger brother, always said the Jersey Devil got him.

Ernest didn't believe in the Jersey Devil. He thought the stories were just that, stories. Tall tales that people repeated until a fictional creation was so well-known that it was an accepted idea, like Santa Claus or the Easter Bunny. Despite whatever historic foundations these myths were based on, they had long ago been turned into flights of fancy.

Ernest stopped for a moment to catch his breath and Hammer, good dog that he was, stopped and sat next to him with his eyes bright and watchful.

"You're a good boy, Hammer," Ernest said, and gave the dog a treat, which Hammer accepted gratefully. The name was so wrong for such a mild-mannered dog, but as a pup he'd found an old wooden handle of a hammer without the head. The dog carried around that stick for months, like it was a bone he'd found, so the nickname stuck.

He had to admit the walk in the woods and down memory lane had tired him, and he decided to head back to his car.

As he turned, a light began to glow, not ten feet from him.

At first, Ernest thought it was the headlights of a truck it was so bright, but a vehicle couldn't drive into this section of the forest.

The dog stared up at the light, cocking its head one way and then another as if trying to make sense of what he saw.

The light grew brighter and Ernest held up his hands against the dazzling illumination. The wind seemed to move all around him, as if he were in the middle of a small tornado.

The light grew bigger, forming an oval that floated in the air about an inch from the ground. It wasn't quite so bright, or his eyes had adjusted to the unexpected radiance here in the dark forest.

Ernest approached carefully, but the dog rushed ahead of him and barked at the elliptical phosphorescence.

"Quiet, boy," Ernest commanded, and the dog ceased his yapping but stood his ground, growling at the circle.

Ernest walked around it. It seemed to be flat, two dimensional. When he moved to the side of it, it vanished, as if it had no depth in the real world.

As he walked further, he stood on the far side of it, and it looked exactly the same: a large flat, egg-shaped hole into... *where?*

Ernest came completely around to where Hammer stood his ground, ready to attack. He moved closer until he was a mere three feet from the glowing oval. He bent and picked up a stone and threw it into the circle of light.

It disappeared into the brightness. There was no sound of it striking the ground.

"Don't that beat all," Ernest murmured. He picked up a short stick, a piece from a broken branch maybe a foot long. He threw it into the circle and it too disappeared. Ernest walked around and peered at the other side to see if it was there.

It wasn't.

He lifted his walking stick, and moved it toward the circle of light.

Hammer growled more ferociously.

"It's all right, boy, calm down," Ernest said, as he gently touched the long staff against the light...and it went in.

It didn't appear out of the other side, in fact, it didn't come in contact with anything.

He pulled the stick out, and a monstrous arm followed it.

With a cry, Ernest stepped back, lifting the walking stick as a defense. The arm was covered with brown shaggy hair. Three clawed fingers reached out, more like the talon of a bird. It grabbed for the stick which Ernest yanked out of its reach.

Hammer leapt into the air, madly biting at the hand, jumping back to avoid the clutching grasp.

"No, boy, no," Ernest cried out.

The dog lunged and dropped back, barking and growling. With remarkable speed, the hand stretched out and reached for the boxer, the claws scratching the animal's side. The dog yelped in fear and pain.

Ernest moved as fast as his legs allowed and brought the walking stick down on the clawed limb, once...twice...

The hand retreated and Hammer backed away in fear, blood flowing from the three slices in his side. Ernest lost his balance, stumbling to the ground in front of the glowing circle.

The clawed hand grabbed his shoulder, sinking into the flesh as Ernest cried out in pain. He held onto his walking stick with both hands.

The arm dragged the hapless man and his stick into the hole which flashed like lightning, as Hammer barked at it again and again.

There was a final flash as Ernest vanished. The opening collapsed into a spinning ball of light before it disappeared altogether. It left a line of burning ground smoldering at the place where the ring of light had been hovering.

Hammer ran in circles around the place where his master had disappeared.

TEN

Called In

I t took half an hour to get back to the truck. Lil had made sure to pick up the obsidian stone and wrap it in the heavy cloth after the strange oval of light disappeared. It had cooled down, the strange heat dissipated.

She shoved it back into her pocket.

After walking about ten minutes, Lil finally took her weapon back from Dennis and returned it into her waist pack holder. It was still warm from being fired, but it no longer felt dangerous. In fact, it had saved both their lives.

Neither of them spoke a word, as they were both on high alert, scanning the area in case there was another attack.

Once they reached the open parking lot and were inside the vehicle, they both gave a sigh of relief, and Dennis hit the automatic lock to secure the doors.

"What *was* that thing?" he finally said.

"Looked like the goddamn Jersey Devil to me," Lil swore, as she unloaded the weapon and moved it to her lockbox.

"But it *can't* be. That's just a legend, a story from hundreds of years ago," Dennis argued.

"Then what's your explanation, Mister Logical?" Lil insisted. "You suggested that since I was on anti-depressants I might be having hallucinations, but you saw it, too."

Dennis gave a loud laugh.

Lil turned to him, annoyed. "I'm glad my medical condition is so damn funny for you."

Dennis got control of himself. "It's not that."

"Then, what is it?" Lil sulked.

"It's just...you...and panic attacks," Dennis reasoned. "You faced a nightmare, pulled out your gun and shot it, like it was something you do every day."

Lil shrugged. "It was strange. I mean, it felt like my hand moved by itself."

"Are you kidding? You went full-blown *Terminator* on that thing," Dennis gushed. "When I saw it, I was so...surprised that I...I guess I was shocked. But Lil, you were fearless."

Lil took another swig from her now almost empty bottle of water. "You were pretty brave yourself, jumping forward and stabbing it with your rifle."

"But what was that glowing circle—that light—"

"I think it was some kind of doorway or," the word struck her, "portal."

"A portal? To where?"

Lil gave an involuntary shudder. "I would have to say someplace other than here. Maybe that hellish place Brian Kent spoke about."

Dennis started the truck and they pulled onto the road, heading back to the shooting club.

Lil's mind was racing. She grabbed the book she had purchased at Batsto Village and began to thumb through it, an idea beginning to form.

"Dennis," she said flipping pages. "What if the Jersey Devil isn't *one* creature?"

"What?" Dennis replied, his eyes on the road.

"This book has stories from 1909 about multiple appearances by the Devil. The weird part was that some people described it as big, like that thing we just saw. But other witnesses said it was only three feet tall. Plus, on the same night it was seen as far north as Morrisville, Pennsylvania, and as far south as Salem, New Jersey."

Dennis struggled to have a rational explanation. "But it has wings, it can fly."

"Dennis, that's seventy miles. A big creature like that? All in one night?"

"Okay, I don't know. What are you getting at?"

"If it were more than one creature, it could show up in all those places. What if it was not just one lone monster, but a species?"

"A *species?*" Dennis repeated. "But what was it doing here?"

"Perhaps those portals have always existed, and it...they...hunt here. It would explain why the Lenni-Lenape called the Barrens the 'place of the dragon.'"

"But why has the Devil gone on these rampages, like in 1909, going to those communities and destroying stuff?"

"What if some of its babies escaped? Think about it, what if a baby...whatever it is...came out of the glowing circle, got lost, and then the mother pursued it?"

"Considering how the one we ran into almost ate us—" Dennis grumbled, just as his phone rang.

"Dennis we have to tell—"

"Hush, Lil," Dennis insisted, as he answered using the vehicle's built-in bluetooth. "This is Decatur."

"Dennis, we've been trying to get in touch with you. This is Captain Hewitt." The voice crackled with authority over the speaker.

"Yes, captain. I'm sorry, I was hiking in the Barrens—"

"And fighting monsters," Lil grumbled.

Hewitt went on, unaware of Lil's statement. "We have another missing person in the Wharton State Forest."

"I'm not in uniform, sir, I'm off today."

"That's fine, Bowman is already there, I need you to back him up. Are you in your truck? Just in case you need to drive those back roads."

"Yes, sir. However, I have a civilian with me."

Lil looked at him aghast and mouthed, "*Civilian?*"

"She's...um...familiar with police procedure, so she might be an asset."

Lil lowered herself in the passenger seat with her arms folded and her jaw clenched.

There was silence for a moment, and then Hewitt finally said, "It's not protocol, but since you were off duty, I'll take any help I can get."

"Yes, sir," Dennis breathed a sigh of relief.

"I'll text you the address. Get there as soon as you can."

"On it, sir."

Dennis ended the call and looked over at Lil, who was much more relaxed.

"So, I'm an asset?" Lil asked, eyebrows raised.

"You saved both our asses in the woods, so yeah."

Lil smiled as they drove down the highway with trees on both sides of the vehicle.

They soon received the text with the location and got there in less than twenty minutes.

They pulled up beside a Furnace Run police cruiser, a small Toyota, and a huge old sedan. The Cadillac was longer than Dennis' truck and must have been from the 1960s.

Dennis and Lil got out and approached the cruiser, where a black police officer stood, looking into the woods. His uniform was crisp, and the shine on his shoes was dazzling.

Jamarr nodded as Dennis approached, and his eyes grew small as he looked at Lil.

"Lil?" he finally burst out in delight. "Lil Slavik? Is that you?"

Lil couldn't help but smile. "Hi, Jamarr. It's been a long time."

"It has," he said, and pulled her into a hug. "Damn, girl you look good."

"Thanks."

He leaned close and said. "I heard about…y'know…what happened. I want you to know that there ain't a cop who wouldn't have done what you did."

Lil had to look at the ground. "I appreciate that, Jamarr."

He put the knuckle of his first finger under her chin and lifted it until her eyes met his brown ones. "You did the right thing."

A part of her wanted to shout, to cry out, "No, I didn't! I lost control and I lost my mind, I was a danger to everyone and myself." But she stayed silent and nodded.

"Can you tell us what happened?" Dennis asked. "The captain only told me it was another MP."

Jamarr turned to Dennis. "The guy's daughter, Mrs. Campbell, is in the woods, looking around. Captain told me to wait out by the road until another officer arrived, as he wanted coverage out here as well as in there. Best as I can tell from what Mrs. Campbell told me about her father, the old man drove out here with his dog this morning and went into the woods by himself."

"Any reason he chose this spot?"

"Mrs. Campbell tells me this was where his house was, growing up. They get worried when the old guy doesn't show up for lunch, and they have a GPS tracer on the old man's car."

Dennis frowned. "Does he have Alzheimer's or something?"

"Actually, the old guy used it to find the car in parking lots," Jamarr chuckled.

Dennis looked at the huge, old vehicle. "How could you misplace this boat?"

"It wouldn't be easy. I met the daughter out here, and we found the dog in the woods, walking around in circles whining. He's got scratches on him, like a bear or something took a swipe at him."

"Where's the dog?"

"Problem is that the damn dog won't leave. She's been trying to catch him since I got here. I came out here to call for backup."

"Your phone didn't work in the woods?" Dennis asked.

"Not even a little, I ended up using the radio in the cruiser. Captain told me to stay in sight until you got here."

"What do you need me to do?" asked Dennis.

"Either keep watch out here or go help Mrs. Campbell."

"Actually, Jamarr, I think since you're in uniform it would be best to stay out here," Dennis considered. "Plus, your shoes look great and I already stepped in mud today."

He held up the leg with the muddy boot to demonstrate.

Jamarr shrugged. "If that's all right with you."

"Officer Bowman," Dennis said and gave a neat salute. "It would be my honor."

This made Jamarr grin.

"Okay if Lil comes with me?" Dennis asked.

Jamarr shrugged. "It's okay with me, and there ain't no one else here. Were you two on a date or something?"

Dennis flushed a bit.

"Actually, we were fighting monsters," Lil said, and took Dennis' arm to guide him to the woods.

"That's not funny here in the Barrens, Lil," Jamarr shouted after them.

They strode a few dozen yards into the woods until they came upon Mrs. Campbell. She was average height and stout, wearing a jogging suit, though Lil figured she didn't do a lot of jogging. A lit cigarette hung from her mouth.

The dog, a boxer, kept looking at an empty spot among the trees, then running around it, whining. There were three gashes in the dog's side, which looked like they had scabbed over. The woman held a leash but it was obvious her efforts to catch the dog had not been a success.

"Trouble with your dog, ma'am?" Dennis said.

Mrs. Campbell looked over and frowned. "You a cop?"

"I'm Officer Dennis Decatur with the Furnace Run Police. I was off today, but nearby so they called me in."

She glared at Lil. "And who're you?"

"Detective Lil Slavik, NYPD." It came out of Lil's mouth before she could stop herself.

"NYPD?" asked Mrs. Campbell suspiciously. "You're a long way from home, ain't'cha?"

"I was…spending time with Officer Decatur, ma'am."

"Sorry I interrupted your date—"

"It wasn't a date," Lil corrected, and flushed. "When did you last see the missing person, ma'am?"

"This morning. We had breakfast, then he said he wanted to go for a walk. I would've gone with him if I knew he was planning to come all the way out here."

"Do you mind if we examine the scene?" Lil asked.

"Go ahead, but he's obviously not here."

Dennis and Lil moved toward the dog which shied away from them, but kept running in circles and barking, as if trying to let them know what had happened.

Lil stepped closer to the clearing, stopped and crouched close to the ground. "Dennis, look at this."

She pointed to a line on the ground. The vegetation was gone along it, and there was a burn mark on the sandy soil.

Dennis frowned. "Isn't that like the one we just saw?"

"Yeah, the ground underneath where that portal appeared was the same way." She reached out her hand.

"Don't touch it!"

"Why not?"

"I don't know, it could be radioactive or something."

Lil pulled her hand back. "Do you have gloves or an evidence bag?"

"I have both in the truck."

"Get 'em," Lil insisted. "I want a sample."

As Dennis stood up and headed back down the path to the truck, the dog approached and began to lick Lil's face. She laughed and gently pushed the animal's large squarish head away.

Lil stood and said to the woman, "If you want to give me that leash, I'll put it on him."

Mrs. Campbell shrugged and tossed the leash to Lil. The dog approached her again, and she attached the leash to the catch on the dog's collar as she patted its head. She stood and led the animal, which obediently trotted beside her.

Dennis walked back carrying gloves and a small evidence bag. He also had a dog biscuit in his hand.

"Is it all right if I give this to your dog, ma'am?"

"Sure, he's gotta be hungry. He's been out here for hours."

Dennis offered the dog the treat. The boxer looked at it doubtfully for a moment, then gently took it from Dennis' hand and wolfed it down.

"What's his name, Mrs. Campbell?" Lil asked.

"Hammer. Look, do we hafta be so formal? I'm Mary."

"I'm Lil and he's Dennis," Lil responded.

"Can either of you tell me what happened to my father?"

"You think he's lost in the woods?" Dennis said.

Mary shook her head. "I can't see how. He had his hip replaced a few months back and can't walk all that far. I'm surprised he made it all the way out here. Then there's the dog."

"The dog?" Dennis repeated.

Mary shook her head. "Hammer would never leave my father out here alone. Plus, he's injured—Oh my God, do you think a bear got my father?"

"Let me look at that," Lil said, and knelt next to the dog to examine the three even slices in the dog's side. The boxer whined as she prodded his flank, but she didn't touch the wound. "It's not too deep, that's good."

Dennis peered upwards at the treetops as he put on latex gloves. "You found him running around that spot between the trees?"

Mrs. Campbell went on, now agitated. "I couldn't get him away, or even get the leash on him. Hammer never listens to me, but he wouldn't run off and leave Pop."

Dennis looked down, then knelt and took some of the burnt soil in his gloved hand and put it in the evidence bag. "Lil?"

"Excuse me, Mary," Lil said as she rose and walked over to Dennis. "What is it?"

"Look at this," Dennis said, as he lifted a small chunk of a green and brown rock. It was about three inches long and only a half-inch wide and a half inch thick. It was covered in dirt and the ends were uneven. One side of it was black.

"Is that glass?" Lil asked, amazed, and took it from him, feeling the weight of it in her hands.

"I believe it is. Do you know how hot it has to get to turn sand into glass?"

"About 3000 degrees Fahrenheit," Lil answered.

"Well, it's cool to the touch," Dennis said and slipped it into the evidence bag.

Lil reached into her pocket and extracted the rock she was carrying. She opened the cloth and they both looked at the black stone.

"That's the rock that became hot?" Dennis asked.

"Yes, and I just realized it became hot when that other portal opened."

Dennis looked at the reflective surface. "Where did you get it?"

"It was something my grandmother gave me. She said she found it in the woods near my parent's house."

Dennis held up the evidence bag with its contents next to the stone on the open cloth. "Looks similar, except yours is darker and polished." Dennis sealed the bag. "Maybe we shouldn't be touching it."

Lil spoke quietly as she glanced back at Mary and the dog. "Those marks on the dog. Could that have been done by that thing we saw?"

Dennis glanced back at Mary Campbell who was patting the dog's head. "Yeah, it's possible. You think it was a different one, don't you?"

Lil nodded. "Species, as in *multiple* creatures. The burnt soil, the fused glass; I think this was another portal. If so, one of those creatures…came out and…took him through it…"

Dennis sighed. "It would explain why the dog stayed here and wouldn't leave."

"Could the dog have tried to protect him? It would explain how he got hurt."

"Shh!" Dennis said as Mary approached, the dog in tow.

"What are you looking for?" Mary said looking at the evidence bag in Dennis' hand. "Is my father buried here or something?"

Dennis stood. "No, ma'am, we're just collecting evidence."

She peered at the bag, becoming visibly upset. "Is that bone? Is it my father's? Did a bear eat my dad?"

"It's glass, Mary," Lil reassured.

"Glass?" This made Mary calm down, but she looked at the evidence bag in confusion. "How could you get glass here in the Barrens?"

Dennis smiled. "That's why we're collecting it, Mary. I think our best approach is to search the area."

"I can't walk much," Mary complained. "I got the diabetes."

Lil spoke up. "First we'll help you get Hammer to your car. The best thing you can do is get him to the vet."

"Well, there needs to be more than just you two," Mary insisted. "For God's sake, if a bear has my father, you need to get state troopers or a search party, or something."

Dennis shook his head. "Mary, it may take hours to form a search party. I think if you talk to Officer Bowman, he can call my captain. In the meantime, Ms. Slavik and I will search for your father."

Mary still looked unhappy. "If I was healthier, I would stay."

"I have no doubt, Mary," Lil reassured her.

"But, you two *will* look, right?"

"We'll search this area right now to see if we have any luck before more people trample the scene," Dennis acknowledged.

Mary had a harsh look on her face that softened, and her lower lip began to tremble. "You think he's dead, don't you?"

"No, ma'am," Lil reassured. "But we think it could go better without the dog to distract us."

Just then, Hammer pulled at his leash which yanked Mary Campbell after him as he headed back to the clearing.

"Strong dog," Lil said, then she knelt. "Here, Hammer. Come on, boy."

The dog turned and brought the hapless Mrs. Campbell along with him.

"Why don't you let me do that?" Lil said and took the leash. "Come on, Hammer."

The dog took a mournful look behind him, and then trotted with Lil along the path.

Dennis walked next to Mary Campbell, escorting her out.

"It's the legs I have the trouble with," Mary complained. "The doctor said I need to give up smoking—"

They were soon at the road, and once Mary unlocked her Toyota, Lil got Hammer into it as Dennis persuaded Mary to call her vet. Jamarr came over and all of them spoke about contacting the State Police.

Mary's vet told her that she should bring the dog right in. So, still unhappy, but at least under control, Mary drove away to have Hammer examined.

Dennis, Lil, and Jamarr watched the car pull away.

"I'm glad you guys came out," Jamarr said. "I'm one of two people on duty, and I got another call, I gotta go."

"We'll go back into the woods, see what we can find," Dennis offered.

Jamarr shook his head. "The state ain't sending anyone for hours."

"Could they do a Silver Alert?" Dennis asked, naming the program designed to help find missing seniors.

"He didn't suffer from dementia or Alzheimer's," Jamarr fretted. "Hell, the old guy was still legally able to drive."

Lil smiled. "We'll keep looking."

"What if you find the geezer?" Jamarr asked.

"I have my police radio in my truck," Dennis replied.

"Okay, that will help."

"If you could write up the initial report and have the captain contact the State Police," Dennis suggested.

"I got that," Jamarr said, and got into the police cruiser and drove off.

Dennis looked at Lil. "Alone at last."

She looked up into his eyes, and saw the passion that rested there, and her breath caught. She turned away, afraid of being lost there when there was work to do. "I'm getting my gun."

Dennis walked to his truck, opened the door, and folded Lil's seat over. "I'll bring the rifle. I promise I won't be surprised this time."

"Do you have a first aid kit?" Lil asked.

"I do. Should I bring it?" Dennis reached in and pulled the backpack he'd used on their other hike. "I mean, if that old guy got sucked into a portal…"

"You should bring it," she said, now trying to avoid eye contact. "Maybe he only fell into a bog."

Dennis nodded as he slipped the bag over his shoulders.

Lil set her jaw and grabbed the lock box. She pulled out the gun and opened the cylinder to reload it. She tried to understand her reaction to her weapon earlier.

Because the last time you loaded it before today, you wanted to blow your own brains out.

Lil slipped the pistol into her waist pack, hoping Dennis couldn't tell how difficult this was for her. "Do you go to many scenes in your civvies?"

Dennis shrugged. "Furnace Run is a small town, and when an emergency happens, we have to be able to move in and help."

"If he did go through a portal, I don't think we'll have much luck finding him."

"But at least we're prepared this time, if we have any visitors," Dennis said, checking his rifle. "Let's go."

They headed back into the woods, both of them on high alert.

This time they knew what they might be facing, and just how dangerous these woods had become.

ELEVEN

A Rescue From Hell

L il and Dennis returned to the spot where the dog had been frantically running and the scorch mark on the ground was obvious.

They walked around the clearing.

"Should we call out his name?" Lil wondered.

"Couldn't hurt," Dennis said and looked at his phone. "According to what the chief sent me, his name is Ernest Fowler."

"Mister Fowler?" Lil yelled out, doubting there would be a response.

"So, do you think one of the Devils got him?"

Lil sighed. "It's the most likely scenario. The dog was injured, probably helping the guy. If there was a portal in that spot, I guess he could have been grabbed and pulled through it."

"So, that's your explanation for the missing persons? They all got sucked into portals?"

Lil looked down at the burn mark. "I'll ask the logical question. What would have happened to us if the thing we saw got us?"

"Both of us?"

Lil shrugged. "Yeah, both of us."

"It appeared to be on its way to that portal. I guess it could have taken us with it."

"That would be my guess. Now think about that Drake guy with the abandoned car. Why did he leave the car out there in the Barrens, with the door open? Where did he go? If he was carried off, it explains everything."

"I'm just trying to get my head around any of this," Dennis said, as he double-checked his weapon nervously.

"Let's add to the weirdness," Lil suggested. "At the other portal, my grandmother's rock got hot."

"Yeah, I saw you pull it out of your pocket. Do you think it has something to do with this?"

"My grandmother said that it's the key."

"I thought your grandmother was dead?"

"She's been appearing in my dreams lately," Lil remarked. "Along with some other scary stuff."

"Let me see the rock again."

Lil fumbled through her pocket and pulled out the cloth with the stone in it.

Dennis drew close as Lil unfolded the cloth, and the stone reflected the light in its dark polished surface.

Lil smiled, and slid the stone into her hand. It felt smooth and cool, and she rubbed it gently. "I always liked this. She gave it to me when I was just a kid and I—"

"Shh," Dennis said and lifted his hand as a signal. "Do you hear that?"

"Hear what?"

"Listen!"

Lil turned her head, trying to catch the sound. It was that odd mixture of an electric hum with a tinkling sound.

"Where's it coming from?" Lil asked.

"Right there." Dennis pointed at the space between the trees with the burn mark. "Isn't that the noise we heard last time?"

Lil looked at the rock on top of her hand. It seemed to be glowing. Lil returned it to the cloth, bent and put the cloth on the ground. She stepped back and pulled her pistol from the waist pack. Dennis was by her side and had his rifle in both hands.

The sound grew louder.

Dennis spoke first. "If something comes through, are you going to shoot it?"

"If we want to convince anyone that the Jersey Devil is real it would come in handy to have a corpse."

The hum grew louder and a beam of light slashed into the forest, as if sunlight had just broken through the trees. Since it was late in the afternoon, the sun was at the wrong angle to produce it.

"If that *is* a portal," Lil worried. "Which side of it should we be on?"

"I'll go to the far side, you stay here," Dennis ordered.

With a nod, Lil moved into position, as Dennis made a circle around the trees.

There was now a ball of light in the center of the beam that was slowly growing larger.

They both moved across from each other, the ball of light between them. Lil countered Dennis as she angled her position to face it. If one of them were to fire they wouldn't accidentally hit each other.

Dennis had the rifle up on his shoulder and was looking down the barrel, one hand on the stock, a finger outside the trigger guard, and the other hand on the fore-stock with the butt in the hollow of his shoulder.

Lil held her handgun pointed to the sky, as it would be easy to lower her arms and fire if one of the monsters came through. She glanced over at the obsidian stone on the ground and it appeared to be glowing brighter, or was that a reflection of the growing portal?

The hum grew louder as the ball of light expanded and flattened to create another oval floating with no visible means of support.

"How is that created?" Dennis yelled over the sound issuing from the circle.

"I don't know," she shouted back.

Both of them focused on the circle, though the light had grown in brilliance to almost blinding. Lil could see a line of sweat trickle down Dennis' nose, and could feel her own underarms grow damp. If one or more of those things came out of that oval, they had to take the creature down quickly.

The monster they'd faced in the woods near Batsto Village had taken two shots from her handgun and kept going. Lil was worried about just how much firepower would be needed to take out these creatures.

The oval was now fully formed and Lil squinted to keep focus on the light in the middle of it. The oval shimmered a bit and an arm came through.

A *human* arm.

The hand was calloused and gnarled: an old man's hand.

"Dennis!" Lil yelled. "This side."

Dennis came quickly around the tree with the gun up. Lil put on the safety with her thumb and shoved the pistol into her waist pack to grab the offered hand and pull on it.

There was resistance, but out of the oval of light came a head and a pair of shoulders.

The hair on the man's head was white, and she could see that the coat was darkened with blood on one shoulder. The old man pleaded, "Help me."

Lil pulled as more of the man's body appeared. He floated horizontal to the ground as Lil strained but couldn't get him through.

Something was pulling back.

Dennis dropped the rifle and grabbed the man's other hand. Lil let go as Dennis took both of the man's hands. Dennis yanked, using all his weight, Lil grabbed the rifle from the ground and shoved the muzzle into the light. The barrel of the rifle disappeared into the oval. She lifted the gun to make sure it wasn't pointed at the old man and pulled the trigger.

The rifle made a loud report, just as Dennis gave one final pull, and the older man flew out of the portal, landing on top of Dennis and sending the pair of them falling to the ground.

One of the old man's pant legs was shredded, and blood gushed from several bad wounds.

She returned her attention to the portal just as a monstrous arm reached out, clutching for its lost prize. She jumped back so as not to be caught by the intruder. The long arm was covered with a brown shaggy fur and had a three-finger talon for a hand. Blood dripped off the claws that had caused the damage to the old man's leg. The arm was thinner than the devil she and Dennis had faced, and much longer as it groped blindly about in the air.

Lil stepped to the side and fired several shots directly into the meat of the arm.

There was a hideous growling shriek and the disembodied arm retreated into the safety of wherever it came from. Lil moved forward and fired into the glowing space again.

"Dennis, cover the stone," Lil yelled.

Dennis had moved Ernest Fowler to the ground and was frantically pulling the back-pack off to get the first-aid kit. He glanced at the rock, where the dark stone was illuminated with an otherworldly light.

He quickly moved over and used the cloth to cover the stone completely.

Lil stood with the rifle ready, waiting for another attack. But instead, the oval shrank.

Dennis got the first aid kit open and began to use a pair of scissors to cut away the pants leg.

"You have to stop it," the old man muttered. "Get me out."

Dennis was pulling on a pair of black nitrile gloves from the kit. "We did, sir."

The oval had now reduced itself to a mere ball of light, and Lil stepped away from the vanishing portal, knelt, and spoke to Ernest. "Do you know where you were, sir?"

He glared at her with a crazed look in his eyes. "I was in Hell," he croaked. "There were monsters." Then he rested his head back and closed his eyes.

"Do you have clotting bandages?" Lil asked Dennis.

"Not a lot of them. Do you think that's a wise choice on the legs?"

"No, for his shoulders. There are wounds on his shoulders."

"Okay, for the leg, I might have to use a tourniquet. Then I'll use the pads on the shoulders. Can you call 9-1-1?"

Lil pulled her phone from her waist pack. "I can't, I don't have a signal."

"Go to the truck and use the police band radio."

"Shouldn't you do that?"

"I've had emergency trauma training. Have you?"

"Not as extensive as that."

"Then you go."

"You probably saved his life," the EMT told Dennis and Lil as they loaded Ernest into the ambulance.

"We're just glad we located him before he bled out," Dennis said.

"It'll be touch and go, but we'll take him to the Atlanticare Facility in Hammonton."

When the ambulance arrived, Lil led the EMTs back into the woods, and they brought a bright yellow "Scoop Stretcher" to pick up the old man. Lil brought out Dennis' rifle and backpack, making sure to retrieve the obsidian stone when she did.

"I'll call it in," Dennis confirmed, taking the rifle from Lil. "I'll make sure the family knows where to find him."

"Good job, officers," the man said as he headed to the driver's door.

Lil gave a small smile. It was nice that the EMT thought that she was an off-duty officer as well. She had missed it.

Dennis and Lil watched the ambulance drive off, the siren loud and clear as it pulled away.

Dennis looked at Lil. "I'd better get you back to your car."

Once the rifle and backpack were stowed, Dennis quickly called the dispatcher and reported that the Missing Person was secured and being taken to the hospital.

They sat inside the vehicle, both of them staring out the windshield.

"You did well out there," Dennis finally said. "I wouldn't have thought of shooting into the oval like you did."

"I figured it was the only way to make whatever was holding him let go. But it's a good thing you were there. I wasn't strong enough to pull him out."

Dennis frowned. "But that was odd—"

This made Lil chuckle. "You found only *one* thing odd?"

"No, what was strange was that after we rescued him, while you were calling for the ambulance, he told me 'it was good we were nearby.'"

"Nearby?" Lil repeated. "What made him think that?"

"He told me he'd only been 'in Hell' for a minute or two, before the circle of light appeared and we pulled him out. It makes sense, if the monster's arm is any indication, that thing could have torn him apart in minutes."

Lil considered this. "Dennis, he disappeared hours ago."

"I know, that's why its odd," Dennis said as he backed the truck onto the road and they drove away.

Back in the cottage at her parent's farm, Lil took a shower, heated another sad frozen dinner, and spent the evening searching for old Native American legends about the Pine Barrens on the internet and placing more pins on her map.

She also made sure to lay out the cloth and uncover the stone. It was cool to the touch again and didn't have that strange glow anymore. She was trying to understand why it grew warm and what it had to do with the two portals she'd seen that day.

She also tried to find the man named 'Ag-well' as the proprietor of trinkets at Batsto Village had called him. Despite multiple attempts at different spellings, including with the name 'Max,' she had no luck.

Finally, she lay down in bed and reread the book she had purchased about the Jersey Devil. About halfway through, her eyelids became heavy and she finally had to shut off the light and go to sleep.

Deep in dreams, she was in the kitchen with her grandmother again. However, this time, instead of being the tiny child, she was fully grown and sitting at the table with a cup in front of her.

It was an old teacup on a saucer, one she had seen her grandmother drink from every day when she visited. She lifted it, but there was no liquid in it, only the leaves in the bottom, forming patterns.

"Tell me what you see," Natalia said from the other side of the table.

Lil jumped and looked across. Her grandmother sat there, looking as she did when Lil was only eight. She hadn't been there a moment earlier.

"I—I don't know how," Lil explained. "You never taught me."

Natalia made a dismissive gesture. She didn't look frightening as in some of the previous dreams, but as her natural self, with her dark curly hair going to gray, and wearing a long mumu to cover her full figure.

"That is because you think too much, here." She pointed to her head as she spoke with her thick accent. "You must look at it from here." Her finger moved to her chest between her ample bosoms.

Lil shook her head. "I can't, *Mami*. I don't have the gifts you possess."

"Bah," her grandmother spat. "There is your head talking again. You use the tarot cards—"

"Those are easier, the meanings are explained in books."

"That is your other problem, too many books," Natalia complained. "Look in the cup, tell me what you see."

"Wet leaves," Lil grumbled.

Natalia slapped the table with her open palm, which made Lil jump again.

"Look carefully at the shapes and the figures made by the leaves. Turn the cup to look from different angles until the symbols become clear." She watched Lil hesitate. "Do it!"

Lil exhaled loudly and turned the cup in her hands. As she did, she could see patterns that resembled things. One of the collections of leaves seemed almost like a dark silhouette of the monster she faced.

"There is a creature," Lil said with fear in her voice, her eyes focused on the cup. "One that I have seen."

"You are drawn to it, are you not?"

"Am I?" Lil said, and glanced up at her grandmother, then returned her eyes to the cup. "It looks like there are bugs."

"Bugs?" Natalia queried. "What kind of bugs?"

Lil shrugged. This whole thing seemed ridiculous to her. "I don't know, ants, I guess."

"A bad omen."

"Something that looks like an arch—or I don't know—the letter 'u' I guess, but it's kind of blurry."

"An unsuccessful trip."

"I think this visit is an unsuccessful trip," Lil muttered.

"Go on," her grandmother demanded.

"One that looks like a cloud," Lil said, turning the cup in her hand.

"That means trouble."

"The male symbol, y'know the circle with the arrow coming off it."

"A man," Natalia explained. "You are working with a man, are you not?"

"Yeah, and a heart, that's all I see."

"Is it near the man?"

Lil looked in the cup again. "Pretty near, I guess."

"Then, you will be lovers."

Lil considered this. "I don't know. I'm not sure."

But now across the table was Dennis Decatur. He was not in uniform but dressed as he had been on their outing the previous day.

He smiled and said, "Why not?"

"Because I can't trust you," Lil admitted. "You cheated on me. I can't get over the feeling that you'll do that again."

She looked up, but it was no longer Dennis across from her. It was another man with brown skin and straight black hair brushed away from his face. There was a pair of horn-rimmed glasses on his nose.

"Perhaps you need to meet someone else," he said, in perfect English with a slight East Indian accent.

She frowned, taken aback. "Who are you?"

"You will know soon enough," he said and rose from the table. He turned and headed for the door.

"Can you tell me your name?"

He reached the door and took the knob in his hand. "It's Max. And we will see each other soon."

He pulled open the door. One of the monstrous creatures stood just beyond the doorway. It was seven feet tall with talons on its hands, the long neck and the face like a horse, yet the mouth was so much longer, more resembling that of an alligator. It gave that unholy scream and grabbed the man by the shoulders with its talons. The dark man cried out in pain.

Huge wings unfolded on its back, and the creature leapt into the air, the man held in its grip.

Lil ran to the door.

The doorway faced the downtown of Furnace Run, as if the house had moved magically to face Main Street. There was a huge red moon overhead that painted the sky a dark scarlet. She could see numerous creatures flying in the air, their huge bat wings extended and flapping, so numerous the red sky was darkened with them. And each one held a struggling person: men, women, even children. All of them dangled in the air, impaled by the clawed hands.

She wanted to run out to the street, help anyone she could, but one of the monsters landed beside her. She looked at the oddly shaped head and body covered in long brown fur. The creature sunk its unholy talons into the flesh of her shoulders as it gave its piercing cry.

Lil screamed as she sat up in bed. She grabbed the covers and pulled them tight against herself. Her shoulders ached as if she'd actually been impaled.

She lay there shivering, knowing that sleep would not return.

TWELVE

An Expert

The digital clock read 5:00 AM, but Lil got up and went into the bathroom to open the prescription bottle and spill out a single *Paxil* tablet, which she immediately took.

She pulled on her robe and got the coffee brewing. Another dream that started with Grandma Natalia but had turned frightening and even stranger than any of the others. The image of the winged monsters carrying off people gave her pause, as if they had emptied the entire town.

Something flashed in her memory.

"An entire town," she said aloud, her own voice shocked her.

A town of people disappeared in the Pine Barrens. Poppa told me about it.

She suddenly had an overwhelming desire to know more and went directly to her laptop to search for Pines Edge.

This brought up several sites that told the tale of the vanished town.

The basic history was this: John Decatur went to North Jersey to work in the fall of 1908. When he returned in late January 1909, the town was empty. It appeared that the residents had left in a hurry but took none of their possessions. He pursued the local authorities, who investigated. They could find no sign of where any of the inhabitants had gone. Over three hundred people had vanished at that time and the only clues were a single gun that had been recently fired, and a message scrawled in chalk on a school blackboard that read:

There is no salvation.

There was conjecture that blamed the situation on everything from secret government experiments to cultists, and one site that theorized it was due to an electrical experiment by Nikola Tesla.

Another site claimed that other towns had reported a vast fire near the location which brightened the night sky red and orange and extended high into the air. Yet, despite the Pine Barrens propensity for forest fires, the location of this fire or any damage caused by it could not be found. This led to the speculation that the cold weather had created an effect reminiscent of the Aurora Borealis, and the residents of Pines Edge had run off in fear and been lost in the bogs of the Pine Barrens.

Lil grabbed her copy of *The Jersey Devil,* as something clicked in her mind.

The middle part of the book was dedicated to January of 1909, when repeated visits of the Devil had appeared in multiple locations in New Jersey and Pennsylvania, often many miles away from each other. It was at about the same time frame as the disappearance of the residents of Pines Edge.

Since this was 2019, that was exactly 110 years ago.

Could something have happened 110 years before Pines Edge's odd circumstances?

Lil wondered where this odd idea came from, but she wanted to see if there might be a correlation. She began another search online for historic references to 1799. She was lucky enough to stumble on the full text of "South Jersey, A History 1640-1930."

It was a huge book, even online, and she made her way through page after page until she reached events in the year 1799.

On one page was a letter that amazed her. It was written by a congressman in the Sixth Congress, one James Schureman. He had a meeting in Monmouth County and was on his way back to Philadelphia by horse and carriage. This letter the Congressman Schureman wrote to his host had been added to the book almost as an afterthought:

"My dear Sir;

"It was a great honor to work together once again, our very long intimacy as fellow-labourers in the same cause. However, a most upsetting occurrence happened as I made my way to Philadelphia from the East Jersey shores. Since my journey was several days in length, I stopped at an inn just outside of the Pine Barrens. I was most distressed that night to see a red light in the sky at a distance and what calumny it bore. This made me concerned there might be a fire within the Barrens that might block my passage the next day when it was most advantageous. I went forth to the innkeeper, and queried him of it, to which he spake, 'That not be no fire, sir. It be the devil out tonight.' I was surprised at the man, for I have oft heard tales of a 'Jersey Devil' but paid them little heed."

"When I continued my journey the next day, the sky was quite clear, and I could sense no smoke. I headed for an inn I knew in a town known as 'Apple Hill.' I had planned to take the midday meal there, but found that the entire town had been deserted. The inn was where it should be and I went forth calling and yelling all about, but there was no reply. Needless to say, I hastened my journey to be far from those strange forests, and I made it to an inn further west by nightfall."

"I alerted authorities upon my return to Philadelphia, but it would appear that no one knows what had occurred, or what did cause the strange lights I had witnessed in the sky."

Lil observed that there was a footnote from the editor that explained that the town of Apple Hill was a famed ghost town in New Jersey and that only "Apple Pie Hill" remained of what had once been a popular summer location.

Lil read the letter a second time. It was so eerily familiar to the Pines Edge story, and the strange fact that it was one hundred-ten years before that famed disappearance. Was it possible that there could be *another* event the same time span before that?

That would be 1689.

That date seemed familiar and she grabbed her notes. She found what she was looking for in her own notes taken from the site that was critical of the Jersey Devil legend. In the history, the skeptics had researched Daniel Leeds, the so called "father" of the Jersey Devil, who lived in Leeds Point publishing his almanac.

Another search with his name and the word "almanac" led to the Princeton Library online database. They had issues of the almanac from the 1600s that had been digitized and put online.

Lil was surprised by this good fortune, but another part of her worried that she somehow was being led to this research.

With a cup of coffee in hand, she sat down to go through the listed almanac entries, until she found a tale that chilled her.

In the fall of 1689, Leeds wrote of a "massacre" that had occurred in nearby Harrisville that year. Women had assembled to assist with the birth of a child, and there was an attack upon them by "Savage Indians." Leeds went on to say how shocked the residents had been, as the nearby Unami tribe was always one of peace.

She went looking for other sources and found one under the title: "The 1689 Harrisville Massacre and the Unami War" written by Doctor Makhesh Aggarwal.

She paused and read the name again.

Could this be the 'Max Ag-well' the man at Batsto Village had mentioned? She went to the bottom of the article and studied the information about the author. There was a photograph of the man, and Lil froze.

It was the dark-skinned man from her dream.

"This is some really weird shit," Lil said aloud.

The biography listed that he was originally from Bombay, India, and suddenly Lil knew why the Native American seller laughed when he said that 'Ag-well' was truly an Indian; he was from India!

She read on and the biography listed an impressive set of credentials, including Cambridge University in England, among others. He was currently a lecturer in Anthropology at Princeton University and Garden State University.

She didn't know what a "lecturer" was compared to a "professor", but first she wanted to read his article.

It read like a ghost story. One strange night, witnesses claimed there had been "red lights in the sky." A woman was giving birth assisted by three friends, when screams rang out throughout the town. Men, overhearing the noise, gathered as a group to protect the women. What they found in that house made them ill. The women and the newborn had been torn apart as if by a wild animal.

Although the men wanted to run into the Barrens and attack the "Savages" that did the deed, cooler heads prevailed.

The next morning, the men of Harrisville, armed with pitchforks, swords, and guns stormed the village of the Unami tribe, bent on revenge.

The Native American village was deserted.

Believing that the natives had fled to avoid their wrath, the group headed further north to the Yocomanshag village, only to find that it was also abandoned.

"According to the writings of the day," Doctor Aggarwal wrote, "the Unami were wiped out by the more aggressive Yocomanshag, who, when they were celebrating their victory, were attacked and killed by the neighboring Amacaronck, who long wanted their lands. This theory is the accepted idea but does not explain the fact that despite many ancient Native American burial sites in the area, the colonists found no bodies. Also, the village's weapons and valuables had been left by the invaders. This truly is one of the oldest mysteries in the lore of New Jersey."

Lil sat back in the chair, her head spinning.

She had uncovered evidence that every one hundred and ten years there were red lights in the sky and a village would be emptied. She was surprised she had been able to go back as far as she did. An attempt to find earlier documentation led to the fact that written records did not exist before the English took over the land in the 1600s.

She pulled up the Garden State University website and searched for Doctor Aggarwal. It included a biography that noted he was an expert in the Lenape language and listed an email address.

She quickly composed an email:

Dear Doctor Aggarwal,

My name is Lil Slavik and I am investigating some odd disappearances in the Pine Barrens. I believe it may have to do with some local legends. I would be interested in talking to you about the Lenni-Lenape tribes in the area and any insights you might have.

Thanks,

Lil Slavik.

She added her phone number to the bottom of the email, and then looked it over. She wished she could add "Detective" or even "Investigator," but at this point she had to admit she was neither. She was just a local girl trying to understand what was happening, and where the monster she'd seen the previous day came from.

Her phone rang and Lil jumped.

It was Dennis.

"Hello?"

"Hey, sleepyhead, you awake?"

She glanced at the time on her computer and saw it was past nine.

"Yeah," she sighed. "I've been up since five."

"Well, I'm about to go on duty. I wanted to check on you."

"How is that man we rescued?"

"Ernest Fowler. He's still unconscious."

"I may have tracked down the mysterious Max."

"Really?"

Lil sipped her coffee, but it was cold. "Turns out he's a college professor, or lecturer or something. I sent him an email. Did you know that there are towns in the Pine Barrens that have mysterious disappearances every one-hundred-and-ten years?"

Dennis chuckled. "Lil, there have been dozens of small towns that disappeared in the Barrens: Ongs Hat, Double Trouble, Sooy

Place. The only thing we have to remember them are parks or roads that have their name."

"I'm talking about towns where the residents all disappeared, like Pines Edge."

"Really? You think it has something to do with that thing we faced yesterday?"

"I think it has *everything* to do with that."

Dennis was silent for a moment. "Lil the reason I'm calling is that I want you to know that in my report I'm claiming that it appears Mister Fowler was attacked by a bear."

"Dennis, you know that isn't true!"

"What do you want me to say? That we pulled him out of an oval of light, away from something that reached out and grabbed him? Come on, Lil, they'll have me committed to the Trenton Psychiatric Hospital."

"But we have to warn people—"

"I agree," Dennis interrupted. "I'll tell the captain that I believe there is a wild bear on the loose, and that people should avoid isolated areas, especially at night."

"What if this is bigger than a few hunters lost to these creatures?"

"What do you mean?"

"I just told you that there is a repeated pattern every one-hundred-and-ten years. What if an army of those creatures attack Furnace Run?"

"What? That's crazy."

"Is it? Yesterday you thought the idea of the Jersey Devil was crazy."

There was a pause as Dennis thought about this. "You might have a point. However, if we can warn people away in the meantime—"

"It won't help. Dennis, we need to be prepared to fight these things."

"Tell you what, I'll come by after work and we'll talk. You can show me what you've uncovered. In the meantime, I'm on duty, I gotta go."

He ended the call without another word. She looked at the phone and sighed. She didn't know what she expected. Of course Dennis couldn't run to his captain and yell, "I saw the Jersey Devil and he's real! We have to evacuate the Pine Barrens!"

He would lose his job faster than she'd lost hers.

Lil went to her bedroom and threw on clothes. She would work with her father with the alpacas and try to think, try to come up with a way she could help.

Was this the reason she'd been having dream visits from her grandmother? Was the cycle coming around again and the possibility of another town, *her* town, being emptied by an attacking force of monsters a real threat?

As she dressed, she considered that maybe Dennis was on the right path. A dangerous animal would scare people away, and the ones that remained would probably arm themselves. But how many people would just freeze up when faced with a nightmare like they had seen? Most of the hunters in these woods knew how to use a rifle, but would they react fast enough if confronted with an actual monster?

She pulled on her shoes as her phone rang. The screen read "unknown number," but she answered it.

"Hello?"

"Ms. Slavik?"

"Yes, who's this?"

"This is Doctor Max Aggarwal. You emailed me this morning?"

"Yes! Thank you for getting back to me so quickly."

"No problem. You are investigating disappearances. Are you with the police?"

"No. I mean, I was an NYPD detective, but now I'm looking into it as a private citizen. A gentleman at Batsto Village mentioned your name, and I read your history about the tribes that disappeared."

"I see. How does the Lenni-Lenape stories help with such an investigation?"

She could imagine the man talking to her, as he seemed so real in her dream. "I may have found a correlation between the tribe's disappearance and other towns that have disappeared in the Pine Barrens." Lil let out her breath as if she'd been holding it. "The man I met yesterday sold me a pin of a *Piasa* bird. He told me the Barrens was once called 'the place of the dragon' by the tribes that lived there."

"There have been many reports of ancient birds that were mistaken for monsters. The Sandhill Crane, which used to be indigenous to the area, had an odd call, and during mating they can be—"

"I saw one," Lil interrupted. How could she be so bold? This guy was probably going to hang up on her.

"*Saw* one?" he repeated.

"A...creature," Lil blurted. "Yesterday, in the forest. I...shot it."

"You shot *what* exactly?"

"Something that looked like the *Piasa* bird, except it had brown fur all over it."

There was a long silence on the other end of the phone.

"Hello?" she finally said.

"Ms. Slavik, it is very amusing that you reached out to me, but I have no time for practical jokes and little interest in Jersey Devil junkies—"

"Doctor, I am not some teenager trying to pull your leg. I would like to meet with you and find out what you know about the Lenni-Lenape legends, to see if those legends can somehow make sense of what I saw."

The doctor inhaled deeply. "Meet with me? And where would you like to do this?"

"Wherever is convenient to you. Doctor, I'm serious. There are hundreds of missing persons in the Pine Barrens over the last year. It may be leading up to something… terrible."

There was another long silence, but Lil didn't interrupt it this time.

The man sighed. "I've been doing research at Rowan College in Mount Laurel. If you could come out here? I would be willing to meet with you for lunch."

"That would be wonderful, Doctor."

"I will meet you at the Ruby Tuesdays off Route 38 at noon. If you are not there by noon, I shall leave and consider this entire conversation suspect."

"Very well," Lil replied, feeling chastened.

"See you then," he said and ended the call.

Lil looked at her phone. The trip would be about forty minutes, so she didn't have to leave until after 11:00. She still had time to help her father, but she had one thing to do first.

She pulled out her lock box and took a few minutes to check her handgun. Once that was done, she placed the box under the passenger seat in her car with the waist pack where she stowed the cloth-wrapped obsidian stone. She wasn't sure why she packed it, but since it grew hot each time a portal opened, it must have something to do with it.

After all, her grandmother told her it was "the key."

But the key to what exactly?

She joined her father in the barn wanting to feed the alpacas and do some grunt work to clear her mind.

"You must understand my concerns," Doctor Aggarwal told Lil a few hours later. She sat in the restaurant, the brown woodwork and green vinyl seats gave the place a relaxed atmosphere, despite the tension Lil felt in her shoulders.

When Lil saw the man, she was a bit surprised that he was exactly the same height as her. In the dream, he'd seemed taller. She also felt his thin frame and studious glasses made him far more attractive than in his quick appearance in her dream.

"Since I wrote that article, based on much research, I have had many people get in touch with me," Aggarwal went on. "All of them think the 'Jersey Devil' was responsible for the death of the women and that the devil was the child born that night. Most of them go on and on about conspiracies and cover-ups."

"I assume many of them were teenagers?" Lil asked. She had taken the time after working the barn to get cleaned up and dressed in denim pants and a simple blouse with a jacket. The ride had been pleasant, the day warm and sunny, and it was hard to believe in impending danger on such a nice day.

"You'll understand that I did some research on you," Aggarwal told her.

Lil lowered her head. "I'm sure you did, and I can completely understand such a choice." She raised her head and stared at him. "But, Doctor, I'm not crazy."

"From what I read, it was suggested that you had a nervous breakdown after that incident. How many died?"

Lil took a moment to answer, thankful she had taken the *Paxil* that morning. "Ten. Including my fiancé and his partner."

Aggarwal nodded his head thoughtfully. "Are you taking anything?"

"*Paxil.*"

"There have been reports of hallucinations—"

"I wasn't alone when I saw it," Lil snapped. "Look, I am not some conspiracy theorist or some wide-eyed kid. I'm a cop. I may have been through a rough time, but I know what I saw. I need to know if there is any information that could help me."

"Such as?" Aggarwal grinned.

"Please don't mock me."

They were both silent as the waitress came by and placed their meals in front of them.

"I don't mean to make fun," Aggarwal conceded. "But put yourself in my shoes. What would you do if someone told you such a story? You *saw* the Jersey Devil? You *shot* it?"

"I shot one of them."

This got his attention. "*One* of them?"

Lil stabbed a piece of lettuce in the salad she had ordered with her hamburger. "From my research, I am operating on the theory that the so-called Devil isn't one creature, but a species. A species that comes from…from…" For a moment she was stumped and then the words the vanishing Brian Kent said jumped to mind. "From a hidden place."

Aggarwal gazed at Lil, and popped a French fry into his mouth, chewing thoughtfully. "A species, you say?"

"Yes, like the *Piasa* bird. There are legends of such a creature in the Midwest."

"I am quite familiar with the tales," Aggarwal said.

"I was not, until I saw this." She indicated the pin of the creature she wore on her jacket. "When I saw this, I realized how similar this creature was to the legends of the Jersey Devil."

"The *Piasa* bird, known as the bird that devours men. In legend it is said that such a creature could easily carry off a full-grown deer in its talons." Aggarwal nodded thoughtfully. "I never really thought to compare it to the Jersey Devil legends, but I must admit that I can see the correlation."

"Perhaps there is a basis for both of these legends."

Aggarwal looked thoughtful. "There are numerous mythical creatures in the native lore, changing from tribe to tribe. Would you have me believe in *Mehuwe*, a man-eating giant? Or the Underwater Panthers, which live in deep water and drown men and women?"

"I'm saying there seems to be a suggestion that there could be creatures, ancient ones, that somehow can move in and out of our reality."

"Look, Ms. Slavik—"

"Can you please just call me Lil? You might think I'm crazy, but we can at least be on a first-name basis."

"Fine, call me Max," he relented. "You think these Devils, or whatever you believe them to be, can move in and out of our reality? And go where, to this 'hidden place' you mentioned?"

"The creature I saw went into a circle of light which closed up behind it. That's why I couldn't bring it down. My argument would hold up a lot better if I could have brought a body to show you."

Max grinned again. "Be hard to fit it in your little car."

This made Lil chuckle in spite of herself. "Yeah, I guess it would."

Max ate more of his chicken sandwich, not speaking, and Lil took several bites of her burger. She was hungry, this was the first thing she had eaten today besides coffee.

Max went on, "There are many stories from different tribes that tell of spirit beings or heroes crossing the borders to the different realms for various reasons."

"What are the different realms?"

Max shrugged. "It varies from culture to culture and tribe to tribe. They all have legends, and so much of it has been lost."

"But what do you know about the Barrens—and the legends about it being the place of the dragon?"

"There is no such thing as a 'dragon' in Lenape lore, that is how the Swedish explorers translated it from the descriptions they received. They met members of the tribe and learned the Lenni-Lenape language as best they could."

"But those ancient people had seen something *similar* to a dragon: a long-necked creature with bat-wings?"

He nodded. "Yes, it could fit the description of either a dragon or *Piasa* bird. But you see, I'm an anthropologist, and the common accepted explanations for the dragon legends is the discovery of fossilized remains from the Jurassic period. Stories were told to explain the large skeletons."

"That makes sense."

"But no remains of a Jersey Devil or a *Piasa* bird have ever been found. Nor are there any remains of Sasquatches or hundreds of other mythical creatures."

"I want to ask you about the tribal disappearances you wrote about in that article."

"The point of the article was the rush to judgement that European settlers made upon the slaughter of—"

"I get it, but did you know about other times when entire towns vanished in the Barrens?"

Max sat back still grabbing French fries and eating them one at a time. "From what I understand, many towns have been abandoned in that part of New Jersey."

"I know, but I mean specific events. The town of Apple Hill in 1799? Then there was Pines Edge in 1909?"

"Is there a point to this?"

"Yes, both those towns the residents vanished, leaving their worldly goods behind."

Max frowned. "You believe this to be a pattern?"

"If we include the date of the tribes you wrote about, 1689, then these mysterious disappearances all happened one-hundred-ten years apart."

He considered this. "Really?"

"And the reports all spoke of a fire in the Pine Barrens that turned the sky red at night. Yet no fire damage could be found."

Max looked shocked, and Lil wondered if maybe she was getting through to him.

"Interesting," was all Max said, not meeting her eyes, but totally focused on his plate.

"Does that mean something?"

"Actually, it does. In researching my article, I located several historic documents not available to the public. I found the diary of a ship's captain, a privateer. He was anchored off the Absegami Islands the night in question. He spoke of a bright red light in the sky and he was, in his words, "grievously afeerd" that the Pine

Barrens were burning. I mentioned it briefly in the article, but I quite honestly thought nothing of it."

"In Apple Hill and Pines Edge all the residents disappeared leaving everything they owned behind. Just like the Native American tribes you wrote about."

Max munched thoughtfully. "Still that doesn't mean they were abducted by Jersey Devils, *Piasa* birds, or even space aliens."

"I know but—"

"It's an amusing theory," Max shrugged. "Now, if you had some proof—"

"You're suggesting I should trap one of these creatures?"

"I'd settle for one of these 'circles of light' you spoke of."

Lil paused. "Okay, how about I take you to one?"

Max eyed her suspiciously. "Seriously?"

"We located one of these portals not that far into the woods."

"How can I be sure you're not taking me on a wild goose chase, or for that matter, abducting me?"

This made Lil laugh. "Why? Are you worth a lot of money?"

"I guess not," he considered. Then he eyed her suspiciously. "What would this entail?"

Lil thought about it. "It's a forty-minute drive, and I could arrange for the other witness to meet us there."

"What's his story?"

"He's a police officer."

"Really?"

"I can give you the address or you can follow me. If you don't like what you see, you can leave."

He casually shook his head. "We'll do both. Quite honestly, my research is not going well, and I could use an afternoon off."

"Let me pay for your meal."

Lil smiled at him, pleased by his willingness to help, and was again amazed that he looked so familiar, so much like the image in her dream. She suppressed a shudder as she recalled how that dream had ended with his being carried off, screaming.

And now she was taking him to meet such a monster...

THIRTEEN

Witnesses

The drive out was uneventful and Lil called Dennis and asked him to meet them at the location.

"I don't know, Lil. Why did you tell this guy about— what we saw?" Dennis complained.

"He's the expert on Native American lore that the vendor at Batsto Village told us about. He wrote an article about a village disappearance in the 1600s."

"I don't see what that has to do with—"

"Just meet us, please. He thinks I'm a nut."

"Great, then he'll think we're both loony. What time will you get there?"

"About another half hour."

"I'll be there," Dennis said unhappily.

Lil sighed as she ended the call and hoped this wasn't a mistake.

Fortunately, the previous day she had made a note of the location where they'd found the old man and had put it in her phone. Mile after mile of the Barrens looked exactly the same, and once the old fellow's big car had been removed, finding the exact location by sight alone could prove challenging.

Once the GPS was programmed, even in the Pine Barrens when the signal dropped, it would guide her and the suspicious scholar to the correct location.

She pulled off the road a dozen feet from the pathway, arriving a few minutes ahead of Max. She quickly secured her pistol in her waist pack. The stone was still in the outer pocket, wrapped in the cloth.

Doctor Aggarwal pulled in behind her. At the same time, an official police car emblazoned with *Town of Furnace Run* pulled off the road across the street, having come from the opposite direction.

Dennis stepped out and joined them, looking totally official in his uniform.

Max got out of his car, seeming a little intimidated. Dennis had six inches on him, and obviously hit the gym a lot more than Max.

Max stepped over to Lil. "He really is a policeman?"

"Didn't I say that?" Lil replied.

Max shrugged. "I wasn't sure of anything. No offense."

Lil nodded. "He's the real thing."

"I'm Officer Dennis Decatur," Dennis said and offered his hand.

"Doctor Aggarwal, but it's probably easier if you call me Max," the scholar said and gave a limp handshake.

"Are you from India?" Dennis asked.

"Originally, yes."

"I thought you'd be, like, Native American."

Max gave that noncommittal shrug again. "I see the irony of an Indian studying Native American lore, but I find the legends and the language fascinating."

Dennis considered this. "You can speak Lenni-Lenape?"

"As well as anyone can, as a great deal of the culture has been lost," Aggarwal explained. "So, your last name is Decatur? As in Commodore Stephen Decatur?"

"He was a distant relative."

"According to the legends, didn't he have a run-in with the Jersey Devil as well?"

Dennis grinned. "I heard that tale over and over again growing up. The story goes that sometime in the first decade of the 1800s the commodore was testing cannon balls here in the Barrens. He saw a creature flying in the air. Since he had a loaded canon, he fired at it and struck the beast, but it just kept on flying."

Lil glared at Dennis, "You never told me that."

"It's an old family legend," Dennis explained. "I didn't see that it had anything to do with…all of this."

Max spoke up. "It is interesting that you, his relative, sees this Devil as well."

Dennis shook his head. "I'll be honest with you. I don't know what we saw yesterday, but it sure as hell looked like the monster out of those stories."

"I told him there's a portal nearby," Lil stated excitedly. "Come on, let's show him."

She started into the woods, the two men following.

Dennis spoke up. "Lil, we don't know if it will work again. It could have been a one-time thing."

Max had to walk quickly to keep up with Dennis' long strides. "This is where you saw the creature?"

"No, that was down near Batsto Village. Something came out of a portal here, however, it was different…"

"What did this portal look like?"

Dennis shrugged. "Like a circle of light. The ground under it was burned, scorched. We found pieces of glass there."

"Glass?" Max repeated. "Are you suggesting that the sand had been fused?"

"That's what we think."

The trio walked a few dozen feet into the woods and came to the small clearing where Lil and Dennis had rescued Ernest the previous day.

"There it is." Lil pointed. "That's the burn mark."

Max looked at the mark. He touched the ground, looking closely at the strange line of blackened earth.

Dennis walked over to Lil and spoke quietly. "Lil, can I ask why you chose to bring him out here?"

She glanced at Dennis. "I...just had a feeling."

Max called out. "This is where this portal of yours appeared?"

"Don't tell him we pulled a guy out of it, please," Dennis pleaded.

"Yes, right in that spot," Lil answered and approached Max. "It was shortly after the stone began to grow warm."

"The... stone?" Max puzzled.

She reached into the front of the waist pack and pulled out the cloth. She unfolded it to show the polished keepsake.

Max regarded the item. "Very pretty, but I don't see what it has to do with this." He wandered over and crouched at the burn mark. "It's hard to believe that this is anything more than a camper who thought he was being funny."

He dug around in the sandy ground, and pulled up a chunk of brown and green material. He stood holding it up to the light. "But you are correct, there is glass here, and it is similar to Trinitite."

Lil reached out and took the piece of fused rock in her free hand. "That's glass from where they did the atomic tests, right?"

"Yes," Max replied. "I've actually seen samples of it, though those are radioactive and you cannot touch them."

"Are you sure you should be touching that with your bare hands?" Dennis worried.

Max took it from Lil's hands and let if fall to the earth. "Perhaps a Geiger Counter would be a—"

A low hum filled the air, which stopped Max in mid-sentence.

"Look," Lil said and held out the polished black stone on the cloth. An otherworldly glow seemed to emanate from it.

"What on earth—" Max started, but Lil pulled him away with her free hand.

"We have to get back," Lil stated, and dragged Max towards Dennis. She placed the cloth on the ground as the stone continued to glow.

"What is that noise?" Max asked, looking around.

Lil moved to Dennis, who unholstered his weapon and drew it in a two-handed grip.

"Why are you doing that?" asked Max, alarmed that Dennis had pulled out a gun. His eyes grew very wide when Lil extracted her revolver out of her pack. "You *both* have guns? Who *are* you people?"

"We should back away," Dennis said, raising his voice to be heard over the steadily rising hum.

"Max, get behind us," Lil ordered.

Both Lil and Dennis, with their attention and their weapons focused on the location where the portal began to glow, stepped back slowly. Max moved behind them, intimidated by the weapons.

Before their eyes, a beam of light poured from above into the spot of seared ground as a ball of light appeared in the center.

"What *is* that?" Max demanded. "How are you doing that?"

"We're in the woods, Max," Dennis hollered. "What do you think we have? Lasers? Projectors?"

The ball of light was growing and flattening out as it had the previous times. Both Lil and Dennis had to squint, and Max held his hand in front of his eyes.

"This is impossible," Max yelled.

"Why do you think I wanted you to see it?" Lil shouted.

The circle of light had now grown to its full height and almost touched the ground at the bottom of the oval, where the nearby grass and leaves began to smolder. As it moved into a flat oval of light the brightness faded a bit.

Max lowered his hand. "Now what happens?"

"If it's like the other times," Dennis stated, "either something goes in—"

"—or something comes out," Lil added.

Both of them kept their guns pointed at the circle.

"Can I throw something at it?" Max said as he moved to the side a bit to see just how thick the oval was.

"You can, but it won't come out behind it."

"Where will it go?"

"We don't have a name," Dennis stated calmly.

Lil spoke up. "I've started to call it the hidden place."

"Indeed?" Max marveled. "And where is that?"

"We don't know," Lil answered. "But we've been told it's Hell."

Both Dennis and Lil had their weapons pointing at the oval.

Max bent down and picked up a rock. He threw it into the circle of light. It disappeared into the shimmering glow.

"You're right. It didn't come out the other side—"

He was interrupted by a loud scream that made him fall back behind Dennis and Lil.

"What was that?" Max gulped.

"Company," Dennis said dryly.

A disembodied arm emerged through the glowing ring, not as large as the arm Lil and Dennis had freed Ernest Fowler from the previous day, but longer than a man's forearm. Dark talons clutched at the air.

Suddenly, a leg stepped out. It was peculiar, with a hoof at the bottom like the leg of a goat or a ram, covered with dense fur.

Then in one quick move, a nightmare leapt out of the opening.

It raised itself up to its full height of seven feet, and with the better light, Lil could see its true appearance. It was covered with a shaggy brown fur except for the hoofed feet and the frightening talons on its three-fingered leathery hands. The neck was long and equine, but possessed no mane leading to the head, from which sprouted a pair of short antlers. They weren't as impressive as a buck or as massive as a moose, but they looked sharp and dangerous. Lil could imagine a man being gutted by those sturdy appendages.

The face and snout were also horse-like, but the mouth opened further than a horse's, though not as far as a crocodile. As its lips curled threateningly, Lil could see the maw filled with sharp teeth. A thick tail swung out of the circle of light and swayed behind it.

The massive creature gave a simple hop in to the air that covered yards in a single leap, and without hesitation, Lil and Dennis both opened fire.

This surprised the monster and it landed badly only ten feet from them and bellowed its cry again.

It crouched and looked at wounds on its chest and leg, almost in surprise. The pair of injuries oozed a green slime. The creature looked at the blood, and moved back, fear in its red eyes.

"Hold!" Lil shouted, taking control of the situation. Dennis held his fire, but his gun was still pointed at the thing, and he was breathing hard.

"What do you mean, *hold?*" Dennis argued, his pistol aimed at the head of their assailant. "I thought you said we needed a corpse to prove this thing is real."

The monster moved back, but instead of the awful scream, it made a whining sound.

"It's wounded," Lil said, also not lowering her weapon. "It knows we can fight back."

"It was ready to attack us without even a moment of hesitation, so excuse me if I lack sympathy."

The creature was moving away, still making the keening sound, and slid towards the portal. Lil rushed to the left and fired at the ground in front of it, the sound of the shot making it flinch back.

"Max, take a picture," Lil cried out, her weapon still leveled at the beast.

"*What?*" Max squeaked.

"Your phone, take a goddamn picture."

The creature glanced around at the humans with its red eyes, sensing that it was cornered. Lil stepped back, knowing a cornered animal was the most dangerous because it would do anything to survive.

"Take the picture!" Lil hissed.

Max struggled with the phone as he got it out of his pocket.

The monster leapt up from its crouch, but not toward Lil, instead it threw itself into the glowing circle. It leaped through, disappearing into the space. Lil rushed toward the glowing circle.

"Lil, no," shouted Dennis, as he rushed forward to stop her.

Without hesitation, Lil shoved her head into the glowing ring, as well as her right arm with the pistol.

The effect was strange, like the way it felt when you put a nine-volt battery on your tongue to test it. Her face and right arm felt tingly.

The place she saw was not of this earth.

The sky was red, a deep blood red crimson, and the air was redolent of sulphur. The ground around her was a dark red clay, with a thin coating of short, scarlet grass and misshapen trees that stuck up with yards of space between each one. Every tree was an ugly, twisted thing without leaves. Only needles poked out of the branches and they were as red as the sky and looked dangerous and sharp, more like long thorns than soft pine needles.

Lil saw the creature running with a limp away from her on the ground that was a good foot below the portal. She raised her gun to fire at it—

—and was yanked back into the clearing, where Dennis pulled her to the ground before she could get a shot off.

"Lil, you okay?" Dennis said.

"Get off me!" she railed and pushed Dennis aside to jump to her feet. The oval was shrinking, and as she tried to catch her breath, she realized that Dennis pulling her out had been the best choice.

Dennis got up, dirt speckling his uniform, and they both backed away from the glowing ring. It grew smaller, until it was no more than a ball of light. There was a flash, and it was gone, leaving only the smoldering earth and the burn mark behind.

"I guess it was a good idea to pull me out of there," Lil conceded. "Sorry."

"It's okay," Dennis said, as he put the safety on and holstered his weapon. "As soon as you stuck your face in, it started shrinking. I thought I'd better get you out before it closed."

"It would be a bad idea to leave my body here and my head there," Lil agreed, as a shiver ran down her spine.

"That oval is hot enough to melt sand, I figured it wouldn't be good for you."

They both turned to face Max, who had not budged from the place he'd stood during the attack.

His phone was now in his hand.

"What...the Hell...was *that*?" Max exploded.

Lil remained calm, checked her safety, and returned her gun to the waist pack. She gathered the small stone that lay open in the middle of the cloth. "We were hoping you could tell us."

She picked up the stone, which was still warm, but no longer blazing hot. She folded the heavy cloth around it and returned it to the waist pack pocket.

"That was completely impossible, creatures do not appear out of nowhere—"

"It came from another place," Lil chided, annoyed by this. "I saw it."

"What did it look like?" Dennis asked.

"Scary. Red sky, twisted trees with thorns for leaves," Lil reported.

"Charming," Dennis replied.

"What is *wrong* with you two?" Max chided. "A freakin' monster came out of a hole in the air!"

Lil stepped toward Max. "And I need you to tell me if there is any tribal knowledge of things like this ever happening before."

Max began to pace, a wild look in his eyes. "Look, I'm an anthropologist and a teacher. I read *books*, I don't fight monsters!"

"We just need to know if there is any—"

"No, no. I can't believe this. This was a trick, something you two concocted as a prank."

Dennis blew up. "You think we *made this up*? And what? Hired Hollywood guys to do the lighting and a seven-foot-tall actor with backwards arms, and got him in a rubber suit? Now, *that's* crazy."

"No, *you're* crazy, both of you, I refuse to believe any of this."

"Doctor," Lil spoke calmly to stop Max's rant. "We really need your help. If you have any insight, it could make all the difference."

He stared at her, breathing hard. The wild look in his eyes had faded a bit. "Okay, okay. I think...this could explain several legends. But, can we get out of here?"

"Why?" Dennis asked. "It's safe now."

"In case it comes back!" Max announced.

Dennis looked at Lil. "We could go to the diner."

"We could," she agreed.

Dennis turned to Max. "Do you like pie?"

Max stared at them in disbelief.

The three of them sat in a booth at the Dine Rite, as Max took another forkful of lemon meringue pie.

"You're right, this is really good pie," Max said and put it into his mouth.

"They make them fresh here," Dennis explained as he took another bite of his apple pie. "People come from miles around just to have it."

"Feeling calmer?" Lil asked Max. She was moving her fork through a slice of pecan pie, but not really eating any.

"A bit, yes," Max said. "You could have warned me."

"I thought I did," Lil clarified. "I told you that I saw one of them."

"But I didn't think it was so...so..."

"Big?" Dennis put forward.

"Fast?" Lil chimed in. "For a large creature it moves fast—"

"*Real*," Max exclaimed. "I mean, I've heard the stories. But we were standing right in front of it and it charged us."

"Good thing I was using a Glock, those nine millimeter bullets hit pretty hard," Dennis assured him. "Stopped him cold."

"Can we not talk about guns, please?" Max stared at his pie.

"I'd think you'd be grateful we had them," Dennis remarked. "Did you see the talons on that thing?"

"You were right." Max shook his head. "It resembled the murals of the *Piasa* bird, only with hair all over it."

Dennis' radio on his belt emitted a sharp tone followed by a crackly voice. "Dennis, what's your twenty?"

Dennis spoke into the radio. "I'm at the Dine Rite. Do you need me?"

"I was told to inform you when Mister Fowler was awake."

"Great," Dennis affirmed. "Can you guys spare me to go question him?"

"Ten-four. I'll inform the captain."

Dennis put the radio back on his belt. "Let's finish up. I have a witness to talk to."

"Can I tag along?" Lil requested.

"Me, as well?" Max asked.

Dennis looked disgruntled as he took another forkful of pie. "Okay, but that hospital room is going to be crowded."

The trio rode in Dennis' police car with Lil sitting in the back because the idea of being behind the caged partition with no way to open the door made Max nervous.

They drove to the Atlanticare Hammonton Health Park, walked to the front desk, and security checked their IDs and issued them paper clip-on badges.

Dennis led them up to the correct floor and into the room of Ernest Fowler.

"Mister Fowler," Dennis said quietly as he approached.

The old man looked up. He had an IV in his arm and there were machines beeping softly, registering his vital signs. His leg was in a cast and suspended a few inches off the bed by a metal rack with strings and pulleys. He wore a large bandage over one shoulder that was barely covered by his hospital gown.

"So, you're a policeman?" Fowler stated, recognizing Dennis. "I was wondering how you got so brave to pull me out of that place."

Lil moved forward. "How are you feeling, Mister Fowler?"

The old man frowned. "And you! I thought you weren't real, just a dream." His eye roved over to Max. "Were you there as well?"

Max started. "Me, no, I just…want to hear what you have to say."

Mister Fowler smiled wanly. "These two pulled me out of that awful place," he said and shook his head. "I didn't know where you came from. You must have been nearby, but I didn't see you."

Dennis had a notebook out and a pen. "Can you tell me what happened?"

"I was walking on the property. You see, that land was where I grew up, where my family's house used to be—"

"Your daughter told us," Dennis confirmed.

"I was just walking along, Hammer and me. Oh! Is Hammer all right?"

Dennis smiled. "He'll be fine. He stayed overnight with the vet, who gave him a strong antibiotic. He might be home before you are."

"Good, good. So, we were walking and there was this light…"

"Any idea where it came from?"

"None. But it grew. It grew into this circle, like those old mirrors that are a big oval? It was like that."

Lil glanced at Max, who looked pale.

"Then this arm comes out of the light, just an arm. It tries to grab Hammer, so I hit it with my walking stick."

"That was very brave of you," Lil said.

Ernest shrugged. "It was after my dog. But I must have gotten too close because it grabbed me, grabbed my shoulder, with claws. Let me tell you, that hurt."

Dennis continued. "And this arm pulled you into the circle of light?"

Ernest nodded. "Yes, and it was strange, I felt all tingly as I went through, like pins and needles in your leg? But this was all over my body."

"It pulled you in. Could you see what the arm was connected to?"

"Yes, it was a giant thing, with hairy arms and eyes that bore into me. It looked mostly human, but bigger and hairier, with very long arms and a big nose that hung on its face. It was kind of like a Sasquatch except it was real skinny, like it hadn't had a good meal for a while. I was in this weird place with a red sky."

"What happened?"

"I had my walking stick, and I hit it in the head with it. The thing seemed shocked that I fought back."

"And you kept that up for six hours?" Dennis asked.

"What? No, I hit it once and it grabbed my walking stick, but it pulled its claws out of me when the circle of light came back." He pointed at Lil. "This lady grabbed me and pulled me out. But that giant, he grabbed my leg with his claws. I think he would've pulled it right off, except that lady shot it." He pointed at Dennis. "Then you pulled me out."

Dennis frowned. "So…you're saying that you were only in that weird place for a few minutes?"

He shrugged again. "If that."

Lil looked at Dennis and whispered, "But it was at least six hours."

Dennis nodded and pulled a business card from his notebook. "Thank you for your cooperation, Mister Fowler, here is my card. Please feel free to call me if you can think of anything else."

The old man squinted and looked at the card. "Okay. And thank you for the rescue, young man."

Dennis turned to the hall and Max and Lil were right behind him.

"Wait, that's all?" Max asked.

"'Fraid so," Dennis said as they walked toward the elevator.

"But he went to another place, another dimension," Max demanded. "You need to test him, get the—"

"We'll talk in the car," Dennis said, as the elevator door opened.

The door closed and it was just the three of them.

Lil looked at Dennis. "This is big, we have to tell people."

Dennis remained silent, and the three of them returned their badges. In a few short minutes, they were once again in Dennis' police cruiser and on their way back.

Lil, behind the partition in the rear, asked, "What are you going to put in your report?"

"Simple. An old man got lost in the woods, where he got mauled by a bear, and hallucinated that he was grabbed by a monster and pulled into Hell."

"But, that's not…true," Max protested.

"Dennis, we have to warn the public," Lil added.

"The public has been warned," Dennis explained curtly. "There is a wild animal loose and people should avoid the Barrens until it is captured. In the meantime, I am not putting on a report that there are flying devils, dimensional portals, or monsters. It will cause a panic or attract a bunch of stupid people who want to see such things."

"But that's not the *truth*," Lil insisted from behind the partition.

"Perhaps not, but I'll keep my job, and be able to help if this gets worse."

"Worse?" Lil challenged. "Hundreds of missing persons? How can it get worse?"

"Look, Lil," Dennis barked. "You lost your job. Do you mind if I keep mine?"

Lil fell back in the seat, crushed by his words. She'd thought they were a team, doing something important, but now she felt utterly alone.

They drove on in silence.

FOURTEEN

Searching The Lore

O nce back at the location, Max stepped out of the cruiser and headed for his car.

Lil pushed past Dennis and headed for her own vehicle.

"I'm sorry, Lil," Dennis called after her.

"Up yours, Decatur," Lil spat, not turning to look at him.

Dennis stepped forward and gently touched her arm, "Lil—"

She yanked her arm free and faced him. "Touch me again, and I'll knock you down, uniform or not."

A grim smile appeared on Dennis' face. "I believe you."

"Right answer," Lil said and crossed her arms over her chest.

He spoke in a calm voice. "I apologize. What I said was harsh. I'm mad about the fact that I have to handle things this way. But if I tell the captain the truth, I'll be put on leave, and then how can we get more information? How can I help?"

Lil was unconvinced.

Dennis opened his arms. "Okay, I could've handled things better."

Lil glanced over to look at Max, who had been watching them. The thin scholar looked away, suddenly interested in the local flora.

She stepped closer to Dennis. "Like you handled things ten years ago with Carrie?"

Dennis exhaled heavily, his own temper rising. "This again?"

"Yes, this again, Dennis," Lil replied. "I thought you changed, but I can't be sure you won't hang me out to dry to save your own ass."

Dennis' jaw clenched.

"Go back to town," Lil said, getting quieter. "Do your job. If you can tell me anything, please do. I'm going to keep investigating and try to find answers."

"Why?" Dennis offered. "If people are warned away—"

"Because something is coming...something...really bad," Lil insisted.

Dennis' temper flared again. "And how do you know that?"

"I have ways," Lil responded, aware of how lame this sounded.

"What, your tarot cards? I remember how you played with them in high school. What? Because you're Romani, and your 'gypsy blood' is telling you so?"

"I should have listened to the tarot cards. Right before you banged Carrie, I drew the Two of Pentacles, the Seven of Swords, and the Tower. If I had read those cards correctly, I'd have known you were a cheating bastard."

"I'm going back to work," Dennis seethed, and went back to his car. Lil watched him get in and drive away. She was aware that her *Paxil* was wearing off. Maybe she should take another to avoid any kind of panic attack.

She turned and saw Max standing next to her car. She had forgotten about him in the heat of the argument.

"I take it you two have a history?" he observed.

Lil hung her head and sighed. "I'm sorry you had to see that." "Relationships are hard."

"Especially when the man is a stubborn idiot," she snapped. She took several deep breaths. "I'm sorry I wasted your time. I'd better let you get back to your research."

"My research can wait, this cannot," Max said and frowned. "Do you really think something bad is coming?"

She thought of the pattern, towns and villages vanishing one hundred and ten years apart, and the repeating nightmare. Her grandmother was trying to warn her. "Yes, I do."

"Can I see your research?"

"If you don't mind coming to my cottage. It's all there."

Max shrugged. "I followed you this far. I am willing to go farther."

Lil smirked. "Not on the first date, you won't."

This made Max look so flustered and his dark face turned a slight reddish hue. "I—I did not mean—"

Lil chuckled. "I'm sorry, Max. I was kidding. I didn't mean to embarrass you."

"Very well. Shall I follow your car?"

Lil pulled out her phone. "I'll text you the address, just in case. It's only about fifteen minutes away."

"Impressive," Max agreed, sipping coffee, when Lil finished telling him about her findings and pulling up the information she'd downloaded from the Internet.

"Okay, so I've told you what I found. Now, I need you to give me any Native American lore that can shed light on what is happening."

"That one-hundred-ten-year cycle after the vanishing of the Lenape villages, then Apple Hill and finally Pines Edge, is intriguing. But the Lenape system tracked seasons and mostly followed the changes of the moon. Now, that old man at the hospital—"

"Ernest Fowler."

"Yes, the creature he describes sounds like a dark entity known as the *Mehuwe*. It was the man-eating giant spoken of in the Lenni-Lenape stories."

"How about the *Piasa* bird? Do you have anything on that?"

"Actually I wrote a paper about it. Would you like to hear the story?"

"I would," Lil replied.

"Tell you what, though. Perhaps I could get us something to eat? It's a long story."

"Umm, okay. I have…um…wine."

Max stood. "Great. I'll get take-out. What do you like?"

"There's an Italian place about fifteen minutes that way," she pointed in the direction of the road. "Amici's, they're pretty good."

"Great," Max said, as he rose. "I'll be back soon."

Max headed out the door, and Lil noticed that it was getting dark. She went to the bedroom and undressed, wrapped the robe about her and moved to the bathroom to take a quick shower, wanting to wash off the dirt from traipsing in the woods.

She put on fresh clothes, a casual top and a skirt. She'd been running around in pants for days, and she just wanted something relaxed for a change.

She stood in front of her mirror, and watched her reflection give her a rueful smile. She'd cleaned up well, especially after the day she'd had. She opened the medicine cabinet, grabbed the bottle of *Paxil*, and stared at it. Her concern grew that she might have nightmares if she took it this late.

She put it back in the cabinet.

Her phone rang, and she ran barefoot to get it.

"Hello?"

"*Lachhi tjiri rat, chaj,*" her father said, giving her a formal evening greeting in Romani. "Since your guest left, your momma wanted you to come for dinner."

Lil sat. "Thank you, *Dati*, but he's coming back. We're working."

"I thought you were working with the *Gorojo* on this mission of yours."

"I am, but this is a professor. He's an expert on Native American lore."

"I saw him. I thought he was Indian, but not that kind."

"He is from India, but we're going over legends that might help. Poppa, I think something bad is coming."

There was a long silence. "Why do you think so, *Chaj*?"

Lil sighed and took a deep breath. "*Mami* Natalia has appeared in my dreams."

Another long pause. "Talk to your mother."

Lil heard muffled voices as if her father was holding his hand over the phone and talking rapidly in Romani to her mother.

"Liliana," her mother said coming on the phone. "You say your Grandma Natalia is in your dreams?"

"Yes, *Daj*, every night."

There was a rapid intake of breath. "How many nights?"

"I'm not sure."

"What does she tell you?"

"She warns me. It's all pretty weird."

"This could be *prikaza*, bad luck. You should read the cards."

"I don't have time, the man I'm working with is coming back with dinner."

"Then after dinner!" her mother insisted. There was a long pause. "This man, what are you doing with him?"

Lil understood the suggestion. Was this what her mother thought, any man she had over was for a sexual reason? It annoyed her.

"Working, mother, that's all. I'm hanging up now."

Lil pulled the phone away from her face and pushed the button to end the call.

She felt the rebel within herself again, the idea that she should seduce Max just to make her mother mad and assert her own independence.

She shook her head.

Who am I kidding? That's not me.

She saw the headlights in her driveway as Max returned. She opened the door and he came in to put two paper bags on the kitchen counter. She shut the door and Max turned to look at her.

"You…got…dressed up. You look fantastic."

She had to admit, she enjoyed this reaction. "I just wanted to get cleaned up. What did you get?"

"Pasta in a pink sauce for me and spaghetti and meatballs for you."

Her eyebrows shot up. "That's my favorite. How did you know?"

Max shrugged. "I would love to say it was my years of study, and my understanding of women, but I just asked the owner if he knew you and what you would like."

This made Lil burst out laughing. "Of course you did. I'll get the wine."

"Only one glass for me, it's a long drive to Mount Laurel."

"So, put out the food, and tell me the story," Lil said, pouring wine into two jelly jars.

"Jelly jars?" Max chuckled as she offered him his glass. "Are you giving me the entire Piney experience?"

This made Lil grin. "How do you know about Pineys?"

"My research focuses on the Delaware Lenape tribes from this area. You have to be willing to talk to a lot of Pineys if you want to hear the local legends."

"Of course," Lil said, and held up her glass for a toast. "To Pineys."

They clinked glasses, and each took a sip. Moving to the table, they slid their laptops out of the way, and sat down to open the aluminum trays that held their individual dinners.

"The story of the *Piasa* bird comes from the Midwest," Max began. "A tribe known as the Illini."

"I'm all ears," Lil assured him as she twisted spaghetti around her fork.

"This tribe had a village near a great river, and the woods had plenty of game to hunt. The chief was named *Watoga,* who was wise and spoke to the Great Spirit often."

"That must have come in handy."

"One morning, the village was filled with the sound of a loud, hideous scream. Out of the sky came a gigantic flying monster. According to the legends, its body was shaped like a horse, with sharp teeth and flames that shot from its nostrils. It had two white antlers on its head and flew through the air on giant bat wings. It had cloven hooves, and arms with talons, and lastly a long, spiked tail that it could use as a weapon."

"This description could fit our Jersey Devil," Lil pointed out as she took another sip.

"I've been thinking about that, ever since I saw that thing this afternoon," Max replied, and gave an involuntary shudder. "Let me continue."

"Go ahead," Lil encouraged him.

"The braves were preparing to go fishing and this creature swooped down onto the beach and carried one of the hapless warriors away. For the next few weeks, the Illini were terrorized by the blood-thirsty fiend."

"So, what did they do?"

"Watoga was in great distress, as the beast seemed invincible. So, he called upon the Great Spirit, and he prayed and fasted. Then he had a dream where the answer came to him."

"A dream?" Lil spoke, troubled by this.

"Watoga called the tribe together and told them his plan. The braves painted their arrows with poison. Then, at night, Watoga and six of his braves hid on the top of the high bluff. When dawn came, only Watoga stood out in the open in full view."

"That doesn't sound like a great plan," Lil scoffed.

"You'll see. The shriek of the *Piasa* bird filled the sky as the winged creature swept into view. It sighted Watoga and dove to take him. Watoga fell to the ground and grasped several strong roots that he had uncovered during the night. The monster's talons bit into his skin, as the six braves rose up from their hiding places and shot poisoned arrows into an unprotected spot beneath the monster's wings. The poison took effect, and the *Piasa* bird released its hold on Watoga and plunged down the bluff, falling into the great river where it was carried away by the rapidly moving water."

"Is that it?"

"Almost. The tribe carried Watoga back to his tepee, and he recovered from his wounds. There was a great celebration and the image of the Piasa Bird was carved into the stone bluff where all could see."

"Where was this?"

"Alton, Illinois. The original carvings were destroyed over a century ago, but there is a re-creation on a cliff in the town. I've seen it."

"What's it like?"

Max sipped his wine thoughtfully. "Impressive. It's 22 feet high and 48 feet long."

"Wow!"

"An interesting side note, in the 1860s, John Russel, an explorer, recorded the tale from members of the tribe. In his research he located a nearby cave filled with human bones, he felt that this proved the legend was real."

"Or the tribe had no place to put dead bodies," Lil added, and finished her wine. "Do you think there could be a correlation?"

Max, who had finished his dinner, put the cheap aluminum dish aside, and pulled up his laptop. "I have a photo of the current representation, and an old drawing from an 1839 German illustration based on the original cliff sculpture before it was destroyed."

Max hit a few keystrokes and pulled up the photographs. The first matched Lil's pin, with bright colors of green on the body and red on the wings, looking more like a Japanese dragon than the creatures she had seen.

He then pulled up the second photograph, which was of a simple hand drawing. This was very different, with the monster having a lumpy body and small curled wings. The tail wasn't nearly as long and was split at the end, and the drawing suggested dangerous claws in its forepaws. The head had antlers on top and a scary look on the face.

"These don't look at all the same," Lil considered. "The second appears much more Native American than the other."

"True. The new one was influenced heavily by modern culture. Of course, there are theories that the original carving was much older. Created by a tribe that lived along the Mississippi valleys called the Cahokia."

"The Cahokia?" Lil repeated.

"Yes. They were a dominant tribe from about 900 AD until about 1200. They used animal pictographs, such as falcons, thunder-birds, and bird men to mark their territory. The *Piasa* design may have been carved as a symbol to let people traveling down the Mississippi River know they were entering the Cahokian territory."

Lil sighed. "So, we aren't much farther than we were?"

"It points to the idea that creatures like we saw today have existed since long ago. The question is, why are we seeing them now?"

"Exactly! That's what concerns me. Why is the creature appearing here? How do those damn portals work?"

"I have no answer for that. But it showed up right after you took out that strange rock of yours."

Lil frowned. "It did, didn't it?"

She stood and grabbed the empty aluminum containers. She took them to the sink and washed the forks and the pans, finally putting them into her recycling bin under the sink.

"I'm having another glass," Lil said, and she pulled her jar off the table, got out the large bottle, and poured herself another drink.

Once she returned the bottle to the refrigerator, she turned and looked at Max. "The stone I had began to glow when the portal appeared."

"That is true, and we weren't there ten minutes," he answered, taking a sip from his still half-full cup of wine.

"And the same thing happened yesterday. I was there when two portals opened in two different locations. Both times the stone got warm and glowed."

"Where did you get it?"

"My grandmother, Natalia, found it, one day on a walk in the woods near here. She had it polished and gave it to me when I was a child."

"May I see it?"

Lil went into the bedroom and quickly located her waist pack, and brought the stone to the table, wrapped in its cloth.

Max reached over and uncovered the stone. "This cloth it was wrapped in, it's heavy, like the kind plumbers use."

"Is that significant?"

"No, it's just that this kind of cloth is fireproof. Perhaps your grandmother knew more than you were told."

"She keeps saying that it's the key."

Max frowned. "Your grandmother is still alive?"

"No...um...she keeps appearing in my dreams."

Max considered this before he spoke. "It was believed that the Lenape shaman could open 'spirit holes,' and traverse to other places. They used rituals that involved stone cairns and special rocks. There are recorded observations of such rituals going back to the 1700s."

"Do they say where they went or what they saw?"

"It's more tall tales than recorded data, I'm afraid," Max sighed, he put the rock back in the center of the cloth, where its polished surface reflected the lights in the room.

"But what happened in my case? Did this rock just happen to show up at the right time? Is there something that makes the rock work when I get near a portal?"

"My theory would be that these portals have been opening, and frequently. That would explain the missing people you told me about," Max proposed. "Dennis mentioned something about you having 'gypsy blood'?"

Lil sighed. "It's not the preferred term, but yes, I'm Romani."

"And you have delved into—what's the proper word—fortune-telling, psychic phenomena?"

"My grandmother Natalia was a great seer," Lil confessed. "People used to visit her from all over the country to seek her wisdom."

Max nodded. "That would make her the 'shaman' for her tribe."

"What are you getting at?"

"Nothing, except the obvious."

"So obvious that I missed it," Lil grumbled.

"It could be that *you* are causing these portals to open when you get near them," Max told her excitedly. "You and this stone of yours."

Lil frowned. "I don't know any Lenape rituals, and I'm not even sure I know what a cairn is."

"That isn't the point. It isn't being a specific kind of shaman, it's the ability to tap into that kind of energy."

"If so, why can't I just…I don't know…conjure a portal out of thin air in the back yard?"

Max shrugged. "The portals might be in specific locations. But today you certainly activated it."

"And a monster came out of it. How did it know to be there?"

"Your guess is as good as mine."

"So, you think the portals are at specific locations, and you need a person with the right mental abilities to open it?"

"All people have a different degree of extra-sensory perception, which could explain why some people went missing while others did not," Max theorized. "People with a certain amount of ESP could have accidentally activated one of these portals." Max stood. "I think I need to get back to my hotel."

She stood as well. "Of course. But, how can I test this theory of yours?"

"I would recommend that you go to the same spot as yesterday, see if you can activate it."

"And you'll come with me?" Lil insisted.

He stared at her, his eyes big. "What?"

"Max, I can't go in alone. I need someone to watch my back, and you saw how Dennis acted after we questioned Mister Fowler."

Max looked upset. "But…I am not…like you. I cannot shoot the creature if you are attacked. I've…never even handled a gun."

"Please, Max. You could video the portal, give me the proof I need."

He looked at the floor, and it appeared that he made a decision. "Very well. If it will help. I must admit, this could have anthropological significance."

"That's true. You could write a paper about it."

Max smiled at this. "A paper no one would believe, even with video evidence."

"Thank you, Max."

"I'll call before I come," Max said and opened his arms to hug Lil.

She stepped into the hug, and had to admit, it felt pretty good.

"I'll see you tomorrow," she said, stepping back.

"See you then," he assured her and without hesitation moved to the door and went out.

"Thank you for dinner," she called after him.

Max got into his car and drove off, as Lil stood there and watched him go. This was good, like her old, normal life, sharing dinner with a friend.

She stepped back into the small cottage and looked at the stone as it lay out on the thick cloth on the table. She sat down and stared at it. Was she the person who made it work? Or was there another secret?

Her eyes were focused on the stone, and she thought she heard a sound behind her. She turned to see an older man with white hair and a round face standing next to her refrigerator, and she gasped.

He wore clothes from another era, a full shirt, a black double-breasted vest, and black pants. The clothes were loose on his thin form, worn from use, and there were multiple patches woven onto the fabric.

He stood with a smile on his face, and he seemed harmless, but Lil jumped up in alarm. He looked at her and held up his hands as if to calm her.

And abruptly disappeared.

He simply faded from view, there one moment, becoming transparent and gone the next. Lil stood with her mouth agape. Everything had happened so quickly that she barely had time to react.

"I'm going insane," she muttered aloud, surprised by how her voice sounded. She moved to where the man had stood, but nothing remained.

It was as if he'd never been there at all.

FIFTEEN

Going In

L il woke up the next day and sighed from relief that no nightmares or strange visitors had occurred during the night. She rose, her muscles sore from the vigorous walking and use of her pistol after so long. It had been the most physical activity she'd done except for farm work.

She pulled the small Hoppe's cleaning kit in the wooden box from a drawer. It had been a gift from Chad, and it always made her feel close to him to use it.

Using cleaning pads and a wire brush, she made quick work of cleaning the weapon, then oiled it carefully, returning it to the lockbox when she was done.

She took a quick shower, then dressed in denim jeans, a work shirt, and a denim jacket, as well as sturdy sneakers. If she was going to be in the woods, she wanted to be ready. She took one last look at herself in the mirror and opened the medicine cabinet. She reached for the *Paxil* and stopped herself.

The *Paxil* prevented the panic attacks but kept her from feeling much of anything too strongly. Yet, the other day, she was almost manic until the panic attack made her crash, and she'd had a hallucination last night, the older man with the white hair.

She sighed and decided that she'd go without it, just in case. If she had a problem, the pills in her handbag would calm her down.

She took her phone from the charger and booted it up. There was a message from Max:

I am awake.

When should I meet you at yesterday's location?

She was pretty much ready, but wanted to text Dennis, to keep him in the loop. The idea annoyed her that she had to check in with him, especially after what he said to her the previous evening.

This was her investigation, not his.

She felt so conflicted with Dennis. He wanted so much for them to be like they'd been years ago, then, on the other hand he could be so difficult, insisting things be his way.

She had not forgiven him for Carrie, but she needed to try to let it go. Her past was in shambles, why did she hold on to his infidelity so strongly?

She did want him and from the look in his eyes he wanted her as well. And there was that kiss, that impulsive kiss, that sung to her heart and made old longings burn with a renewed fire.

No matter how conflicted she was about her feelings, Dennis was too valuable a resource to cut off. She sent a text:

Going to yesterday's location to do more research.

Thanks.

She quickly texted Max and told him to meet her in an hour and sent it just as her phone rang.

It was Dennis.

She took a deep breath and tried to focus. "Hello, Dennis."

"Lil, you're not thinking of going out to that place alone, are you?"

I can if I want to.

"No Dennis. Max is meeting me there."

"Max? That's your idea of backup?"

"I'm *his* back up, Dennis. I have the gun and know how to use it."

Dennis paused. "Is he still here? Did he spend the night or something?"

Lil felt her hackles rise. "And what if he did? That's not any of your business, Officer Decatur."

Dennis went silent, and a part of Lil felt triumph.

"You're right, Lil, it's none of my business," Dennis said quietly. She could tell she struck him deeply. "I just want you to be safe."

She immediately felt guilty. "Dennis, I'm not anyone's plaything, got it?"

"I know, Lil," Dennis said, still sounding wounded.

"Look," she sighed. "I just wanted you to know what I'm doing. I'm not asking permission."

Dennis voice was calm. "I know, Lil. I just worry, okay?"

Lil calmed down and spoke quietly. "You could've just said that first."

"I know, I know. Dammit Lil, I just want to talk to you the way we used to talk. Hell, ten years ago, it's like we could read each other's minds."

"It can't be like it was, Dennis. We've both changed."

"I'd just like to know where to start."

She stood outside her cottage, and for a moment she felt an overpowering affection for this man. He was flawed and his temper was as fiery as her own, but she could hear it in his voice. He wanted to make it right between them. He wanted to sweep the years away and go back to the time when it was just her and him.

She also knew that was impossible. Too much had changed.

"I—I don't know, Dennis. I think I have to solve this situation first."

"It's easier to fight monsters than talk to me?"

"To be honest, it's easier to fight monsters than make *any* plans right now."

"Okay," he muttered, unhappy with this answer. "Then go get 'em, Lil. Please let me know anything you find."

"I will, Dennis."

She ended the call and went into the cottage. She packed her purse and grabbed her lockbox, and got into her small two-tone car to drive out to the location.

It was another pleasant day, surprising for March, where the weather could be beautiful one day and cold and dreary the next. But the sun was shining, she drove with one window open, and she was warm enough in the denim jacket.

The roads in the Barrens were all the same, trees on both sides and two lanes of blacktop, unless she pulled into one of the small sandy side roads that criss-crossed through the woods. But those raised the danger of getting caught in a large pothole or pool of water too deep for her small car.

She pulled up about ten minutes early, and wished she'd stopped for a cup of coffee. Instead she grabbed a bottle of water from her back seat.

She checked her pistol, loaded it, and put it in the quick release holster in the waist pack. In another pocket she made sure the stone was there and added her phone to the pack. She surprised herself by grabbing a handful of bullets that she put into an extra pocket and zipped it tight. The waist bag was getting a bit heavy, but she felt it might be wise to carry more bullets.

She stuck her water bottle in the fabric belt, and locked up the car as Max's car parked on the opposite side of the street. The thin man came out of the driver's seat, dressed in denim and sturdy clothes as well. He carried a full oblong bag with a strap on his shoulder.

As he drew near, Lil noticed that he had been careful in the way he'd styled his hair. He drew close and offered a hug, which Lil accepted, and caught the scent of a cologne on him.

Max had cleaned himself up to impress her.

They parted and she made a point to say, "You look really nice today."

"So do you," the scholar said, as his hands went stiffly to his sides.

This got a grin from Lil. "You don't work with a lot of women, do you?"

"Oh yes, I do," he responded, not meeting her eyes. "It's just that they are not as attractive as you."

"That's a nice thing to say," Lil told him, and focused on what he carried. "What's the bag?"

"A tripod to hold my phone," he boasted. "I want to get video, and this has a bluetooth remote control."

"That's a good idea, but we'd better set it up out here," Lil surmised. "If there is any possibility that I can activate the portals, we have to be ready to take video the moment we get to the location."

He nodded at this. "Good point."

He took the bag off his shoulder and unzipped it to pull out a folded tripod. Even so, the bag still seemed to hold something within it that Lil couldn't see. "I really enjoyed having dinner with you last night."

She smiled. "So did I. But I think I owe you an apology."

"For what?" he asked as he opened the tripod and extended the legs.

"I don't want you to get the wrong impression."

He continued his work, pulling the stand to its full height. "So, you and Dennis?"

"No…well…maybe," she fretted. "Right now, it's me and no one."

"I read about your fiancé," Max confessed as he removed the phone from his pocket, and began to manipulate it into a bracket at the top of the support. "I'm really very sorry."

"Thanks," Lil said, her jaw set. Emotions were hitting her a lot harder without the *Paxil*.

"He must have been quite a man," Max added as he locked the phone in place.

"He was," Lil said, surprised that a single tear trickled down her face.

Max looked up and was dismayed. "Oh, I made you cry. I—I did *not* mean to do that."

"I'm fine," she said and wiped at her face. "I better be, because I'm your back up."

"Excuse me?" Max said, confused.

"Sorry, it's something I said to Dennis. Since I have the gun, I'm backing you up."

"I think we are 'backing up' each other, are we not?"

Lil grinned, relaxing a bit. "Yes, I guess we are. Are we all set?"

"Aye, aye, captain," Max said jovially. "I am ready to get photographic proof that this stuff is real."

"It would certainly help our case," Lil agreed.

They moved into the woods following the barely discernible path. It had helped that a lot of people had tramped it down over the last few days, from Lil and Dennis, to Mrs. Campbell and the EMTs.

As they approached the clearing, Lil pulled her pistol, and aimed it at the ground.

"Where do you want to set up?" Lil asked.

"Over here," Max called out, and pointed to a tree opposite the portal site. "It should be far enough away, so that nothing will happen to it."

"Let me give you Dennis' cell number," Lil insisted, as she held the weapon in her left hand, and took her phone out of the bag with her right.

"Why?" he asked.

"We're backing each other up, right? What if something happens to me? Or my phone?"

He nodded. "Of course, that makes sense."

She read the number out loud and Max put it into his phone, which was difficult with it locked in the tripod. He nodded when it was done.

She returned her attention to the clearing and the line of scorched earth. "It's a pity you don't have a weapon."

"Oh, but I do," Max conceded, and pulled the bag off his shoulder. He unzipped it and pulled a baseball bat out of the bag. It bore a logo with the words "Louisville Slugger." He held the wooden implement in a batter's stance and waved it several times in the air.

"I stand corrected," Lil smirked.

"What's more, it is ash wood, which was sacred to the Lenape. They used it to make the shaft of their arrows."

"We'll take any help we can get," Lil assured him.

She moved to the line of burnt grass in the clearing and stood at the ready, the pistol now facing the sky.

Time seemed to slow down as Lil stood near the location of the portal. She was almost quivering in anticipation, while a part of her felt nervous, another part felt exhilarated, in her element. It was odd to experience this dichotomy of emotion.

She tried to center herself and focus, telling herself it was just the fact that she quit her *Paxil* this morning.

After about a half hour, she lowered her weapon, her muscles tiring from holding it upright. Max stood near the tripod with his phone, and had put the bat down, seeing that it wasn't needed.

Finally, Lil walked over to him. "Well, this certainly gets rid of the idea that I was the catalyst."

Max sighed. "It was only a theory," he said and scratched his neck. "Why don't you try taking out the stone?"

"Do you think that will work?"

He shrugged. "Have you taken it out each time?"

Lil reached into the pack and pulled out the cloth. "No, the first time it just got hot and I had to pull it out of my pocket before it burned me. The other time, Dennis and I wandered around, we touched the fused glass..." she stopped and her mouth fell open.

"What?"

"The glass. Both times, before the portal opened someone touched the fused glass on the ground. Dennis and I on Sunday, and you, yesterday."

"That's right, and I took it from your hand and dropped it right before that hum started."

Lil's jaw clenched. "Let's try that now."

She slipped the gun back into her waist pack and moved to the blackened line burnt into the ground. She pushed her hand into the sandy soil and rooted around, pushing the grainy dirt around until she touched something hard. She pulled a piece of dark green translucent rock out of the ground and held it up for Max to see.

"What do I do now?" Lil asked.

"I don't know…maybe concentrate on it."

Lil nodded, stepped a few feet back, and stared at the small rectangular piece in her hand. She also retrieved the polished stone with her other hand.

She continued to look at the dirt-covered glass she'd pulled from the earth. "Am I doing it right?"

"I'm an anthropologist, not a shaman."

"Well, I'm no damn shaman either," Lil grumbled. She exhaled in exasperation and threw the rock back at the discolored line on the ground.

Instantly the polished stone in her other hand began to glow with the same unearthly gleam as the previous day. She placed it on the ground and backed away from it, retrieving her handgun from her pack.

Lil moved quickly to Max, and there it was. The strange sounds Lil had heard the other two times the portal had appeared: a deep hum with tinkling reverberation. She and Max exchanged a glance as he grabbed his bat and shouldered it.

The hum grew in volume, and a beam of light appeared, striking the scorch mark in the clearing. The ball of light began to form in the middle of the air.

"That did it," Lil exulted. "Turn on the freakin' camera."

With a start, Max lowered the bat and hit the switch on the remote, and then moved to look at the screen. "We're recording."

He joined Lil, the bat in a two-handed grip again. Lil pointed her gun at the ball of light.   The light began to grow, just like the other times. It expanded and stretched out, gaining size and volume. After a few short minutes, it was the full size of the previous portals.

They both stood at the ready with their weapons raised.

Nothing happened.

"What do we do now?" Max asked in a loud whisper.

Lil looked determined. "I want to look in there."

"In there? What if there is a *Mehuwe* waiting to grab you?"

"Then, he'd better be bullet-proof," she threatened. "If you see that circle start to grow smaller, pull me out right away."

Max nodded nervously. "I don't know about this, Lil."

Lil moved forward cautiously towards the portal. She approached and looked up and around at the treetops. When the first portal had opened, it attracted a creature who wanted to go into it, as opposed to the previous day when the Devil had come out.

She was about a foot away, the circle of light undulating in its strange hypnotic way.

She turned in a slow circle, eyes still up, and she moved close to the shimmering surface and carefully inserted her left hand, the grip on the gun firm with her right hand.

The feeling of electricity ran up and down her arm, like a mild electrical shock or pins and needles from a limb gone to sleep. She took a deep breath, and plunged her face and head through the opening.

She opened her eyes to the hellish landscape, with the twisted trees adorned by the sharp thorns, but there was no creature near the portal. It was darker than the last time she looked in, and the sky was a dark maroon. She let go of her breath, and found she could breathe the air with no trouble, except for the pungent smell of sulphur that permeated the atmosphere.

Maybe the creatures had all gone to sleep, but she considered that they might only come out at night.

She looked down and could see the same oval on this side as well, shimmering in the same way. This reassured her, as she could see if it grew smaller and leave if she needed to.

Lil was ready to pull herself back out, not wanting to risk staying there too long and attracting any of the denizens.

She started to lean back only to be body-slammed by something large and heavy that shoved her through the portal and threw her through the air a good five feet.

With reflexes that had not lost their edge, she rolled over, the weight of the handgun still clutched in her right hand.

She looked up, and standing over her was one of the Devils, as big as life, and twice as hideous. It looked down at her and made its ugly screeching cry, as it raised one of its sharp talons.

She brought the pistol up and fired two rounds into the hideous misshapen head.

It fell back as green fluid leaked out, its arms flailed in the air, and the large tail swung over Lil, almost hitting her. She rolled away as the creature made piteous noises and fell to the ground.

"You *can* be killed, you bastard." Lil said, as she rose to her feet, the gun still trained on the monster.

Then with a sudden awareness, she glanced around at the dark sky and deformed trees. The portal was still open, and she rushed towards it, not wanting to be trapped in this place.

The fallen creature was in the throes of agony. Its large tail swung and took her legs out from under her. She fell to the ground, did her best to roll quickly and point the gun at her adversary.

But, that had been its final response, and it lay unmoving and silent. Lil looked up, but the portal was shrinking rapidly.

"No, no, no," she chanted, getting to her feet and moving toward the opening, but it was far too small for her to fit, and she stepped back from it.

A baseball bat flew through the shrinking hole and plunged to the dark red earth next to her. She stared at it, the words 'Louisville Slugger' facing upwards.

She turned her attention to the portal which had now become nothing more than a ball of light.

Then it was gone.

SIXTEEN

Left Behind

On the other side of the portal, Max had been nervously pacing, the bat on his shoulder. It had been so bizarre for him to see Lil's body on this side of the circle of light, while her head and left arm vanished into it, like some kind of magician's beheading illusion.

He kept his eye on the portal in case it began to shrink. The outer edge had been hot enough to turn sand into glass, and he could see the earth at the bottom smoldering. If it were to shrink, that hot circle could easily burn her head off, and that idea terrified him.

The screech that pierced the air was so shocking, it spun him in a circle holding the bat with both hands.

He moved protectively toward Lil to pull her out of the portal.

The sound of wings thundered in his ears and he looked up just in time to see a huge creature fall from the sky, huge bat wings open and blocking the sunlight.

Max backed away as the creature landed. He gaped at the long head, the wide mouth bristling with sharp teeth, and the wings folding down as the long tail moved from right to left as if with a mind of its own. It had two short arms that bent with a backward elbow and sharp talons on the end of the three-fingered hands.

Max stood rooted to the spot, face-to-face with a nightmare.

However, the creature reared back, gave another scream, and leapt toward Max.

Max, finding a courage he didn't know he even possessed, moved into a batter's stance and brought the heavy bat past the threatening talons, hitting the charging beast in the side of the head with all his strength.

He felt the blow up both his arms. It was like taking a hammer and striking a brick wall. The creature was knocked aside from its charge and its overlarge head fell to the side.

It made a whimpering noise of pain and backed away, shaking its head to recover from the blow.

"You want me, come and get me," Max screamed. He stepped toward the creature, his fear so strong that his mouth tasted of iron.

He was shocked to see fear in the thing's red eyes and instead of attacking, it turned and rushed toward the portal.

"No!" Max howled as the monster pushed into Lil, knocking her completely through the portal in its headlong rush to escape.

Both Lil and the Jersey Devil disappeared.

At first Max stood there, his mouth open, frightened and amazed. What should he do, go after them? He looked from the circle to the tripod with the camera. If he went in, who would be here to sound the alarm?

Just as he worried about this, the portal began to shrink. He rushed towards the glowing circle and shouted, "Lil! Lil, can you hear me?"

It was collapsing at an impossible rate of speed. Not knowing what to do, he impulsively took the bat and threw it through the shrinking hole, being careful not to touch the portal himself.

It went through and was gone, and he hoped it landed near Lil.

A moment later the portal was only a ball of light that vanished as suddenly as it had appeared.

The forest around him seemed darker without the portal of light, and Max looked down at the smoldering ground, not sure what to do. He stumbled his way back to the tripod and fought to remember how to stop the video.

Once the camera was off, he yanked the phone free from the tripod, and pushed the number to call Dennis.

No signal.

"You've got to be shitting me," he cursed, and rushed down the path. He stumbled over the unstable ground and was careful to not trip. He reached the paved road, where he got a very weak signal, but it was enough.

He pushed the button.

"Decatur," said a professional voice on the other end.

"Dennis, it's Max. You have to come right out here!"

"Is everything okay?" Dennis said, fear in his voice.

"Lil has disappeared!" Max looked up the empty highway towards the town of Furnace Run.

SEVENTEEN

Alone Or Not?

L il looked at the ground where the edge of the portal had touched it. The thin burn mark on the ground was on this side as well, and it was smoldering.

With a glance to make sure her adversary was indeed lifeless, she approached the spot. She wanted to search through the red dirt and to try to see if there was one of the fused glass pieces that had opened the portal in the Barrens, but the ground was still far too hot for her to even get close to, let alone touch. It was more like a red clay than the sandy soil in the Pinelands.

She looked up as noises came from overhead. She glanced again at her dead attacker and rose to her feet, opened the cylinder of her pistol and ejected the two empty cartridges, replacing them with fresh rounds.

It made sense that there were creatures here that would consume the corpse as surely as there were scavengers at home. She felt a dark terror, trying to imagine the creatures that ate the dead in this place. She wanted to avoid those at all costs.

She bent, picked up the baseball bat, and returned the pistol to her waist pack. Crouching low, she began to make her way through the barren forest. She was glad there was little underbrush, only the scrubby trees, a few fallen branches, and the short red grass that seemed to be in patches all over the ground. This allowed her to move noiselessly on the clay.

The light from the portal had been the main source of illumination, and she had to move slowly to feel her way as she went. She remembered that there were large thorny branches and knew if she ran face-first into one of those, it would do a lot of damage, so she stayed close to the ground.

She thought she understood why the monsters would have red eyes. They must possess a certain ability to see in this dark landscape. The first time she had peeked through a portal it had been brighter. Did they have day and night here, like at home? And if so, why did time flow differently in this place?

She hesitated, as she didn't want to wander very far from the location of a known portal but a noise caught her attention…the flapping of wings from the location she'd just left. She paused and listened again, as sweat prickled on her face.

Could the monsters track her by smell? Or did the sulphur stench eliminate that ability?

She worried about a panic attack, as this would be a really bad time for one.

Why didn't I take the damn Paxil? My purse is in my car on another plane of existence. Why didn't I bring the pills with me?

She heard the flapping of multiple wings and the sound of large bodies landing on the ground. Her eyes slowly adjusted to the dark, so looking back, she could make out shapes moving near the place where the dead Devil lay. Several large silhouettes were moving in the distance, as squawking noises came from their enormous beaks. She could just make out their large heads moving on scrawny necks. They appeared to be fighting over who got the tasty bits.

The largest one moved to the fallen creature, ducked its head, and lifted it with a tearing noise, pulling away with hanging flesh in its beak.

Lil looked away and swallowed repeatedly, the urge to vomit powerful. She had to fight it, it would give the predators a way to track her.

It was clear she couldn't return to the spot with the portal, at least not now.

Instead, she looked in the opposite direction. She could see more with each passing moment, and she considered pulling out her phone and using the built-in light. She quickly dismissed that idea. It would be an invitation for the creatures of this ravaged land to find her easily.

Staying low, she moved away as silently as she could, still hearing the sound of ripping flesh and the noises of the feasting carrion-feeders.

The ground rose uphill, and that was good. She needed to get to a higher plane where she could survey the area for threats and assess her situation.

She was uninjured, and had the bat and a gun, which gave her a tactical advantage. She had successfully shot two creatures in two days, and both had appeared unaware of the fire power of modern weapons.

Considering the one hundred-ten-year cycle, the advancements made in firearms could certainly surprise any of her adversaries.

Why didn't it work in 1909 for Pines Edge? They had been sure to have rifles and handguns. Or did the sight of these creatures so shock the citizens of that small town they didn't have time to defend themselves?

Another thought occurred to her. Could it be that the attack was so overwhelming the residents had been unable to stage an adequate defense?

She reached what she felt was the top of the bluff and leaned against a tree, using the thick trunk as cover. She held the bat over her head as she straightened to catch any of the branches before her head did.

Once at her full height, she paused, feeling dizzy. This was odd, she'd never felt dizzy in her life. It had to be the tension, the fear of attack, and her mind was overwhelmed.

Bad enough she was in this foreign place, but now she worried her thinking was muddled. She took several deep breaths, the taste of the sulphur in the air bitter on her tongue, and she gazed around.

She was on a bluff and the land sloped down around her. From what she could see in the darkness, the hill led down into a valley beyond. Even though there were many of the misshapen trees, she could still see between their branches.

She looked back to where she had come from and although there were no longer cries from the creatures, she could still hear the sounds of flapping wings combined with the noise of ripping and tearing. The feast was in full swing, and there were probably a dozen moving bodies in the distance.

Her gorge began to rise again and she remembered the bottle of water on her belt. She untwisted the cap and took a small swallow as a shiver went down her spine. She returned the bottle to the webbing on her belt, knowing that if this was her only supply of potable water, she had to make it last.

She looked out at the sprawling land before her. It went on for miles and miles, rather like the Pine Barrens itself. There were several rolling hills and odd buttes that jutted out of the land, appearing as huge, hulking shapes in the semi-darkness. No roads interrupted the vista, although several clearings broke up the continuous cover of trees. She could see no man-made construction, no buildings of any kind.

In a clearing in the distance, Lil caught the sight of a flickering orange light and her breath caught in her throat. Was that a *fire*? She looked again, as it appeared small and contained.

She listened intently as a sound came on the faint breeze: *drums.*

Lil took a huge breath. Could that be people? She didn't think drumming would be a sound the Jersey Devil would make.

She stared at the distant flickering flames. From what she could tell, it was in a clearing right next to a giant mesa, which stood straight and tall in the middle of the open land, a huge mountain with a flat top and steep sides.

She didn't want to leave this area where a portal had been. On the other hand, if there were people, it seemed a logical place to go. What if it wasn't people, but an intelligent race of creatures like the Devil? She would literally be walking into a place where there would be no escape.

She didn't have many options.

She crouched low and began to descend the hill, keeping the direction of the place she'd seen in her head.

As she moved into the lowlands, she proceeded quickly from tree to tree. Although she had not seen any of the winged creatures, she wanted to make sure that she wasn't open to being attacked. She headed in the direction she had observed the fire, with the sense that it was about a mile to reach it.

Her muscles ached from being in a crouched position, but she maintained her movements. Her body was damp with sweat, and she felt slow and clumsy. She had been thankful that there was little underbrush in the woods, as she made no noise as she advanced. But here in the lowlands, the spaces between the trees opened up more, without even tall grass to help hide herself. All that could be seen was the short red grass that didn't grow as tall as in the meadows of her home.

She surmised that very little grew in this place.

She was making progress and scanned the sky when she reached another tree, not that she could see much through the branches and the thorny needles. On her move to the next tree, a muscle spasm went through her leg. She paused and stretched for a moment, waiting for the spasm to pass. It was probably caused by crouching and the additional weight of her waist pack.

The fire was closer now, blazing up in the dark night. The flame was contained by large stones placed around it. It burned next to the open mouth of a cave in the side of the mountain.

The fire and the ring of stones were so close to the cave opening that it would be very hard for one of the overlarge devils to slip past it and get into the underground chamber. Or if it did and there were more than one, they would have to attack in single file. This made it a very considered and defensible position. Only a thinking being could have planned this.

She ducked low and continued on her way, weaving across the open area between the trees to make her path unpredictable.

Another grove was in front of her, and she paused there to catch her breath. She was now a collection of aches. Looking out again, the clearing before her seemed to be growing brighter.

She turned to look behind her and gasped.

The biggest full moon she had ever seen was rising in the distance. It was absolutely huge, at least ten times larger than at home. On the horizon, it was a bright reddish object that illuminated the path ahead of her.

It certainly looked like the same moon she'd grown up with, but as it rose, she could feel herself growing lighter, as if the closeness of the satellite shifted the gravity and lightened the heavy constraints she'd felt since arriving.

In the distance, a chorus of otherworldly shrieks and howls chilled her blood. The cries were preternatural and savage, the call of the predator as it prepared for the hunt.

She was the prey.

This realization got her moving and she ran on, this time upright and hurriedly, not bothering with stealth. There was no time for furtive movements, as the monsters were being awakened by the rising moon.

She was certain they would be hungry.

She continued her journey towards the open flame, which was easier to spot through the trees as she went, the baseball bat held in both hands, ready to strike. It could be easily thrown aside and replaced with her pistol.

She moved into another grove of trees as she heard wings overhead. Not the mere flapping of one or two pairs as silent as a bat, but the sound of dozens of wings, and the wild screeching was louder and more insistent.

Had they caught her scent? Or could they detect her presence through some impossible sense beyond the five that limited her?

She stayed low in the grove. The creatures would have to land beyond the trees, due to the sharp thorns that grew instead of the much gentler pine needles. A creature landing in one of the trees would be torn apart.

It was growing even lighter now as the massive moon continued to rise. It reflected more of the scarlet color of the atmosphere, making the sphere look bloody and frightening.

She reached the clearing that opened to the area around the cave. It had to be at least a hundred yards and completely open, though there were some small plants that stood up straight from the earth, in carefully cultivated rows.

There was no way to get to that cave and the safety it offered except over that open field.

She tightened her jaw, peered up at the sky, and saw nothing flying directly overhead, though she could still hear the sound of wings somewhere near. She broke into the clearing at a dead run.

A hideous scream came from overhead, and she could hear it coming closer. She was still too far away, so she slid to a stop and turned with the baseball bat raised.

The flying monster was almost upon her, huge and charging, its frightening talons aimed for her, the mouth open and the ferocious teeth bared, saliva slipping from the sides of the open maw.

It charged at her, teeth gleaming in the red light. Using the power of her turn, she struck the monster in its head with the bat and all her strength.

The creature tumbled aside and collapsed, but the talons of one clawed hand ripped into her shoulder and cut into her flesh.

The creature hit the ground hard and struggled to return to its feet.

Lil tossed the bat aside and extracted the pistol in one practiced move. She put two shots into the creature's head right between its equine eyes.

Above her, more screams echoed with the sound of more flapping wings. She turned and ran towards the fire, towards safety, and the monsters howled with their horrifying call of the hunt.

She sensed another creature diving down at her, and as its cry grew closer, she dove to the ground, rolling over to see one of the monsters as it fell on her. Lil would have been crushed except that its claws landed on either side of her thin frame, holding up the creature above her. The long body hair smothered her, and the animal stink filled her nostrils, as the monster lifted its head and opened its mouth to bite down on her.

She fired the gun, two shots in a row, hitting the enormous creature's head.

The head exploded in a rush of green gore that spurted over Lil, drenching her face and dripping into her mouth.

Sputtering and screaming, Lil slid out from under the thing as it lost its strength and collapsed to the ground.

Spitting, she rose to her feet, her vision blurred as what felt like an electric shock travelled through her brain and she collapsed back to the dirt.

She shook her head and looked up. The fire was not that far away. She had to get there. She struggled to rise to her knees as another electric shock travelled through her, blinding her with a flash of white light.

She had to make it, had to move, if not she was dead, it was that simple. She ran, the flashes of light going off every few seconds, causing her to stumble. She got to her feet in time to see one of the Devils diving down upon her.

She raised the weapon and fired her last two shots into her attacker. Green blood washed over her as the creature shrieked and fell sideways.

I have to keep going...

She attempted to take a step, but fell to the ground, the electric shocks making her muscles convulse and taking the strength from her legs. She rolled over to look up and see numerous monsters flying overhead.

She knew she had to reload the gun to shoot the bastards, but she kept being blinded by the flashes of light, and the pulsing of the odd electric current through her body.

Her vision grew dark, and she knew that the monsters would come down and take her, and she would be eaten alive.

I failed you, Mami Natalia.

The creatures flew low, diving down to attack, but she heard voices. A human voice yelled out in a language she'd never heard before. Sharp sticks appeared over her and a man's voice shouted words she couldn't comprehend.

Just as she blacked out.

PART III:

CONVERGENCE

EIGHTEEN

Artist's Retreat

S am Welling wandered over the train tracks on his way to paint. He carried his supplies in the worn pack, the reassuring weight felt good against his back. He was an artist, but a most specific type. His focus was graffiti, though he preferred the better name: Street Art.

It paid nothing. It was pure. Art for art's sake. Creating a mural that would impress his fellow artists and visitors gave him a high that drugs or booze never could.

He had travelled and studied the works of some of the greats. He had gone to Granada, Spain to watch El Niño de las Pinturas work, and helped him secure his location for an outdoor presentation using the side of a building. He'd gone up to Canada, and worked with StreetARToronto on the famed Graffiti Alley, a backstreet filled with colorful murals, that had become a major tourist attraction. He had painted in the Market District in San Francisco and the back streets of Brooklyn, New York.

His work was so good that his murals and designs were often left up for years, until another new artist painted over them. He was now on a mission to reach every famed graffiti location in the country and leave his mark in all fifty states.

He'd driven down in his smart car to Pasadena, New Jersey, to find a specific location hidden in the Pine Barrens. He could have done a location in Trenton or even Camden, both of which contained abandoned buildings that would work as a suitable canvas, but today, he'd sought the ruins of the Brooksbrae Terra Cotta Brick Factory.

The original building was built in 1905 by a man named William Kelly, who wanted to create terra-cotta bricks using the unique soil found in the Barrens. Before the factory went into production, Kelly died. Disputes over his will caused everything to cease, and the entire location fell into ruin.

The remaining walls of the abandoned site attracted artists. At first only a few, but over the years, more and more creators came here to make the battered walls a place of beauty.

As he walked up the path, the tagged areas appeared while he was still far from the actual structures. Trees along the path were decorated with brightly colored designs and skillfully prepared logos that represented different artists. He could see the remaining stone walls upright ahead of him in the path, and the bursts of color around him continued.

Rocks on the sides of the path were painted, even a small ground plant with sharp, pointed leaves was not spared. The green plant was now an explosion of aquamarine, purple, and red. Sam thought the paint might be killing it, as it was drooping and unhealthy.

But what a way to go, as a thing of beauty.

He now approached the walls, four standing about eight feet tall, and several low ones, that must be the remains of the foundation that formed the factory and its different rooms. There was an active stream nearby, which was necessary for the brick-making process.

Sam walked past the short walls and examined one of the taller ones, looking over the designs and colors. Some artists had merely painted a name in the classic overlarge, puffy letters, but in a palate of interesting colors. Others used tight hard messages or names with the characters simple and stark but the background behind them clever and shaded.

He was glad he'd made this his choice, as there was the work of hundreds of artists, who had all come to leave a little something for the next voyager to see.

He went to the side of the buildings that faced away from the path. This would be a better choice, not something you would see as you approached, but a hidden gem that an explorer would have to seek out.

Art for the sake of art.

He wandered to the far side of what appeared to be a longish tunnel that extended for the length of the lost factory. The roof of it had collapsed and left debris so that this hall could not be entered, but Sam knew what it was.

This would be a drying tunnel for unfinished bricks to harden before they were 'fired.' At one time, wooden shelves lined both sides of it, from the ground to just inches from the ceiling, and layer upon layer of bricks would have filled those shelves. A large fan, powered by a steam engine would have been at the end of the tunnel to move the air past the bricks to speed the process.

Sam liked to do his research before he came to a site, and this was no exception. He read about brick-making before he came, so that he could fully appreciate the place where he wanted to create his work.

The tunnel seemed the perfect location, and he set down the backpack and began to pull out multiple cans of spray paint.

He put on his headphones, pumped some tunes, and picked up a can to begin his work.

The lighting was changing. He hated when the light shifted, but he had done projects long into the night, so he would adapt.

He turned to find this new light source and was shocked to see a ball of light floating about three feet off the ground, no more than ten feet away.

He stepped towards it but shielded his eyes from the brightness as he approached. The ball was growing, and Sam stepped back quickly. He was familiar with stories of 'ball lightning' yet he couldn't imagine that would occur on such a clear day.

He slipped his headphones off as he could sense a loud hum in the air. It sounded like it originated from the light itself.

The ball continued to grow and flatten out into an oval of light suspended an inch off the ground. The center seemed to move and shift as it glowed.

Sam reached down and picked up a small rock. With trepidation he threw it into the oval. It disappeared into the pool of light.

After a moment, the rock flew out of the oval back at him. Sam bent and picked it up. It looked like the same rock, and it was not hot or changed in any way.

But he couldn't be sure.

He picked up a can of spray paint and coated the rock with a little red paint. Not much, but enough so that he could recognize it if he saw it again.

He tossed it into the circle of light. Once again, he did not see or hear it drop to the other side.

After a few moments, a rock flew out of the circle and landed on the ground.

A rock with red paint on it.

There was a line in the fresh paint, like a finger had smeared it as it was picked up.

Sam stared at the circle of light, but it was swirling and it looked like something was coming through it. First, a hand appeared. Well, not really a hand, more like the talon of a bird, but larger than any bird Sam had ever seen.

This was followed by another talon, and arms. But the arms were about the thickness of a branch and covered with a fine hair.

All at once, a creature hopped out of the oval and stood before Sam, who jumped back in shock.

His fear passed, as the creature was only about three feet tall with large eyes, and it looked around, appearing more afraid than Sam was.

He knelt to look at it as it glanced about blinking its large red eyes, as if the sun was far too bright for it.

This was an animal he'd never seen before. It had stubby legs, covered in golden hair, that led down to hooves of some kind. Its upper body was like a person, but the long neck and elongated face suggested a pony more than anything else, yet the ears were floppy, like some breed of dog. The forearms with the sharp talons had elbows, but they were backwards, more like the forelimbs of a four-legged animal. A long tail curled behind it, making gentle sweeping movements.

As if to prove this, the creature leaned forward and put its claws to the ground, making it appear to be the size of a large dog.

It unfolded a pair of bat-like wings and shook them out, and then folded them close to the body again.

"I have *so* got to get a picture of you," Sam said quietly, not wanting to scare the creature. He reached into his bag to get his camera and found one of the protein bars he carried with him.

Moving slowly, he brought out the bar and held it up.

The creature eyed him suspiciously, but its ears perked up in curiosity. He carefully unwrapped the treat, his movements slow and deliberate. Then he held it out.

The animal sniffed the air with its large nostrils and the eyes widened in excitement.

"It's okay," Sam said softly as he held it out. "You can have it."

The creature opened its mouth slowly, exposing a wicked maw of sharp teeth. It took a hesitant bite and moved quickly back as it chewed.

The eyes grew wide again. The creature obviously enjoyed the taste.

Sam took the rest of the wrapper off, and put the packaging on the ground with the bar resting on top of it. Then, with his camera in hand, he stepped back to the wall he'd been about to paint.

The creature delightedly moved forward and, resting on its haunches as it picked up the bar in its odd hands, it brought the treat to its mouth to continue eating.

Sam lifted his camera, but the creature was in silhouette from the light of the oval. He slowly stepped away in a large circle around the little animal, as the strange beast stopped eating to look at him in alarm.

"It's okay, it's okay," Sam soothed, as he positioned himself near the oval of light, and raised his camera again.

Once he stopped moving, the beast went back to eating the morsel as he snapped off several photographs. He would have to do some serious research to find out what this creature was, as it was unlike anything he'd ever seen before.

The beast finished the treat and snuffled its long snout on the ground to see if any bits remained.

"So, where did you come from?" Sam asked, his back to the oval of light. "And where is your mother?"

With an unnatural scream, talons sank into the flesh of his shoulders.

Sam cried out, his camera falling to the ground as pain coursed through him. The creature he'd just bribed jumped up and down with excitement.

Sam turned his head to see a much larger version of the animal towering over him, saliva dripping from the mouth filled with those large, sharp teeth.

Sam screamed as he was pulled through the portal. The small creature followed eagerly and dove through the opening.

A moment later the oval shrank into a small ball of light and disappeared, leaving a dark line of burnt soil where it had been.

NINETEEN

Under The Red Moon

L il's eyes fluttered open. She came awake to see the gray stone of a curved ceiling far above her. She raised her head and glanced around the room, her breath catching in her throat.

Where was she? How had she gotten here?

The stone ceiling curved into stone walls, and she decided that she was in a cavern. Near her was a rough-hewn table made of red wood. Upon it, sat an old-fashioned lantern with a glass globe and a burning wick. This is what supplied enough light for her to see as the room had no windows, no openings at all, except a tunnel.

The room itself was amazing, tall and curved, and as best as she could tell, carved out of solid rock. But, she could not see what tools could have made it, as the walls were smooth and almost polished in their beauty.

She was lying on a woven mat that did little to make the ground under her any softer, but at least she had not been left in the dirt. A fur blanket rested on her, made from the skin of some animal. From the long coarse hairs, she couldn't fight the feeling that it had once been one of the Devil creatures. She looked at her left shoulder where she'd been wounded, to see that brown grass was wrapped around it like a bandage.

She slowly stood up and looked over at the table. The wood was indeed a dark red like the trees and the tabletop appeared to be one solid horizontal slice of a mammoth trunk. There were four tall chairs made of wood with seats woven from some reedy plant.

A man's head appeared at the tunnel and looked at her. He was an older man with white hair and a round face. He stepped into the room wearing clothes from another era, a full shirt, a black double-breasted vest, and black pants.

It was the man who had appeared briefly in her cottage the previous night.

Lil stared at him in shock, unable to speak.

He smiled. "Hablas Español?"

Lil shook her head in surprise.

"Do you speak English?" he attempted.

"English, yes," Lil gasped, finally able to produce a sound.

"Ah! Good, that will make things easier. I wasn't sure since you were colored."

Lil was surprised, and a bit put off by his choice of the word 'colored.'

He went on, "Welcome to *Nkantahkink.*"

"Is that where I am?"

"Yes. From my knowledge of the language it simply means 'hidden land,' but it is as good a name as any. How are you feeling?"

"I'm fine, and I'm not Hispanic. I'm Romani."

His eyebrows went up. "Then you're a gypsy?"

Lil stood up straighter, still not sure how she should react. Was he even there, or was this another phantom? "We...um...don't like that term."

"Oh? I'm sorry, I meant no offense," the man said, as he moved to her. "May I help you to the table?"

Wanting to make sure he truly was there, she offered a hand which he took and escorted her to one of the tall chairs.

"You're real," she said.

The man frowned. "Was there any doubt?"

"Yes," she confessed. "You appeared in my kitchen last night."

"Really?" He seemed amused by this. "I was unaware that I traveled anywhere."

Lil pushed herself up as the chair was as tall as a bar stool, if not taller. The chair creaked as she sat, but was comfortable enough.

The man pulled himself up on a chair as well. "I believe introductions are in order. My name is Albert Thompson."

She nodded. "Lil Slavik." Her hand went to her waist pack, to find it was missing. "Where are my things?"

The man opened his hands to suggest he meant no harm. "Your possessions are quite safe. We recovered your pistol and even your cudgel."

"Cudgel?" Lil repeated, unfamiliar with the word.

"Yes, the one inscribed 'Louisville Slugger'?"

"That's a baseball bat."

"Ah, I thought as much, but it has been many a year since I saw a baseball game."

"Thank you for...um...rescuing me," she said tentatively. "You did rescue me, didn't you?"

"Oh, there were many of us involved."

Lil indicated the webbing of grass on her shoulder. "I also appreciate the bandage."

"It is woven from a healing plant we cultivate here and is perfectly safe. I know, I was a doctor when I lived in Pines Edge."

"*What?*" Lil leaned back in her chair. "That's impossible, that town was abandoned over a hundred years ago."

Albert paled a little at this. "That long?"

"Yes, Pines Edge was found empty in 1909."

Albert looked at the floor. "May I ask what year of the Lord you come from?"

"Year of the—you mean, what year is it?" Lil replied, confused.

"Indeed."

"It's 2019."

He thought about this before answering. "This is troubling."

"Why?"

"Because I have been in this place since 1909."

Lil stared at him as if he were insane. "That would mean you're, like, a hundred-and-fifty years old."

"Only one-hundred-and-forty. I was born in 1879."

Lil's mouth fell open. "How can that be?"

"Time passes differently in this place. I was thirty when I arrived. I thought I was about sixty at this point, but it is hard to tell," Albert sighed. "The *skòntay* disrupt time in ways I can only guess."

"*Skòntay?*

"Yes, the glowing ovals of light that link this world and the one we both came from."

"I just call them portals."

Albert shrugged. "*Skòntay* would translate to doorway, so it would appear that we are close enough." He held up a wineskin he'd been carrying. "I brought water."

"Is it safe to drink?"

"I've been drinking it a very long time," he said and held it out.

Lil took the wine skin and poured some of the water into her mouth. It was clear and possessed a slight sulphur taste, but she really needed it. Once finished, she handed it back to Albert.

"Perhaps I can explain things," Albert said, taking back the wineskin. "We heard your gunfire, and the *ilaok*, the warriors, ran out to protect you and bring you within our caves. It is not common for one person to kill three of the *Piasa*."

"Is that their name?" Lil blurted. "It's what they call them in the Midwest: the *Piasa* bird."

"The 'bird' part was an addition. The people who live in this land call themselves the *Clova*. The name *Piasa* has been used for many generations."

"We call it...them...the Jersey Devil."

Albert leaned back and nodded. "Ah yes, I can recall those tales. I am sure you know, since you've been here, that those legends were very wrong." He met Lil's eyes. "I have to ask you, how did you arrive here? You came with a weapon and are quite adept in its use. I must say you seemed prepared."

Lil sensed the easiest explanation would be the best. "There's been a rise in missing persons in the Barrens."

Albert frowned. "Was your husband one of the missing?"

"I'm not married. I'm a cop."

Albert appeared surprised. "A *woman* police officer?"

"What's wrong with that?"

"I have no idea the way things are done in your time. But in my day, it would seem inappropriate to allow one of the fairer sex to be in such a violent and dangerous occupation."

Lil grinned. "Things have changed since 1909."

"So it would appear," Albert said wistfully.

"As to how I got here, I was pushed through a portal by a *Piasa*. I wasn't able to get back through before it collapsed."

Albert considered this. "I assume you dispatched *that* creature as well?"

"Yes, and I had to run because I heard whatever you have for vultures here, and I didn't want to meet them."

"A wise precaution. The *Mòchipwis* are not something you want to run into. They are a large red feathered monstrosity, rather like an overlarge scarlet vulture. But their talons and sharp beak make them quite formidable, especially if they think you want to fight them for their meal. I must tell you that there are very few people who come through a *skòntay* and survive long enough to find our camp."

"I can believe that."

Albert stood and picked up the lamp by a handle. "It would be best if I introduced you to the people who actually saved you. The chief has requested to speak to you. Come, let us go."

Lil pushed herself up from the table. "When do I get my things? I need to get back."

Albert smiled. "After you meet with the tribal elders. It would be impolite to meet them with a weapon. And you may need to rest, you've been injured. Please follow me."

"But I—"

"Doctor's orders," he said and headed down the nearby tunnel, carrying the lantern aloft.

Lil followed, looking around as best she could by the limited light of the oil lamp. The passage was also quite smooth and the ceiling at least ten feet from the ground. They walked for a few minutes in silence before entering an enormous cavern. The space went on as far as the eye could see, and the roof above them was twenty or thirty feet high.

In front of them was, to all appearances, a Native American village with multiple wigwams, and stout frame buildings covered in hides. The structures were scattered around the large encampment, with small campfires burning in front of several of them. The cavern carried the smell of woodsmoke.

"Most of the camp is sleeping now," Albert explained. "Always the best choice during the full moon, when the *Piasa* are on the hunt."

He led her through one of the well-trodden paths and approached a large wigwam at the center. He stopped outside and turned to Lil.

"Inside you will meet the chief of these people. He is called 'Chinkwe' and he will want to know how you arrived here. I will tell him what you have told me, but he may have questions."

Lil nodded, as Albert politely called out, speaking words in the strange language again.

He received a reply, placed the oil-lamp on the ground, and gestured for Lil to follow as he entered.

As she stepped in the room, five of the tallest men she'd ever seen stood before her. They were at least seven feet tall, and thin. They had good sized noses and strong cheekbones. To Lil's eye, they appeared to be very tall Native Americans, yet there was a strange shape to their heads, that suggested a divergence somewhere along the genetic path.

They were dressed in long leather robes, from what animal, Lil could only imagine. There were sections of the garment that were woven and trimmed with many beads of different colors and patterns, some quite elaborate. Colored designs were hand painted or embroidered at the waist and the hem: a red moon, black birds, even a *Piasa*. Moccasins covered their large feet and were as red as the leather of their clothes.

The man in the center wore the most elaborate outfit of all, a heavy robe adorned with beads, with colored patterns of many animals, and a large headdress made with long dark red feathers. The unusual plumes were larger than any bird's plumage Lil had ever seen. Each feather seemed to have a skeletal structure, bony and sharp.

They stood within a circle of rocks with a small campfire in the middle that offered warmth and light. The wigwam abounded with huge shadows of the men that leapt and shifted as the fire flickered.

Nothing Lil had done or seen had prepared her to be standing in front of these tall, imposing figures, and she felt terribly small and completely unsure of herself.

"It would be best if you sat," Albert suggested and pointed to a place within the circle of rocks.

Not knowing what was proper etiquette, Lil gave a clumsy bow to the chief and sat, trying to breathe deeply and calm herself.

The tall men lowered themselves into a cross-legged sitting position as Albert spoke in that unfamiliar tongue.

She heard her name 'Lil Slavik' in the mix.

The men sat and listened, then the chief held up his hand. He said several words to Albert who nodded and turned to Lil.

"He said you were most brave to fight the *Piasa* by yourself."

Lil wanted to respond but was afraid to say the wrong thing. "Um...please, tell the chief I am honored by his praise." She then added in a whisper, "Are his people Native American?"

"Hm? No, actually the *Clova* are a much older tribe. Generations ago, members of the Unami tribe appeared here, and they intermarried. Over the years, the *Clova* took on many of their customs and much of their language."

"That's the tribe that disappeared!" Lil gushed and turned to her host, realizing that Albert had not told him her response, and she fell silent.

Albert spoke quickly in the strange language and the Chief nodded. Then the chief gave a rapid fire statement to Albert, who turned to Lil.

"The *Clova* as well as the *Piasa* and *Mehuwe* are preparing for the *Wenchimtin*."

"Is that a festival?"

"Not in the least," Albert said quite seriously. "It is the 'coming together,' the time when our two worlds become one for a night. You might call it, a 'convergence.'" Albert opened his fingers to interlock them, as if to illustrate his words. "The chief and his warriors have found…the remains of many of your people who ended up in our world."

"Did any of them make it to this camp?"

"I am afraid not."

Lil lowered her head. "I'm sorry to hear that."

"The chief understands you are a mighty warrior woman, who burns with an inner fire."

This made her look at her impressive host. "Um…thanks?"

Albert spoke to the chief, who nodded and replied. He returned his attention to Lil. "If you wish to go back to your world, the chief has offered to have you escorted with strong warriors once the moon goes down and the beasts are sleeping."

The chief spoke some more and Lil recognized his use of the word *Wenchimtin:* the convergence.

Albert spoke up. "The chief wishes to tell you that the time of the *Wènchimtin* is very soon, and you must warn the people of your world."

"You mentioned that time is different here."

Albert nodded. "You and I shall discuss what is to be done. Please bow to the chief."

Lil faced the man, rose to her feet, and bowed. "Thank you, chief."

The chief nodded, a smile on his face. He said some other words, and Albert answered as he pulled aside the flap of the wigwam to escort Lil out. She followed with one last look at the tall men. Even sitting, their long legs and arms were disconcerting.

Albert picked up the lantern and led her in the direction of a different tunnel from which they came. It was then that Lil noticed that the walls of the central cavern were littered with many similar openings and other tunnels.

"You will be able to leave once the moon sleeps," Albert announced as they walked. "Two warriors and I will accompany you in the morning. Meanwhile, you should have food and try to rest."

Lil tried to look down the tunnel they were in, but the light of the lamp was very limited in dispelling the gloom. "Are we going a different way?"

"Hm? Yes, I am taking you to my abode to eat. You can stay there and rest."

"Why aren't you in the village in the big chamber?"

"That is only for the tribal elders and their families."

Lil stopped. "Well, you look like an elder. And you look very good for one-hundred and forty."

He turned back to smile at her. "But I am not of the tribe. I will always be an outsider, despite my many years here."

"What's your story, Albert? How did you end up here?"

The older man began to walk again. "I was there when Pines Edge was attacked."

"Wait, you were *attacked?*"

"I told you of the *Wènchimtin.* It is when the two worlds come together."

She caught his arm, and he paused. "I don't understand."

He looked down the dark tunnel. "Not here, we can discuss it in my home."

He turned and they continued until he took a side tunnel that opened up into a large room. It was not as large as the huge cavern, but it was much bigger than the small room in which Lil had awakened.

There were blankets hung from ropes to make different sections. The blankets were handmade and Lil felt the rough fabric. It was a similar plant that had been used to make her bandage, a weed carefully dyed and interwoven into breathtaking designs. There was the smell of a wood fire, and Lil saw a small hearth, not more than a hole carved into the rock. The smoke was carried out and did not fill the room.

Around the room was simple handmade furniture, including a round table like in the other room, with the same style of primitive chair. The difference was that of the six chairs, three of them were the regular height of a chair in her world.

Albert placed the lantern on the table and went to the fire to warm his hands.

One of the blankets moved aside and a tall woman entered. She wore a simple red 'buckskin' dress, though it had a few patterns on it. Her graying hair was wrapped into two pigtails on both sides of her handsome face, and there was a red ribbon woven into the hair. She smiled at Albert and spoke to him, and then bowed politely to Lil.

"This is my wife, Walania."

"I begin to understand why you didn't go back to Pines Edge."

This made Albert smile. "It is one of the reasons. Please sit. Walania will bring you cornbread and stew."

"You have corn? Here?"

"It does quite well in the soil of this place. The tribe has grown it for a long time. When the Unami came, they carried seed with them."

He took off the wineskin and sat at the table, pulling out a long-stemmed pipe and a worn pouch. He put a bit of tobacco in the pipe and grabbed a piece of kindling from a hide bucket near the floor in front of the fire. He lit the stick and touched it to the bowl of the pipe and puffed until the tobacco lit.

Welania brought them both carved stone bowls of a stew that smelled wonderful. Along with it, in woven fabric, were two pieces of cornbread. She put down crudely carved stone spoons.

"Thank you," Lil said, and Walania smiled and went back behind the blanket.

"You must forgive my wife. She is shy around strangers."

Lil tasted the stew. It was hot and good, and there was a meat in it she didn't recognize and didn't want to ask about.

"Why is she shy?"

"You noticed how tall the men were in the chief's home? The *Clova* are all like that, seven feet tall and taller. That changed during the *Wenchimtin* when the *Unami* were brought here."

Lil broke off some of the cornbread and chewed it thoughtfully. "Wait...they were *brought* here."

"I'll explain that more in a moment. The *Unami* were Indians —"

"We call them Native Americans in my time."

"Oh? Well, their customs fascinated the *Clova*, and they adopted many of their words and ways. The two races intermarried, and most of the children grew to be over seven feet tall."

"But not Walania."

"In every generation there are those who are of average height. They are often treated with contempt by the tribe and many times do not marry."

"But *you* married Walania?"

"I did, and now we come to my tale. I was a doctor in a small town in the Pine Barrens. At that time, I was married with two children, and was a respected member of the community."

"Then came this 'convergence' you spoke of."

"Yes," Albert said, puffing on his pipe, his food ignored. "Imagine you are living your life, perfectly ordinary. And at twilight, a strange red light fills the night."

"Red? Like the sky here?"

"Yes, only it was like last night. A blood red moon, larger than any you could imagine, appeared. And *things* flew out of the sky...and attacked. Things that look so much like devils you felt that the gates of Hell itself had opened, and Armageddon was outside your window."

"That would be difficult," Lil agreed, caught up in the story.

"Hundreds of those monstrosities flew out of the night sky with a screeching sound as they descended upon our town. There were gunshots and people screaming, and the monsters' cries of victory. My wife and boys ran into the woods to be safe. I didn't know that it wasn't our woods anymore. It was these woods, *here*."

"You mean anywhere you went in your town, you ended up here?"

"During the night, dozens of the doorways opened and surrounded our town. Any direction we ran, we ended up here. The monsters burst into people's houses and carried them away. No one was left behind, even the bodies were taken to…feed upon."

Lil found that her appetite was gone and pushed her food away. "What happened to your family?"

"When we were set upon, I had an old pistol and shot one that attacked me, but the *Piasa* carried off my wife and sons." He stared at the bowl of his pipe. "I can still hear their screams."

"How did you find this tribe?"

"The same way I suppose you did. I saw the fire outside the cave and made my way to it. The *Piasa* and *Mehuwe* were far too busy feasting on the citizens of Pines Edge to bother with me. The tribe was not surprised, as this had happened before and they expected it."

"How did you communicate?"

"There were people who had been brought over in the previous *Wenchimtin*, and some were still alive back then."

Lil paused for a moment before she said, "The people from Apple Hill?"

Albert's eyes lit up. "Yes, yes indeed. You know of them?"

"The town was abandoned in 1799 and was very similar to Pines Edge."

"How have you found out these things?" Albert marveled.

"On the Internet," Lil admitted, then was aware that Albert had no idea what that was. "It's like a—" she struggled for the word "—an encyclopedia, it has a lot of information."

Albert looked confused but went on. "There was an older gentleman. He had learned the language and even taught the tribe's shaman English. He was very old, didn't last more than a year after that. But the shaman, Talleyia, and I became fast friends. I helped him with my medical knowledge and he taught me how to use the native plants to make medicines and bandages."

"Why didn't you try to get back to Pines Edge? You know, let the world know what happened."

"Because after the *Wènchimtin*, the portals were closed for a long time. I stayed with the tribe and met Walania. My life is here."

"I can see that," Lil agreed.

"That is why *you* must go back and warn people, prepare them. The *Wènchimtin* is coming and there will be no way to return when it ends."

TWENTY

Searching

"Well, that's just fine!" Dennis huffed, after he watched the video of Lil and the Devil vanishing into the portal.

"What do we do, Dennis?" Max asked.

Dennis looked at the little man in annoyance. The statement Lil had made when he asked if Max had spent the night ran through his mind.

"That's not any of your business, Officer Decatur."

He felt it *was* his business. The only thing he'd wanted was for he and Lil to be as they had been, reunited after the years of separation, and this Indian dweeb showed up and ruined it.

On the other hand, looking at the video, he couldn't see what Max could have done differently.

Dive in after her, he thought. But he knew it would've been a foolish gesture. If both Max and Lil were on the other side, Lil would have to protect the pair of them from God only knows what.

Lil had her gun and could take care of herself. But, he worried that Lil had been pushed in the portal by the Devil creature. What if the thing had wounded her, or worse? Even if they could open the portal, would there be the chance that all they would find was a corpse, picked clean by one of those fiends?

That thought was intolerable to Dennis.

"I need you to go over how you opened the portal again," Dennis said, taking charge. "You told me that Lil did something with a piece of the fused glass. How does that work?"

"I don't know, she held it then threw it back to the spot it came from."

"Which caused that rock of hers to glow?"

Max nodded. "Yes, and then there was that weird hum and the portal opened."

"I get it." Dennis pulled on a pair of leather gloves from the pocket of his uniform jacket. He rooted through the sand and pulled up a small, glassy rectangular stone.

He moved away from the clearing, walking backwards, his eyes on the portal location.

"Now what?" he asked Max.

"Throw it in."

Dennis gave a level underhanded throw, the rock clunked to the sandy soil inches from the burn mark.

He walked over to the small polished stone that lay on the heavy black piece of cloth and picked it up, holding it out.

"Do I concentrate on it or what?"

"How do I know? Lil's the one who did it."

"Okay. If it opens, I'll keep the stone when I go in."

"What? Are you out of your mind?"

"I have to find Lil. If I'm not back in one hour, call the Furnace Run Police or the State Police."

"Um…sure." Max rolled his eyes.

Dennis held the small stone and focused his attention on the rock. It was still slightly warm, as if the stone had not yet completely cooled from the last time the portal had opened.

Inside his mind he repeated, *Gotta get to Lil, take me to Lil.*

He opened his eyes.

The two men stood there and waited...and waited.

Finally after ten minutes, Dennis covered the stone. "It doesn't work."

Max visibly relaxed. "Maybe you did something wrong?"

"Like what?"

"I don't know," Max whined. "Throw the first rock again."

"Fine!" Dennis spat, pocketed the cloth with the stone in it, and went back to the line to pick up the fused glass piece again.

"Maybe you have to hit the line," Max suggested.

"It's not a freakin' game of horseshoes," Dennis grumbled, picking up the rock a second time.

"Maybe it's your glove. Lil touched it with her bare hand."

Dennis considered this a moment. That wasn't a bad idea. Shaking his head in disgust, he pulled the glove off his right hand and held the rock tightly, focusing on Lil a second time.

The small stone seemed to grow warmer in his clenched hand. At first he barely noticed, but as he held it, he could definitely sense the warmth that radiated from the rock. Dennis stepped about two feet away from the line and lightly tossed the rock right on it.

The sound of wind rushed all around them, and Dennis moved back several steps and pulled his weapon to raise it toward the portal location.

A sudden burning warmth came from his pocket.

With a shout, he pulled his pocket inside out, the small cloth landed on the ground, and the stone rolled out, glowing.

What looked like a beam of sunlight shone down from above and the ball of light appeared in the center. Max gave a cry of excitement that Dennis could barely hear above the loud hum.

He moved to the small man, and again swept the trees to make sure no unexpected visitor arrived.

"Remember what I said: one hour," he told Max.

Max checked his wristwatch. "You got it."

The ball had begun to flatten out and form the elongated oval that hung in midair.

"Is there a trick to this?" Dennis asked.

"Trick?" Max repeated, confused.

"Yeah, a way you have to go in."

"I would advise jumping or stepping through, as you don't want your feet to touch the outer rim of the circle, which is hot enough to fuse glass."

"Right, that makes sense," Dennis agreed. He returned his glove to his right hand, bent, and wrapped the glowing stone in its cloth. He pulled his sidearm from the holster, and shoved the rock in its place, where it lodged near the bottom. "All right, I'm going in."

"Good luck," Max shouted over the din.

Dennis, suddenly not feeling all that brave, walked up to the glowing circle. He was sure that going through all at once would be a better choice than sticking in his head or his hand, as he had no idea what would be on the other side.

He took a deep breath, ducked his head, and hopped into the circle of light. It felt like he was being touched by a low-level police stun gun, as quivers of electricity ran up and down his body.

He landed on his feet and raised his head to a red world, gnarled and twisted trees were all about him, covered in red bark that matched the scarlet sky.

Out of the corner of his eye, he saw a flash of white to his right. He ducked, fell to one knee on the ground and raised his weapon.

Hanging from a nearby tree was the skeletal remains of one of the Devil creatures. The body was stripped of flesh and organs, and all that remained was a skeleton held together with the remnants of muscle and sinew. The folded pair of bat wings on its back appeared to be untouched by whatever had stripped the flesh so effectively. The head lay on the ground nearby, disconnected from the rest of the skeleton and thrown aside.

Dennis gave a sigh of relief and lowered his weapon as he surveyed the area around him. The air was warm and there was a sulphuric smell to it.

Carefully, turning to the right and left with his pistol extended, he approached a small pond.

It was a circular lake that reminded him of the famed "Blue Hole" in the Barrens. That small body of water was supposed to be bottomless and unexpectedly cold.

He turned again and looked around. The red clay soil was thinly covered by red grass about an inch high. However, the grass in this clearing had been trampled flat.

He lowered his weapon and turned his back to the pool to take a closer look at the skeleton hanging on the tree. The bones were still covered with the remnants of red meat and looked well chewed. On the ribs of the big creature there was a large hole where something punched into the chest to feed upon the internal organs. But near this large opening was a much smaller one, that looked like it could have been made by a bullet.

He glanced around, and his eye caught two bullet casings on the flat crimson grass. He began to smile. Lil had beaten the creature and had stopped to reload.

He wanted to call out to heaven, gesticulate up to the sky. She was alive and had dispatched the monster that put her here. Then, he stopped and glanced around again, with fear in his heart.

Where was she now?

Dennis heard water dripping behind him and what sounded like a human voice in the distance. He turned his head just in time to see a giant snake rising from the small pool behind him. It was bending back its head in preparation for a strike. The thing towered over him, at least ten feet high and on its head were a pair of horns the size of a grown bull.

With a cry, Dennis turned and fired three shots at the creature, the sound deafening at this close range. The monster fell back away from the noise and the stinging bullets. It made an inhuman cry and thrashed its tail, sending water flying from the round pool. The creature quickly sank back into the pond and disappeared.

Now soaking wet, Dennis watched it, amazed that such a large creature could fit in such a small round lake.

A voice called out again, and he turned, his pistol raised, his breathing fast.

Lil came out of the trees, in denim pants and a denim jacket, perfectly fine. A rush of joy filled his heart as he saw her, but just as quickly terror took over as she was followed by two enormous Native-Americans carrying spears.

He raised the gun as Lil lifted her arms and yelled, "They're friends, they're with me."

For a moment Dennis was confused, but he complied and lowered the weapon.

Lil rushed ahead, running now, and fell into his arms. Dennis held his weapon but hugged her with his free arm and kissed her hair over and over.

"God, I thought I'd lost you," he murmured.

Overwhelmed, he bent to kiss her, but suddenly noticed the portal rapidly closing.

"Lil!" Dennis shouted. He released her to frantically move towards the circle of light, but it had already collapsed into a ball which faded away as he watched.

Dennis walked over to where the portal had existed, but it was gone, leaving nothing but a smoldering line in the red dirt.

The tall warriors approached, carrying their long wooden spears and accompanied by a white-haired man with a walking stick.

"Lil, is this the man you told me about?" the older man asked as he approached, a slight smile on his face.

Lil looked like she was trying to compose herself. "Yes, it is. Dennis, I have someone you need to meet."

Dennis turned to face them, glancing up at the pair of giants.

The man examined Dennis' uniform from head to foot. "My, you truly look like a policeman."

"Um...thanks?" Dennis replied as he gazed up at the tall warriors. "Who are these guys?"

The two men inclined their heads and said some words to each other in a tribal language.

The older man spoke. "Forgive my lack of manners, sir. I am Albert Thompson, and these two warriors have been escorting myself and Lil here to try to return her to your world. These gentlemen are impressed that you frightened off the *Mëxaxkuk*."

"The *what*?" Dennis frowned.

"That serpent from the lake. It has killed many men."

"The warriors are members of the Clova tribe, Dennis," Lil gushed. "They have an entire civilization here."

Albert remained serious. "You both must return to the Pine Barrens, for a great danger is about to fall upon you, all of you."

"What?"

Lil took over. "It's called *Wenchimtin* or the convergence. This world connects to ours and these monsters have free rein to come and go as they please."

Dennis still glanced at where the portal had been, trying to wrap his head around everything that had happened. "I don't understand."

"I'll explain it when we get back home," Lil insisted. "We need to let the captain and the State Police know." She then turned to Albert. "So, how do we open the portal on this side?"

"The portals open and close randomly here. My plan was to bring you here and wait, as the portal would open eventually."

"Is that what has allowed these creatures to hunt on our world?" Dennis asked.

"That is correct. There are many such portals, and the *Piasa* are attracted by the noise they make," Albert told them. "To open the portal with intention can only be done on your side."

"Why?" Lil gasped.

"I am not quite sure," Albert said. "But I believe it has something to do with the soil and the heat of the portals."

"The fact that it fuses the sand into glass?" Lil asked.

"Indeed."

Dennis smiled and reached into his holster to pull out the black cloth and put away his weapon. "Will this help?"

Lil's eyes grew wide. "You brought it!"

Albert drew near, as Lil took the cloth and exposed the dark polished stone to the light.

"Where did you get that?" Albert wondered.

"My grandmother found it on a walk in the Barrens," Lil said. "She had it polished and gave it to me when I was a child. She told me it was 'the key.'" She looked at Albert's careworn face. "I'm sorry. With this you might have been able to leave here years ago."

Albert smiled. "My life is here. My wife and my tribe. But you must go, warn everyone, prepare them for battle."

Lil went to Albert and hugged him. "Thank you."

The older man stood back. Lil took the cloth and slid the stone into the open palm of her bare right hand. She closed her eyes and stroked it with her left.

Immediately the ball of light hovered over the line of burnt earth and began its slow growth. The two tall men took a step back in amazement, murmuring in their language.

Dennis looked up at the two men and each of them raised their overlong spear in a salute, just as Albert lifted his walking stick in the same gesture. Lil gave a bow and returned her attention to the expanding portal.

"We'll have to go through one at a time," she said to Dennis.

"I'll go first. The portal might attract something on our side," Dennis offered.

Lil reached into her pack and retrieved her revolver. "Good idea to go in armed." Then she added in a teasing voice. "You can still go first if you need to be macho."

Dennis grinned. "No need. I'll back you up."

Lil turned. "Albert, please thank the chief and your tribe."

"Godspeed, Lil," Albert replied.

She took several short steps and hopped through the ring of light.

Dennis nodded his head to Albert and followed her.

"Lil," Max yelled as he rushed forward and took her into a hug.

Lil returned the embrace, and then pushed him back gently. "I need my gun arm free."

Dennis stepped through the portal with a smile on his face.

Max shifted back and glanced around nervously. "Did one of those things follow you?"

"No, they usually only attack at night," Lil explained. "But on this side, they can hear the sound and it attracts them. The *Piasa* come here to hunt, but they always seek to return to *Nkantahkink.*"

"Nkanta-what?" Dennis asked, he was looking up and around for any incoming attackers.

"*Nkantahkink,*" Lil repeated. "That's the name for the Hidden Land according to Albert."

"That is the Lenape language, I recognize it," Max marveled. "But who is this Albert?"

"One of the people who live there," Dennis reported.

"There are *people* there?" Max frowned, then glanced over at the clearing. "The circle, it's closing."

Lil and Dennis both looked to the circle of light, which was rapidly collapsing in on itself. Once it faded, they both put their handguns away. She put her hand on Max's shoulder. "Thanks for getting reinforcements. Sorry I left your bat over there."

Max shrugged. "It was only a bat."

"How long was I in there, Max?" Dennis demanded.

"About half an hour, I guess."

Lil nodded. "More important, how long was I gone?"

Max thought about it. "I guess in total, about two hours for both of you."

"I stayed there overnight, I slept," Lil said shaking her head in amazement. "Then I was escorted to the portal in the morning. I had to have been there for over eight hours."

"How is that possible?" Max asked.

"I don't know," Lil pondered. "Albert said that time was different there."

"I think the old guy would know," Dennis agreed.

"That's the thing," Lil revealed. "He looked about sixty or so? Turns out he's a hundred-and-forty."

"What?" Dennis blurted.

"He's been in that place since 1909, the time of the last *Wenchimtin,*" Lil explained.

"It's a good thing I brought the stone or we couldn't have opened the portal," Dennis said.

"How do the Devil creatures get here, then?" Max asked.

"From what Albert told me, the portals open and close randomly, the number of occurrences increasing until the convergence. Then they don't open again for several years."

"When is this convergence?" Dennis asked.

"Soon," Lil intoned. "It could be as soon as our next full moon."

"I hate to bring this up," Max pointed out. "But...that would be tonight."

The three of them stood staring at each other.

"It looks like we have a serious problem," Dennis growled.

TWENTY-ONE

Alerting

"I don't give a good goddamn about this video you showed me," Captain Hewitt stormed.

"But captain," Dennis pleaded, "you saw what happened. That creature, Miss Slavik disappearing into the portal —"

"Yes, you got footage of the Jersey Devil, good for you! Looks more like a guy in a rubber suit and some cheap special effects. Now you want me to declare a state of emergency and ask the governor to call in the National Guard?"

"Captain," Lil spoke up. "We're not trying to fool you. There's more than one of those creatures, there are hundreds, maybe thousands of them. If they descend upon Furnace Run—"

"I've heard enough of this bullshit," Hewitt exploded. "Take this so-called proof you have to the media, see if they give a damn. I have a police force to run and I can't be bothered with wild tales about devils and other worlds." He turned to Dennis. "And Decatur, you're off-duty until further notice."

"But captain—"

"Look at the bright side, officer. You'll have plenty of time to hunt down your monster. Now, clear out, I've got work to do."

They left Hewitt's office silently, and Lil and Max waited outside the station house until Dennis had a chance to take off his uniform and change into civilian clothes.

"I'm sorry, Dennis," Lil consoled him when the big man came out.

"I knew it was a long shot," Dennis lamented. "Who is going to believe the Jersey Devil is real and about to attack our town with an army?"

Max nodded. "Taking it to the media would be useless. They'll just dismiss it like your captain did."

"You're right," Lil agreed. "With digital effects, you can create almost anything. Anyone who looks at it will just figure it's a clever fake."

"What can we do?" Max asked.

"I have guns, rifles. If we could get a group of people together…" Dennis stopped talking and stared into space.

"What?" Lil asked.

"People with guns," Dennis said, and turned to Lil. "My hunting club."

"Yeah," Lil said, getting excited. "The Hung Eagle Club!"

"It's Tall Eagle, Lil."

"I don't care if it's a scrawny buzzard. We need to talk to them."

Max cleared his throat. "Do you really think they would help?"

"We have to try," Dennis affirmed.

Dennis made several phone calls while Lil and Max waited by the truck. Soon, the trio all drove their cars to Lil's cottage to drop off their vehicles and ride with Dennis in his truck.

Lil took a few minutes and ran to talk to her father.

"Poppa," Lil said as she went into the barn and found him brushing one of the alpacas.

"What is it, *Chaj*?" he said, not taking his eyes off the contented beast.

"My dreams were right. Something bad is coming. I think it's coming tonight!"

"What are you talking about?" Her father turned to face her. The tall animal looked at him, annoyed that he stopped stroking her.

"I don't have time to explain. But you need to be safe. You need your gun tonight for the full moon."

"These are the dreams you spoke of with your grandmother Natalia?"

"Yes, and I think many Jersey Devils are coming!"

Her father frowned. "There's more than one?"

"Yes."

He stood there unmoving, and the animal finally pushed against him, and he began to run the heavy brush over its coat again. "If your grandmother Natalia warned you, then your mother and I will be armed."

"I need to go."

"Where will you be?" Her father stepped away from the animal and looked at her, worry creasing his face.

"I have to fight them, stop them. They are coming to do what happened to Pines Edge."

Fear crept into his eyes. "That bad?"

"I think so."

He put his hand on her shoulder. "Come home to me safe, *Chaj*."

She nodded and headed out to Dennis' truck, where Max was already in the back seat. She got in and shut the door. She shook her head to clear it.

"What's wrong?" Max asked.

"While I was in the Hidden Land, this weird thing happened," Lil confessed. "It was like electricity in my head, and I passed out."

Dennis glared at her from the driver's seat. "You didn't tell me that."

"You were busy fighting a sea serpent, Dennis."

"What?" Max yelped.

"Don't worry, I won," Dennis assured Max.

Lil went on blithely. "Anyway, my head feels strange."

"Lil, I know you were taking anti-depressants," Max pointed out. "Did you stop taking them, suddenly?"

"I didn't think I needed them…"

Dennis spoke up. "What are you getting at, Max?"

"When you cease taking antidepressants, some people experience what they call 'brain zaps.' They can be quite severe."

"How can I stop them?" Lil demanded.

"Keep taking the antidepressant," Max suggested.

She looked at Max in the back seat and then glanced over at Dennis. "No."

Dennis looked at her. "Lil, we need you at your best tonight."

"I know," she responded. "The *Paxil* helped me through a very rough time. But I have a feeling if we're going to survive, I need to be there, all there, feeling everything, even the bad stuff. With the *Paxil*, I was in the world, but emotionally, I was vacant."

Dennis nodded. "Okay. We have one more stop to make before we meet them."

"Where?" Max asked from the back seat.

"My place. We need more guns."

Dennis' living quarters were on the second floor over an empty storefront on Main Street, a short drive from Lil's. The trio raced up the stairs and into the apartment, where Dennis opened a large gun safe hidden in a closet in the bedroom. The safe contained an impressive cache of rifles, pistols, and even a shot gun.

Dennis placed the weapons on the bed along with ammunition.

"Were you expecting something like this?" Max worried, shocked by all the firearms.

"I like guns," Dennis stated flatly. "You'll take the shot gun."

Dennis picked up the single-barreled weapon and placed it in Max's hands. Max seemed surprised by the weight of it and held it clumsily.

"I'd rather not," Max declined, looking at the weapon with wide eyes.

"I'd rather you didn't as well," Lil said. "But, we're fresh out of baseball bats."

"Look, this will make up for any lack in accuracy," Dennis assured. "Just don't kill any of my friends."

With a curt nod, Max got a better grip on it and tried to hold it in a more useful stance. Lil pointed out the safety and explained how the rifle was loaded, as Dennis got a pair of cloth shopping bags and loaded boxes of ammunition into them.

Lil came over and picked up a small green rifle with a squarish stock and a large suppressor on the barrel. "Is this a Kel-Tec?"

"It's the RDB Hunter, good rifle," Dennis said, as he quickly went over his inventory laid out on the bed. "Just be careful, as it ejects shells downward. So you don't want to…um…"

She held it up, looking down the sight. "Don't hit myself in the tits with the hot brass?"

"Um…yeah. You can have it, I like a longer rifle, anyway."

"Compensating for something, Dennis?" She gave him a teasing grin.

Dennis smirked. "You would know, Lil."

"Can we please get going without comparing the size of our guns?" Max looked from Dennis to Lil and back again. "Cause I'd probably win."

Dennis grumbled. "I forgot the chaperone was here."

Dennis bundled the rifles into gun bags, and the rest he wrapped in towels. Soon, they were carrying out weapons to the truck. During one of the trips, Dennis pulled a pair of what looked like walkie-talkies off a charger in the corner of the living room.

"What's this?" Lil asked as Dennis brought one of the radios to her.

"Handheld GMRS Radios. They have a thirty-six mile radius."

They headed down the stairs, each with wrapped bundles. "What do you use these for?"

"When I go hunting with a friend in the Barrens. They work when the cell phones don't."

Lil shook her head. "Leave it to you to have these."

"Keep it with you," Dennis advised.

They loaded the wrapped parcels in the back seat of the truck.

"First aid kits?" Lil asked.

"We'll probably need them as well," Dennis agreed, indicating two white packs stowed in the truck.

Lil looked at the red crosses on the backpacks solemnly. "I think you're right."

A few short minutes later, Dennis parked next to the cement block building. Several other pick-up trucks were there as well.

"Not an overwhelming number," Max fretted. "Does everyone here drive pick-ups?"

"They're the best vehicle for the sugar sand roads in the Barrens," Dennis explained. "I know there aren't a lot of people, many are still at work, but we need to get the word out and these people can do that."

The trio went in through a side door, into the dark room with the large bar. Sitting at the different tables or standing near the bar were about ten people, eight men and two women. Dennis fist-bumped and greeted people, calling them by name.

"Everyone," Dennis said, using his strong voice to get their attention. "This is Max and some of you know Lil Slavik."

One guy stood up from a table. He was average height and a bit stocky with brown hair and a matching mustache. "Lil, we went to high school together. Tim Harkness."

Lil brightened, "Tim! Wow, it's been a long time."

They went around the room introducing each other, and Lil was pleased to see the dark face of Jamarr Bowman.

"Nice to see you here, Jamarr," Lil said as she gave him a hug. "Is anyone still working tonight? The captain sent Dennis home."

"Julie Hogan is on, and it seemed like a slow night. I'm here because Dennis said it was important. What's this all about?"

Dennis raised his hands to get everyone's attention. "This is Doctor Max Aggarwal, and he has a video to show you. It looks like something made in a special effect studio, but it's not. It's real."

Over the next half hour the group watched the video of Lil disappearing into the portal and the creature that pushed her there.

Tim spoke up first. "Come on, Dennis. This has to be fake. It's some kind of digital thing, like all those superhero movies where the good guys are fighting an army of aliens or robots."

"I know," Dennis said raising his arms to keep the group quiet. "But I'm telling you, this was filmed right in the Barrens, right here in Furnace Run."

Lil stepped forward, opened her coat, and pulled her blouse down at the shoulder to reveal the woven bandage. "Dennis, pull off the bandage."

Dennis frowned "Are you sure?"

"They want evidence, I have it right here."

Dennis carefully pulled at the dressing, which was woven from thin strips of a gray plant. Lil gasped as it was removed from her flesh.

Just under the clavicle bone were three long scratches neatly spaced. They had scabbed over, and stood out in dark contrast to her dusky flesh.

Murmurs went through the room.

"Christ, Lil," Dennis hissed. "Why didn't you tell me?"

Lil spoke up. "This was done to me by one of those creatures, by those claws they have. I was lucky it struck me where it did, a little higher and it would have cut my throat."

Dennis replaced the odd bandage, and Lil pulled her blouse back into place.

Tim looked around the room. "Okay, let's say we buy it. There are more than enough of us to take out this creature."

Sounds of agreement were voice by several people.

Dennis looked to Lil.

"It isn't just one creature," Lil advised. "When I went through that circle it took me to a hidden place where there are hundreds of them. The truth is, the Jersey Devil isn't one creature. It's a species."

Tim raised his hand. "How many of those circles—or whatever —do you think there are?"

Jamarr agreed. "Good point. If we can post people in the right places—"

Lil interrupted. "There are people in that world, and this has happened before. I was told that on the full moon, that place and Furnace Run will become one. It won't be a matter of portals, it will be *many* wide-open passages between the two worlds."

This caused a flurry of murmurs throughout the group.

Lil moved until she was near the bar. "I don't completely understand it myself, but there is a pattern. Every one-hundred-ten years a town disappears in the Barrens. You've all heard of Pines Edge? Or Apple Hill? Those towns weren't abandoned. The people were attacked by those…things."

The group was silent.

"You said on the full moon," Jamarr mentioned quietly. "The full moon is tonight."

A woman stood. She had long grey hair and a sturdy body in a flannel shirt and jeans. Her hands were strong and her face, careworn. "Dennis, if this is true, we got to get the army or the national guard or something." This suggestion received noises of approval. "You need to take that video to Trenton, show it to the governor."

Tim spoke up. "I don't know, Molly. Those politicians don't know Dennis."

Jamarr spoke up. "Dennis, did you show that to the captain?"

Dennis nodded.

"He thought it was a fake, am I right?"

"Yes, which is why I'm off-duty now," Dennis explained. "But look, we have to warn people. I mean, we're all Pineys here. Everyone we know has at least one weapon. We need to defend ourselves, defend our town."

Molly spoke up again. "Dennis, if I start calling people and tell them the Jersey Devil is about to attack, they're going to laugh at me."

"Good point," Max murmured.

"What if we tell them it's not the Jersey Devil," Jamarr responded. "Tell them it's something else."

"Like what?" Dennis asked. "The story so far is that a dangerous bear is loose."

"We have another problem," Lil revealed. "When this convergence happens, the sky turns red."

"We can tell people there's a fire in the Barrens," Tim pointed out. "That's common enough."

Murmurs went through the room and several heads nodded in agreement.

Dennis glanced about and finally said, "A fire is a good explanation. That leaves the question: how do we get people to arm themselves?"

Lil held up a hand. "A fire could cause the animals to flee. The story is we have a killer bear. If it panicked, it could rush into town."

"People would be afraid for their kids and their pets," Molly confirmed.

"That's not bad," Jamarr agreed. "That would give us an excuse to block the main road."

"For protection?" Tim asked.

Dennis nodded. "To keep the bear from going into town. We could even tell people that we need guns to scare it away, and only intend to shoot it if necessary."

Tim piped up. "Yes, but will the police chief let us do that?"

"That's a good question," Lil said and looked to Dennis.

"I think we can work it," Dennis suggested. "We park our vehicles in the parking spaces at each end of Main Street, and if there's trouble, we pull the trucks into the street and form a barricade."

"You do know these things can fly, right?" Lil stated.

"Shit!" Jamarr cursed. "This just keeps getting better."

There was a small amount of nervous laughter in the room.

"But it happens tonight, right?" Tim asked "When?"

Dennis looked to Lil.

"Okay, I know this is all very strange, but time is different in the Hidden Land," Lil explained. "But I believe in my heart it will be tonight. And it should be around sunset or the rising of the moon."

"What's your proof?" Tim challenged.

"Our only evidence is that video, Tim," Dennis said simply.

Molly stood, her phone in her hand. "I've been looking it up. Sunset is at 7:13, but the full moon rises tonight at 6:28. And it appears that tonight is something called a 'super moon' where it's closer to the earth than at any other time of year."

Another murmur went through the room.

"That can't be a coincidence," Lil stated with a look to Dennis.

"Here's the plan," Dennis proposed. "First of all, call people and let them know the bear story and that there is a fire in the Barrens. Then, we'll get our trucks to each end of Main Street. We only have about two and a half hours until nightfall."

The group nodded and everyone pulled out phones, moving to different parts of the room to speak to people and attempt some privacy.

Lil moved to Dennis, who was standing near Max. "Dennis, I think I have to be at that portal we found at sundown."

He frowned. "Then I'm going with you."

"No, you need to be in town and organizing the group. With Jamarr you can cover both ends of Main Street."

"You can't be there alone. You saw that sea serpent that almost got me. You need eyes in the back of your head, or someone to watch over you."

"I will go with her," Max volunteered.

"You?" Dennis growled. "You didn't protect her before."

"He attacked a *Piasa* with a baseball bat, Dennis. You saw it on the video," Lil affirmed. "I think that's pretty impressive."

"Besides, *now* I have the shotgun," Max said.

"Just don't shoot Lil," Dennis chided.

"That is where I need to be, Dennis," Lil insisted.

He took Lil by the arm and escorted her to a corner away from Max. "Where is this coming from? Visions from your grandmother?"

"It's just a feeling, Dennis. That's why I wanted to stop taking the *Paxil*. There's something…like a higher force…trying to guide me, tell me what I need to know. That drug got in the way of that."

"Higher force," Dennis argued. "What? Your gypsy powers telling you the future?"

"I'm a *part* of this. The stone, the way it can open the portal. I need to be there when this happens."

Dennis' jaw was clenched, and he couldn't meet her eyes. "I… just…don't want to lose you."

She reached out and touched his cheek. "Dennis, I don't know about us. I don't know about anything right now. I know I'm feeling attracted to you, after a long time of feeling dead inside. But...I don't know if that's enough."

"I want to be worthy of you, Lil. That was my mistake, years ago. I just assumed you would always be there. Now, I want to earn your love and even more, your respect."

Lil nodded and sighed. "Let's get through tonight in one piece, and then we'll talk, I promise. Now go, call people, make a plan and defend our town."

Dennis nodded. "I'd better make it a good one."

As Dennis strode away, pulling out his phone, Lil muttered to herself. "Please do or Furnace Run is dead."

TWENTY-TWO

Preparing

L il rode in Max's car, watching the setting sun as they drove west.

Dennis had driven them back to Lil's cottage, where they picked up Max's small SUV. It was a better choice than Lil's car, as it might be able to handle the terrain of the back roads in the Barrens, if necessary. The weapons were wrapped in towels and hidden from view. Dennis had also insisted that they take one of his first-aid kits.

Lil spoke as Max drove. "Once we get there, I want you to fire the Remington to get used to the recoil."

"Great, now I'm *Rambo*," Max fretted, obviously nervous.

"The best thing about a shotgun is that with enough distance you just have to point in the general direction and fire. It's a twelve gauge and Dennis gave us a box of heavy game load. A direct hit will take out one of those bastards but from a distance it will only wound them."

"Got it."

"You can load seven cartridges and you have to pump the lever each time before you pull the trigger."

"Okay."

"And if worse comes to worst, it's sturdy and you can swing it like a baseball bat."

This finally got a smile from Max. "At least I know how to do that."

"You'll do fine," Lil reassured him.

"I'll try," Max replied, and they drove in silence for a while. "You know that Dennis is in love with you, right?"

Lil sighed. "I don't know if he loves me or is in love with the memory of what we once were."

"What do *you* want?" Max asked. "I mean, once this is over."

"I don't know. My old life, my old goals…all of them are gone."

"You're resourceful, Lil. You'll think of something."

"How about you? I pulled you away from your research."

"My research seems so unimportant now," Max mused. "I think I want to change my focus on the Native American lore to study these different creatures and their legends. Perhaps I can find out if more of them were real or not."

"That might help people be prepared."

"There are also many stories of portals that shamans used for travel to other worlds. The Lenape practiced many rituals, especially in this area. If I could find one to activate—"

"We're close," Lil interrupted, looking at the road. "Pull over."

They got out of the SUV and Lil opened the trunk. Max caught her arm. "Lil. I want to thank you for making me a part of this. This is the most exciting thing I have ever done."

Lil nodded, as the memory of the dream of Max being carried off by one of the monsters flashed through her head. "Do me a favor. Don't get killed."

They quickly unloaded the car. It took two trips, one for the weapons, which they kept covered with the towels until they were in the woods. The second trip Max did alone, as Lil watched the weapons with her own loaded gun drawn. Max returned with several battery powered LED lights and also brought the first-aid kit.

"How long will the batteries last?" Max asked, as Lil set one up.

"A few hours," Lil reassured him. "I've been to the Hidden Land, there was a huge full moon, much bigger than here. If we do converge, it will be bright enough to see without lights."

"Aren't you afraid the lights will attract one of the *Piasa*?"

"We need to be able to see and the light might blind them," Lil stated. "Now let me walk you through how that shotgun works."

Lil quickly showed Max how to load the cartridges in the Remington and instructed him to carry extra shells in his pockets.

"If you hold it away from your body, it will slam into you and bruise your shoulder," Lil explained, showing him how to hold it correctly. "If your cheek is on the side of the stock, it won't hurt you. If you move it to the back, it will break your jaw."

"I don't think I can do this," Max worried.

"You can. Remember, lean with a leg forward. If you lean back you'll get knocked off your feet. Now, pump the lever and fire at that tree over there."

Max nodded, took a solid stance, pulled the lever back, and pressed the weapon into his shoulder. He sighted down the barrel and gave the trigger a pull.

The shot rocked the air and a chunk of the tree exploded into particles.

"Holy shit," Max muttered as he lowered the weapon.

"Good. Now put the safety on. You have to pump it every time to eject the old cartridge and load a new one."

"Okay, okay," Max said nervously.

"How was the recoil?"

"Not bad, I can handle it."

"I'm going out into the street and calling Dennis to see how he's doing. We have about an hour until dark."

"I'll be here," Max said and turned to watch the clearing.

Lil walked out of the woods and across the street. She only had one bar on her phone and she wondered if the devices would work at all once the convergence occurred.

She had a feeling phones would be useless.

She called Dennis.

"How's it going?"

"Good. We've got an assembly of trucks here, all parked in the spaces. And Jamarr has a team at the other end of town. If we need to, we can pull them into the street to block the road pretty quickly. We also have our weapons covered but accessible if we need them—"

"*When* you need them," Lil interrupted.

"So far, no one from the police has bothered us."

"I have a feeling our cell phones won't work when it happens," Lil advised.

"*Another* feeling?"

"Yes," Lil said. "I'm going to turn on the radio you gave me. Can you let Jamarr know about the possibility that the phones won't work?"

"Okay, I'll power up my radio, so at least you and I can talk."

Lil ended the call and crossed the street to head back into the woods. The road ran east to west, and was the only clear space between all the trees. In the east, she could see the full moon as a faint shadow in the sky as it rose from the horizon. She turned around to look west at the sinking sun which turned the atmosphere a reddish hue as it descended.

If they didn't succeed this would be the last day for Furnace Run.

She continued walking and found Max sitting with his back against a tree, the rifle across his lap.

"How are you two getting along?" Lil teased.

"I don't know," Max speculated. "She scares me, like most women."

"We aren't scary, we just need to be treated correctly. Besides, you have a certain charm."

Max shook his head. "I spend too much time with books. I have prided myself on my learning, on what I know. Now, I just feel I'm not up to the task."

Lil grew solemn. "We never know all that we're capable of until we are pressed into it. You read about my fiancé, right?"

"Yes."

"It was a tough bust. We went in with four detectives and thought we were just going to arrest one drug dealer who would spring for bail and be back in his apartment the next day."

"That wasn't what you found, though."

"No, he had a freakin' army with him. I honestly had never been so scared. But I saw Chad get hit, I saw him fall, and something happened, something broke in me. I lost all emotion, and just started taking out the shooters, one by one."

"You weren't scared anymore?"

"I became a cool, calculating thing. I lined up each shot and took out men, one after another, and finally they were all down, except for Paulo. I should have waited for backup, I shouldn't have gone in there. But I didn't care, I was dead inside. So, I walked in and Paulo throws down his weapon and says, 'I surrender.' And then he smirked at me."

"Smirked?" Max repeated.

"Yes, like this was all a big joke, like he didn't care that his guys had died or that he killed cops. I knew and he knew that if I took him in, he would get a high-priced lawyer and it would get him off. So, I shot him, just like that."

Max sat silent, looking at Lil.

Lil looked at the ground and muttered, "I guess *I'm* the actual monster in these woods."

Max opened his mouth to say something, but the radio in Lil's hand crackled and Dennis' voice came out. "Lil, it's Dennis, over."

Lil depressed the button on the side of the box. "I read you, over."

"I called Jamarr, and he's got about fifteen people with him. I have about twenty, over."

"Max and I are situated at the portal, over." Lil said.

"I'll call when something happens, you do the same, over."

"Got it, over," Lil said, and attached the radio to her belt. She unwrapped the Kel-Tec Semi Automatic from its towel and pulled the magazine, which she began to load with bullets.

"I don't think you're a monster, Lil," Max told her from where he sat. "I think you are very brave."

Lil finished filling the magazine and slid it into place. "Well, NYPD doesn't agree with you." She pulled out a second magazine for the gun and began to load it.

"Maybe they were wrong."

Lil shook her head as she continued to load. "No, they weren't. I lost control. I would've shot anyone who came in that door. That made me a danger to the public. I didn't deserve the badge anymore."

Max looked around. Long shadows filled the forest surrounding their area, lit by the battery-powered lamp. "I still think you're amazing. I mean, you went into that portal, visited that Hidden Land, and you came back."

Lil put the second magazine in the pocket of her coat. "Max, I may have to go in there again."

"You said it closes after tonight, maybe for years."

Lil nodded. "Then if I go in, I'd better get my sorry ass back out."

Lil walked over to Max, put her back to the tree, and slid down to sit near him. "You're a good guy too, Max, but get away from the books now and then. I mean, you're a scholar and I know you love it, but it's good to come out and be in the world as well."

"It's easier to hide in research," Max said. "Then I—"

An unearthly scream filled the air.

"Eyes to the treetops," Lil barked, as she rose in a crouch and sprinted to a different tree. She put her back to the bark and scanned the sky. Max stood, and he pumped the shotgun which sent the empty first cartridge flying out of the side. He kept his finger on the trigger guard and clicked off the safety.

They scanned the sky, but nothing moved.

"Hold your fire unless it comes at you," Lil shouted.

Another screech rang out, louder and closer than the first. Lil's hands were sweating as she gripped the rifle.

There were the sounds of something crashing through the trees, branches being broken and large wings flapping.

Not twenty feet away, just outside the pool of light, a dark shadow landed with a crash, snapping branches fell around it. It stood tall, its large bat-like wings extended. making it appear larger and more threatening.

It leaned its head back and made its fearful cry as it moved into the clearing, extending its wings and flapping them a few times as it did.

Lil had a bead on the creature with the Kel-Tec, and her finger was just outside the trigger guard. One quick movement and she could fire at the creature.

She was puzzled that, instead of attacking her or Max, the creature moved into the center of the clearing and walked to the burnt line on the ground. It folded back its wings and bent over to run one of its claws through the dirt.

Lil watched the shaggy creature as it bent. It didn't have a waist and needed to pivot its hips to lean forward.

The talons of its forepaw scraped through the soil as it lifted one of the fused chunks of glass from the dirt. It held it and stood up, again spread its wings and screeched.

"Don't shoot," Lil ordered Max in a low voice. "I want to see what it does."

The monster stepped away from the burnt line. It held the fused glass in one claw, and began to stroke it with the other. Since the eyes were on either side of its large head, it kept turning its head left and right to watch the clearing.

Lil's mouth fell open. She stood there in shock, the weapon still aimed right at the monster, as this thought burned through her brain:

It knows how to open the portal.

This wasn't the mindless instinct of a savage creature. It was trying to activate the portal, and had *learned* how the portal worked.

This changed everything. It wasn't merely a monster to fight and destroy, but a creature that could process information and come to a rational conclusion.

The ball of light materialized in the middle of the air just above the spot with the burned soil and began to expand.

Lil looked over to Max, who was standing with his back to the tree and the rifle pointed at the enormous fiend. But it seemed totally uninterested in either of them and kept its focus on the growing portal.

In about a minute, it had opened to its zenith, and the flat oval hung in midair. A claw came through and with a quick leap, a second *Piasa* came through, ducking low as it went and then standing up to its full height and unfurling its folded wings.

Suddenly, both creatures turned, one faced Lil and one faced Max, and the one that held the glass rock threw it at the floodlight.

The light was knocked off its small stand, which sent the beam shooting off in another direction as, with a cry, both monsters leapt at them.

The thundering blast of the shotgun went off, and Lil fired not one, but three bullets into the second creature which hurled itself in her direction. The suppressor on the barrel of the gun reduced the report to a mere "thwack—thwack—thwack."

The creature fell, but its forward momentum continued toward Lil, who spun to the side of the tree, just as the monster's talon lashed out and one claw ripped at the sleeve of her jacket and into the flesh of her arm.

Lil cried out and pulled away, so she didn't fall with the creature. She looked back as Max pumped the shotgun and fired point blank into his downed monster's head.

Green blood and gore leapt into the air and rained down on Lil as she moved further behind the tree. She glanced out of the other side to see if anything else came through the glowing portal.

She put the weapon strap on her shoulder and held the wound with her other hand.

"Are you all right?" she hollered as Max was on the other side of the tree.

There was another loud shotgun blast, and then Max said. "Yeah, I'm fine. The creatures are dead."

He came around the side of the tree. His glasses had green blood dripping from them, and there were pieces of hair and flesh on his clothes and face.

"I'm wounded," Lil said.

"Come to the light, let me see," Max said and gently led Lil to the fallen light, which he sat upright. Lil kept her eyes on the portal, still floating in the air, undulating in its disquieting way.

"It's not too bad," Max said, as Lil pulled her denim jacket off the arm. Max quickly pulled a pair of surgical scissors from the kit and cut her sleeve away.

Lil grinned. "It looks like you really are *Rambo*."

Max picked up the roll of gauze and looked at the two fallen creatures, unmoving on the ground. "Damn straight."

Lil hissed as Max put an ointment on the wound and wrapped it, quickly and efficiently. "Did you see what it did?"

"I saw. It knew about the rock," Max said as he worked.

"You're the anthropologist," Lil stated. "What does it mean?"

"It shows that they are *not* just mindless predators. The first one had a strategy, to get…backup. This displays metacognitive self-awareness and the ability to plan."

"You sound like you admire them," Lil said as Max cut the gauze and put white adhesive tape over it.

"I would love to study them," he gushed, and then looked over at the fallen *Piasa*. "I mean, if they didn't want to eat us."

"That does make studying them more difficult," Lil said, and pulled her jacket back on over the dressed wound. She pulled out the radio. "Lil to Dennis, over."

"I'm here, Lil. Anything happening? Over."

"One of them landed and opened the portal, do you copy?"

"Wait, what?"

"One of the creatures landed, ignored Max and me, picked up one of those fused glass pieces, and used it to open the portal. It waited until another Devil came through before it attacked. They're both dead. Dennis, these things can *think*." She paused for a moment and then added, "Over."

"You two all right? Over," Dennis sounded worried.

"We're fine, but did you hear me? They can think and plan, over!"

"That can't be good, over."

"Lil!" Max shouted. "Look at the portal."

Lil turned to see the shimmering surface of the portal moving, quivering as it turned a deep blood red.

Lil stared at it. For a moment she saw her grandmother Natalia in the center of the oval. The old woman looked right at her and in a voice that echoed in Lil's head said, "Run."

Then the old woman was gone. The red shimmering oval looked like it was on fire. The ground where it touched smoked and smoldered, even hotter than before.

"We have to run," Lil blurted.

"But the lights—" Max attempted.

"*Run!*" Lil screamed, jumped to her feet and ran as fast as she could with Max right behind her. The red light pulsed behind them and she glanced back as a blaze of fire surged toward where she and Max had been standing. The flame blackened and burnt the ground as it expanded in a scorching line through the old dead grass to the base of the trees.

Lil was sure it would set the forest ablaze.

The line of fire reached the lights and the battery pack exploded in a shower of sparks as the flames washed over it.

The strange otherworldly red light was expanding, pushing its way into their reality, rising higher and higher into the sky.

She kept running with Max behind her.

They were almost to the street when Lil stopped and turned, with Max gasping, bending at the waist with his hands on his knees.

"Are…we…far…enough?" he puffed.

Lil stared back at the place where the portal had formed. The darkening sky appeared to have been torn open by a jagged triangle of red light shining through it. Overhead she could see part of the blood-red moon larger than anything anyone had ever seen on earth.

Except maybe the residents of Pines Edge and Apple Hill long ago.

A cacophony of screams and screeches filled the air. Max and Lil both covered their ears against the tumultuous noise.

Hundreds of flying creatures darkened the sky, wings flapping, long necks outstretched, and clawed hands at the ready.

Lil looked up at the teeming airborne creatures as Max lifted the shotgun.

"No," she told him, and pointed the barrel of the weapon at the ground. "If you fire up at them it will do little damage, and it will attract them to attack."

Max made a curt nod, terror in his eyes.

Lil pointed to the nearby grove and moved in under the cover of the trees' canopy of branches and needles, looking up at the flying creatures.

Lil reached for the radio on her belt, to find that it was gone. "Dammit!"

"What's wrong?" Max said.

"I lost the radio. We have to go back."

"Are you insane?"

"We have to warn them."

Max nodded and they both began to move, glancing at the sky. "If they don't know, they'll find out in about ten minutes."

They walked about twenty feet, Lil's eyes on the ground as Max scanned the sky overhead.

"There it is." Lil pointed to the radio on the ground ten feet from them.

Flashes of light appeared in her eyesight, and the strange electrical buzzing began in her head.

No, not here, not now.

With the rifle in both hands she moved forward, just as she saw something that looked like a tree moving in the same direction.

It was a creature over ten feet tall, with brown shaggy fur on its arms and legs, but the chest and head were hairless. The face had exaggerated human features and a huge, hanging nose.

Lil recognized the long, hairy arms from her rescue of Ernest Fowler.

"It's a *Mehuwe*," Max cried out as Lil looked up at the giant bearing down on them. Flashes of light continued to make it hard for her to see. She fought back the weakening effect and lunged forward.

She lifted the gun at the creature and fired three shots. It looked confused as each slug hit home, struggled for its footing, just as Lil rushed forward to rescue the radio in case the lumbering colossus were to fall on it.

The behemoth fell to one knee, the brain finally realizing that the body had been damaged.

Max pumped the shotgun, firing right at the creature's chest, which exploded in green blood and twisted tissue. The blast from the shotgun knocked it over and it collapsed against several saplings, crushing them in its fall.

Max looked down at the deceased creature. Though very tall, it was thin and ribs showed through the layers of skin. The misshapen head bore a small pair of antlers and the exaggerated arms lay sprawled open, making the giant look even larger. It lay in death with its mouth open, which showed a row of vicious, pointed teeth.

Lil grabbed the radio, a pounding headache running through her brain as Max yelled, "We have to go."

Lil rose unsteadily to her feet, still disoriented. She had to press on, this was just a 'brain zap', it was temporary and it would pass.

Max helped her along as she pressed the button on the radio and yelled, "Dennis, they're coming!"

TWENTY-THREE

Attack

In the center of town, Dennis pointed to the sky. In the distance, there appeared an opening in the dark. As it expanded, it revealed a portion of the huge, blood red moon as it slowly rose in the distance, bathing the land under it in a red light as bright as fire.

Dennis pulled his phone and speed dialed Jamarr, who instantly picked up. "Do you see that, Jamarr, to the east?"

There was heavy static over the phone as Jamarr spoke. "I see… we are…set for—"

The call ended abruptly. Dennis looked at the phone. There were no bars to signify that he was getting a signal.

"Damn," he muttered. "Lil was right again. I should have gotten more radios."

All the streetlights as well as any illumination from businesses suddenly shut off. The entire town plunged into darkness, except for the radiance of the exposed red moon that hung behind the enlarging crack in the sky.

Tim stood next to Dennis staring at the red moon in awe. He pointed at shapes with flapping wings in the distance. "What are those, birds?"

Dennis' jaw tightened. "No, that's a *lot* worse than birds." He turned to the crowd of men and women. "Everyone grab your weapons, something's coming our way."

One plump grizzled man, Frank, pulled a double-barrel shotgun from the bed of a truck. He looked up at the sky and muttered, "That don't look like no wild bear."

Dennis' radio beeped, and Lil's voice crackled through. "Dennis, they're coming!"

He grabbed the radio. "We see them. You two still all right? Over."

"We may have to evacuate. This seems to be the epicenter, over."

"Then get away, we'll make our stand here, over."

Dennis turned to the crowd and spoke loudly. "Folks, the facts are this. Our town is about to be attacked, and we have to defend it. Those aren't birds flying this way—"

"What the hell are they?" a nervous man shouted out.

Dennis raised his arms to get everyone to quiet down. "You know those stories you heard growing up about the Jersey Devil? I'll tell you, I don't know any of the truth behind them, but those things flying towards us look a hell of a lot like those stories. But they *aren't* supernatural and they *can* be killed. If we don't stop them, this town will be as empty as Pines Edge."

A murmur ran through the group. Everyone knew the story of Pines Edge as well as the legends of the Jersey Devil.

"We need to use our vehicles as a shield. Pull them out into the street to make a barricade."

The others nodded and Dennis got into his truck to move it into the center of the street. Soon, others added their pickups and four-by-fours to effectively block the road.

Dennis glanced at the other end of town and, in the darkness, saw multiple vehicle headlights in the distance. He hoped that it was Jamarr getting his group to block the other end of Main Street.

The men and women got themselves behind the vehicles, now all armed. People were loading their weapons, and the man with the double barrel shotgun was filling the pockets of his hunting vest with cartridges.

As they stood ready, a police car pulled in front of the barricade with the headlights on and the red and blue lights flashing. Julie Hogan stepped out of the car in full uniform. She was a pale redhead whose face was loaded with freckles, her hair rolled in a bun under her hat. The red and blue lights silhouetted against her skin making her appear to change color from pale blue to pale red.

She walked over to the barricade and called out with her southern drawl. "Dennis Decatur, what the hell are y'all doin'? I know you're here, I recognize your truck."

"Julie," Dennis called out, moving so he could be seen over the bed of the truck, the alternating lights flashing on his face. "You've got to get behind here. Grab the shotgun from the car!"

"What are you talkin' 'bout?" she demanded, and a dozen arms pointed at the sky behind her. She turned and looked at the opening in the night sky and the portion of the giant red moon that was exposed.

"We know about that," she announced. "Now everyone, there's no need to panic. We've had a power outage, and it's just a super moon. I need you all to clear the roadway for emergency vehicles —"

"Julie, that's no fucking super moon," Dennis shouted. "Get behind the barricade!"

"There's no need for such language, Dennis," Julie chided and she glanced back at the sky and frowned, the dark silhouettes drawing near. "What kind of bird is that?"

"The kind that can kill you, Julie," Dennis shouted. "Get your shotgun."

She hesitated for only a moment, then she ran back to the police car, yanked open the door, and pulled a shotgun from an overhead rack in the cab of the vehicle, just as the first of the flying monsters landed next to her, with a "whump" as its hooves hit the ground.

Every one of the citizens were armed, they all held a weapon, but at the first look of the nightmare creature everyone froze on the spot.

Julie turned from the car, looked up at the massive creature; the bat wings on its back, its maw open, the taloned claws held in an aggressive stance on the backward elbows. She let loose a primal scream of fear, which became a cry of pain as the monster sank its talons into her shoulders and lifted her into the air with incredible speed for something so large.

Dennis was the first to gather his wits and had his Savage 64 FXP in his hand. With a simple squeeze, several shots hit the creature, and its head exploded in a mist of green blood and gore.

Julie fell to the ground as she was released from the lifeless claws, still screaming.

The winged hellions were landing, some in front of the barricade, some behind it, and some just kept flying overhead. The shock that had incapacitated the group had lifted, and they were all moving, aiming, and systematically firing their weapons.

Frank fired one barrel at a creature that landed behind him, and the massive thing fell, just as he turned to fire his second blast at a charging *Piasa*.

Tim was using a lever-action rifle, firing and levering a new bullet into the chamber as quickly as he could.

Dennis rotated, taking out landing creatures around the group, trying to give the others a chance to fire and reload.

Molly slid between the trucks that formed the barricade, grabbed Julie under the arms, and dragged her behind the trucks. There was blood on both of her shoulders and green goo on her face from the creature that had clutched her. She was wild-eyed and panting from the pain.

"What the fuck was that?" she groaned, her concerns about language gone.

"Just lie there, Julie. We got you," Molly said.

The fighters at the far edge of town were also firing and Main Street sounded like a war zone with the crack of gunfire and the screams of the creatures as they attempted to attack.

"What's going on?" Julie moaned.

"It's the end of the world," Molly told her as she grabbed her gun and rose to fire at one of the creatures.

In the woods, Lil and Max had again returned to the grove of trees as more of the flying monstrosities came out of the expanding portal. The flaming line on the ground stopped moving as the speed of the expansion slowed, but the rip in reality tore steadily into the sky, revealing more and more of the huge red moon.

"What do we do?" Max demanded. He was breathing hard with panic in his eyes.

"Reload," Lil growled, as she replaced the magazine and frantically shoved bullets in the one she just removed. "Look, we can't take out the *Piasa*, because they're flying and hard to hit. But the lumbering giants are slow, and we can stop them."

"Okay, okay," Max panted. "That sounds like a plan."

"We have to assume that since they can think and plan, there might be intelligence behind the attack. If so, we have to get them to retreat."

Lil finished reloading her magazine as Max shoved the last cartridge into the slot in the bottom of his shotgun and clicked the safety off.

"How do we do that?" Max asked, as he looked around.

"You're the anthropologist, you tell me."

Max looked up in the sky then down at the slain giant. "Lil, what we are seeing now resembles sharks on a feeding frenzy, when predators are overwhelmed by the amount of prey available."

"But you saw the one that waited until it had backup to attack —"

"Yes, but this is like a large school of fish and the *Piasa* are like sharks. The intense stress causes sharks to enter a frenzied state. Think about it! The convergence has to be a stressful situation, and if they can communicate with others of their species, they know that humans are easy prey."

Lil nodded. "I guess in the past, they've always conquered an unprepared group and fed upon them. Today they're meeting resistance, maybe for the first time."

"But if they're in a frenzy, resistance will only increase their bloodlust."

"So we should just surrender, and let them take us?" Lil demanded.

"Of course not. The point is that there is no way to reason with them—"

Lil pulled out from behind the tree to fire several shots past Max, which made him cry out and slam himself against the tree.

Max turned to watch a second *Mehuwe* stumble and fall to the ground, more than twenty feet away. He had not seen the lumbering giant approach. It fell to the ground mortally wounded, making a hideous sound as it lurched and fell, several wounds in its chest spurting green blood.

Max turned away from Lil as a large Devil landed with the sound of breaking branches. Sticks fell as it leapt forward with amazing speed, and rushed them with a shriek. Max barely had time to raise the shotgun and fire, which threw the creature off its feet and onto the ground, while smacking him against the bark of the tree from the recoil.

A different kind of scream filled the air and both Max and Lil raised their weapons, spun and scanned the red sky for the source. Overhead, a huge red feathered monstrosity soared past, and Lil could swear it was the size of a small plane.

"What the hell is that?" Max shouted.

"I don't know," Lil shouted back. "I didn't do a full inventory when I was over there. I was too busy running and hiding."

Lil caught a flash of red feathers and pulled Max against the tree.

Walking into view was a bird, extending a pair of red wings in a threatening gesture of dominance. It stood over six feet tall, and scarlet feathers covered it, but these feathers contained an obvious skeletal structure, giving them a bony look.

She realized where the feathers for the chief's war bonnet had come from when she had met the tribal elders.

The red bird had an uncovered head, black as pitch, and a huge hooked beak with a nasal cavity protruding on top.

That beak could do serious damage as a weapon, and Lil held the rifle at the ready in case the creature charged them.

The giant feathered menace looked over at the pair of them, but was not interested. Instead it was focused intently on the first giant they had dispatched.

The bird looked around to make sure that there was no threat, and with its enormous beak, tore into one of the wounds on the chest of the dead *Mehuwe*. It then shoved its entire head into the chest cavity.

"Ugh," Max said, turning away. "I'm gonna be sick."

Lil also could not bear to watch as the creature dined, and the duo went to the far side of the tree away from the carrion-feeder. "Those must be the vultures from the Hidden Land, I think they're called *Mòchipwis*. I guess they would be part of this as well, it would explain why no corpses were found in Pines Edge."

"Nice to know the monsters clean up after themselves," Max moaned.

"We have to get out of here. The dead will attract these things, and they might think we're competition for the food."

"Or if they're hungry enough, they might attack us even if we're alive," Max fretted.

"Come on," Lil said. She crouched low and began to move quickly away, with Max right behind her. As they moved from the grove of trees they heard two more of the giant vultures landing and begin feasting on the remains of the *Piasa* Max had shot.

They went several hundred more feet and hid at the base of another large tree, far enough away so they didn't have to watch the monster buzzards enjoying their meal.

Lil pulled her radio. "Dennis, can you read me, over?"

"Yes, over," came Dennis' static-filled reply.

She depressed the button. "You have giant vultures coming. I don't know if they attack people, but they are eating the fallen *Piasa*, over."

Static came back over the box, until finally she heard Dennis. "You're breaking up, did you say vultures?"

"Ten-four, vultures, big ones, all red."

More static came with his reply. "We'll keep an eye out. The radio is—"

His voice fell away under a cacophony of static.

"Do you need us to join you in town, over?"

Nothing but a loud hissing.

Lil repeated the request. "Do you need us to join you in town, over?"

"No, stay there, let us know what you can, over."

She hung the radio on her belt. "Doesn't seem like anything else is coming out of the portal right now."

"Maybe they come out in waves," Max offered. "I mean, first it was the Devils, and then the giants."

"Sounds like a football game instead of the apocalypse," Lil muttered.

"What should we do?"

Lil considered this for a moment. "Let's move closer to the portal location, if any more *Mehuwe* come through we take them out."

"What about the vultures?"

"They don't seem interested in us. But if we can take out any stragglers, it will help."

"You're not planning to go in there are you?"

Lil looked up at the rip in the sky and the huge red moon. "The Hidden Land is no longer hiding, Max, it's here now. I don't know if we can avoid it, even if we want to."

They moved into the woods and began to travel in a circular path to avoid the red vultures.

They crept cautiously through the trees, alert for any unusual noise or movement as they went. In only a minute or two, they reached a black line of smoldering grass.

Peering up at it, reality was disjointed. On this side of the burn mark was brown grass and green pine needles and underbrush. Beyond it, the ground and the trees were red, with short red grass in patches, and a dark mist swirling within it. The trees were not in the same place and it looked as if two photographs of different locations had been glued together badly.

Max indicated the red area. "Is that *Nkantahkink*?"

"Yes. But the mist is new. It wasn't there the last time I went in."

"Maybe that was the signal for the creatures to come through," Max surmised. "Do you think this is as big as the portal gets?"

She looked up at the rip in reality that rose high into the night sky. "I don't know. Don't step on the burning area, it might be hot enough to melt your shoe."

Lil gave a short hop over the smoking soil, and turned back to Max.

"Any problems?" Max worried.

"No, and I didn't even get that weird pins-and-needles sensation, like when I went through the portal before. Come on!"

Max nodded, made a small jump, and landed on the dark red clay next to Lil. Soundlessly, they pressed on through the colored mist, alert to any attack. "How will you know when we are at the original portal location?"

"Doesn't matter," Lil replied. "We're in their world now. Our mission is to take out the things that don't fly, so they don't get into our world."

"So those giants, the *Mehuwe*. They seem to resemble the Algonquian legends of the *Wendigo*. A giant, cannibalistic creature, with long arms and covered with hair."

"Good to know what we're up against, I guess," Lil said, then raised her arm to stop their forward motion. She crouched low, her weapon raised, and Max did the same.

Tall figures moved through the mist up ahead, several of them.

Max pointed his shotgun, ready to fire.

Lil's hand moved to the trigger of her weapon. One of the figures approaching had feathers on it, but then she saw a shorter silhouette in the mix.

She quickly reached over and pushed the barrel of Max's shotgun to aim at the ground.

"No," she whispered. "These are friends."

"*Friends?*" Max hissed.

Lil lowered her weapon and stood to call out. "Greetings!"

"And greetings to you as well," a jovial voice called back. "Lil, is that you?"

"Yes, Albert. We're here in the mist," Lil said and gestured for Max to stand.

Albert came through the smoke, his white hair shining. Behind him, the tall warriors stood, several held bows with arrows notched, and several held spears that stood seven feet tall. It was a mixed group: some males with long hair, some with mohawks, two of the warriors with bows were women with long buckskin dresses.

Lil moved forward and met Albert, whereupon she hugged him, much to his surprise.

"Oh my," he said and pulled back. "We saw the mists this evening and knew it was the time."

"It was brave of you to come. I mean all of you."

"There was little risk to us," Albert said. "All of the predators are on your side this night."

"I was wondering why more of the *Mehuwe* did not come through," Lil stated.

"The warriors and I have been stopping them. Should we continue?"

"Yes. Let me give you my pistol," Lil said, reaching into her waist pack.

"Is that wise?" Albert asked. "I am not well-acquainted with your firearms."

She held up the rifle that hung from her shoulder strap. "The rifle is more effective, but I think you'll handle the pistol better."

Albert gently touched Lil's rifle. "Yes, that is a bit imposing."

Lil handed Albert the pistol, and then gave him the extra bullets which he put into his pockets.

"If you can guard this portal, I can go help the others fight the *Piasa* in town."

"We can guard here, Lil. But I must warn you, as the night goes on, more portals will open in different locations throughout this area. That is what happened in Pines Edge. We focused on one location and then others opened up and we were surrounded."

Lil grew serious. "If you want to return to New Jersey, this is your chance, you know."

Albert frowned. "Leave my wife and my people? I cannot."

Lil looked at Albert, his threadbare clothes repaired multiple times. "Can your warriors defend this location without you?"

"They have been fighting the *Piasa* long before I arrived."

"Then come with us. You might be able to help defend the town. That is where they are attacking now."

"How far is it?"

"Ten miles."

"Such a long way, will we make it before the night is over?"

"We have a car."

His eyebrows went up. "A motorcar? That would be most efficient."

"Then come with us," Lil said and turned to Max.

"Give me a moment," Albert said and walked over to one of the tall warriors who wore a large war bonnet. He spoke to him as Lil looked over to see Max conversing with one of the giant women. She was almost two feet taller than the little man, but they were speaking in the same language, and she smiled down at him.

Suddenly Albert was at her side. "Your friend is quite proficient in the Lenape language. But some of his pronunciation is terrible."

Lil yelled over. "Max, we have to go."

Max nodded, waved to the warrior woman, and fell into step beside Lil and Albert as they headed out of the woods.

Albert spoke up. "I understand you have a motorcar, sir."

"Yes," Max agreed. "Are you coming with us?"

"So it would appear."

"Max, the warriors are going to protect this portal, so we're joining the others in town," Lil explained.

"However, young man, the path may be treacherous. More portals will open as the night progresses."

"How many?" Max worried.

"Well, there's this one," Lil said, "and I'm aware of one near Batsto Village, but those are the only two I've seen."

They reached the highway and Lil stopped to observe the large opening to the east. The trio then looked to the west, where numerous small lines of red were poking up above the treetops from different locations, each glowing with the red light of a portal.

"Yes, I think this will make things a bit tricky," Max gulped.

TWENTY-FOUR

Second Wave

L il sat in the passenger seat of the vehicle with Max driving, and Albert in the back seat.

They were not making much progress.

The two main roads to town had been cut off by portals that filled the roadway. These were rectangular but shot up high into the sky. They were wide enough to shut off the simple two-lane road due to the trees on both sides, making using the shoulder impossible.

They had stopped directly in front of one of the wide portals, looking for a way to pass.

Max looked at Lil. "Can I just drive into it? Maybe it's still our world on the other side."

"We can't." Lil said, "If this opens in the Hidden Land, there are no roads there. We wouldn't get far."

"How else can we get to town?" Max asked.

Lil considered this. "There was a dirt road through the Barrens about a mile back. Let's use that."

Max shook his head. "I don't know if my car can get through those sandy roads."

"I don't see that we have any choice."

Directly ahead of them, a claw appeared at the portal.

Max gave a cry and shoved the car into reverse, just as one of the *Piasa* stepped through. It stared at the vehicle, its red eyes bright in the beams of the headlights.

"Stop, Max," Lil ordered.

Max hit the brake, and the car stopped suddenly. The monster was shielding its eyes as best it could from the dazzling headlights.

"Hit the high beams," Lil ordered and opened her door. She stepped into the street as she raised her weapon from the sling on her shoulder.

The creature gave its blood-curdling scream as Lil fired off three rounds in quick succession.

Green blood burst from the monster and with a gurgle of surprise, it fell to the ground.

Lil lowered the rifle and returned to her seat. "Okay, turn us around and get us back to that roadway."

As Max turned the car and drove, Albert said, "You seem quite versed in the use of that weapon, Lil."

"At the police academy I did well in sharpshooting."

"They have a school for peace officers?" Albert replied. "How amazing."

"Here's the turn," Max said, slowing the car. "Are you sure about this, Lil?"

"I can't think of another way to get to town," Lil said.

Max nodded and moved slowly onto the white roadway.

Albert leaned forward to look at the one lane sandy trail in the car's headlights. "That is what the roads were like in my day."

"Not a lot of cars in 1909?" Lil asked.

"We only had one motorcar in Pines Edge. The mayor owned it," Albert said. "As the town doctor, I was looking into one, but the price was far too extravagant."

The car moved forward slowly, the trail only lit by the headlights. The ride was bumpy as the trail was pockmarked with potholes and depressions, some of which were filled with water.

The dark forest was all around them, and it all had an eerie red glow, the result of the overlarge red moon's reflected light.

"I can see why people thought there was a fire in the Barrens during the last convergence," Lil speculated, as she looked out the side window at the red-hued vegetation.

"Do you have any way to communicate with your fellows?" Albert asked.

"I have a radio, but it's working less and less as the night wears on. Basically we're cut off—"

Max pulled the car to a stop as they faced the end of their road and had to choose to go right or left. Beyond the road in the woods was another rectangular portal that rose from a pool of water with an opening to another pool in the red landscape beyond. All three of the occupants looked at it with concern.

"Head left Max, towards town," Lil advised, her eyes focused on the portal.

Max started forward, turning to the left, as Lil noticed something moving. A long tube seemed to be rising from out of the pool of water.

"Max, I think you want to move it," Lil advised.

What appeared to be a tube now possessed a large scaled head, but with flaps where ears would be. It leaned back like a snake getting ready to strike.

Before Max could drive away the creature sprang forward, lightning quick. It hit the passenger side of the car and lifted the right side of the vehicle off the ground with the power of the impact.

Lil's side of the car fell back to earth so hard her teeth clanked together painfully.

"Move it!" Lil yelled to Max.

With a screech of wheels and sand kicking up in a plume of dust, the car jerked forward, leaving the giant serpent blinking its eyes and looking surprised.

Albert looked out the back window.

"I believe it is confined to the water," Albert confirmed, as the car bumped and jumped across the unstable trail.

"Man, this car is a lease," Max complained. "What the hell was that?"

"We call it a *Mëxaxkuk*," Albert explained. "They are quite dangerous and quick."

"How many different creatures do you have over there?" Max stated, visibly shaken.

"Quite a few, I'm afraid. That's why we live in caves."

"There should be another turn, back to the main road," Lil observed.

"How do you know that?" Max asked.

"I grew up here. As teenagers, we drove into the Barrens all the time," Lil said.

Her mind flashed back to when she and Dennis had given themselves to each other here in the Barrens, so long ago. That night, the Pinelands had seemed safe, a loving embrace of trees and nature. Now, it all seemed hostile, the blood-red light flickering through the trees, and danger at every turn. This was not the Barrens she knew and loved. It was an alien place that had forced itself upon her world.

Max turned the car on the next pathway, and then yanked the wheel to pull the vehicle out of the way of a large water-filled pothole in the center of the trail. He got back to the middle of the track and headed forward, going under twenty miles per hour, a speed the rough route allowed.

More portals were appearing in the woods around them, and soon there would be no more *there* and *here*, but only a continuation of the red landscape forced upon them.

She worried about her parents, and the small group of warriors in the center of town. How could they win against an enemy with overwhelming numbers, as well as claws and teeth designed to rend human flesh?

The headlights flashed on a break in the trees ahead, and an exposed paved roadway.

A *Piasa* stood in the middle of the sand-covered path.

"Holy crap," Max shouted and stomped the accelerator.

"What are you doing?" Lil yelled.

"Getting us to that road," Max explained, his teeth bared in a grimace.

He hit the creature going about forty miles per hour. The huge animal was knocked off its feet as Max reached the pavement, pulled the wheel to the right, and jammed on the brakes, just as the airbags deployed.

Albert, who had not been wearing a seat belt, was thrown to the floor in the back.

"What were you thinking?" Lil bellowed.

"We made it to the road, didn't we?" Max said, pushing the deflating airbag out of his way.

"You could have damaged the car. We need it to get to town. If this happens again, you stop and I shoot it!"

"If you could argue later, please," Albert pointed out. "The *Piasa* is getting up."

Lil pushed open her door which squealed with the sound of creaking metal. "Let me show you how this works."

She stepped out and raised her rifle as the creature got up to its feet, but it had been wounded by the collision. It raised only one of its claws, and made the horrible scream of attack.

"Shut the hell up," Lil jeered, as she let fly a burst of gunfire. The beast fell to its knees, gurgled, and collapsed to the ground, dead.

She got back into the car and pulled the door closed with a creak. The door sprang open again, and Lil used more strength to force it closed.

"Your hood is bent," Lil told Max.

"I noticed that," Max agreed.

"Drive."

The vehicle lurched forward but didn't stall, and they were headed towards their destination where she could see creatures flying in the air above the silhouettes of the buildings in the center of town.

It took a few tense minutes, but soon the small SUV with a crumpled hood and a dent in the passenger door pulled up to the barricade on Main Street. Max, Lil, and Albert got out, crouched low, and with weapons in hand headed to the barricade.

Lil moved right next to Dennis, who asked, "Why didn't you let me know you were coming?"

"Radio stopped working," she said, and pulled it off her belt. "Testing."

Her voice came through the radio on Dennis' belt with no static.

"Works now," Dennis said as he lifted his rifle and peered through the scope to take a bead on a *Piasa* as it flew overhead, firing several shots. The monster fell from the sky and landed heavily on the macadam with a loud noise, cracking the pavement.

"I wish we could get that radio to Jamarr," Dennis said. "We can see their headlights and hear the gunfire, but we don't know how they're doing."

Lil looked past him at the other group of trucks. They were on the same road, and she could see the barricade of large vehicles and shots being fired, but the people were small, and in the red moonlight, hard to see.

Lil turned back to Dennis. "Maybe Max can drive it there. Take side roads to the other end of town."

"That might work," Dennis agreed.

Tim, Molly, and the others were firing at the *Piasa* that flew low, but many of the beasts were now landing on the roofs of the downtown buildings, and moving out of sight.

"Why are they doin' that?" Dennis asked, pointing at the building as another *Piasa* landed and crouched low.

"They're calming down from the frenzy of the attack," Max remarked.

"Agreed," Albert said. "In their natural habitat, they prefer high places from which they can strike."

"These monsters can think," Lil explained. "I would say they've landed on the roofs to watch us, and they can hide if we fire upon them. Once they see a lone unguarded person or we run out of bullets, they'll attack again."

"The damn things are too smart," Dennis cursed.

They looked down the wide road that ran the length of the town. It was littered with the bodies of the large flying creatures, a dead dog, killed by one of the monsters, and the unmoving body of a woman the monsters had dropped.

Lil turned to Max and handed him her radio. "Can you drive down a side street to the other end of town and give this to Jamarr Bowman? You met him at the hunting club."

"I remember," Max agreed. "I can if my car still runs."

"Then do it, please. We can fight better if we can talk," Lil assured. "We'll cover you."

Max dashed back to the car which started with a grinding sound which didn't sound good. He drove off as more of the Devils landed on the roofs and hid from sight.

Another police car, a large utility vehicle, pulled up with lights flashing to park next to the sedan Julie Hogan had driven.

The vehicle stopped and Captain Hewitt himself jumped out with a riot shotgun in hand. He moved fast to get behind the barricade and join Dennis.

"Good to see you, captain," Dennis yelled. "Have you called for back-up?"

"Phones are out as well as the power," Hewitt explained, panting from the exertion of getting to the barricade. "Even the police band radios aren't working for shit, nothing but static."

He looked over at Lil. "Dennis, Ms. Slavik, I guess I owe you an apology," Hewitt said, then turned to fire as a *Piasa* flew past, missing it.

"You can apologize if we're all still alive at the end of this," Lil replied, her eyes on the sky.

A huge Devil flew down to land on top of the vehicle Hewitt had just vacated. The captain lifted his shotgun and fired, which knocked the creature off the car and it collapsed in a heap on the ground. Molly ran over and shot it in the head.

"So, no communications?" Dennis asked. "We're on our own?"

"Looks that way," Hewitt said, scanning the sky. "What's going on, besides all Hell breaking loose?"

Dennis sighed. "Not going well, sir. We've been overrun by several of the monsters who carried off two people who had come out of their apartments to see what was going on."

"Damn idiots," Hewitt muttered.

"So far most of the fighters at this barricade are uninjured. Julie Hogan was grabbed. We saved her, but she's injured."

"How is the ammunition holding up?" Hewitt asked.

"Ammo is running low, and there seems to be no end of the *Piasa*, who are now hiding on rooftops."

Hewitt frowned. "What did you call them, *Piasa?*"

Lil spoke up. "There's a tribe of people where they come from, and that's the name they use."

Dennis looked up to see none of the Devils attacking. "They've all taken shelter, except those damn vultures that Lil had warned us about. Those only circle high in the air. I think they don't like the gunfire. What are those called?"

Albert spoke up. "They are called *Mòchipwis,* but I must confess I believe it is the same word used for a common vulture."

"And just who the hell are you, buddy?" Hewitt asked, looking Albert up and down.

"Albert Thompson, sir," the older man claimed.

"He's from the Hidden Land, captain," Lil explained. "He was abducted from Pines Edge in 1909."

"What? That's impossible!" Hewitt sputtered.

"Quite possible, I'm afraid," Albert insisted. "I must advise you that the creatures arrived ready to strike, no doubt using the element of surprise. Since you have reduced their numbers, they appear to be preparing for a more systematic attack."

"Captain, we need to drive them off the roofs," Dennis said.

Hewitt looked up at the buildings. "Some flash-bangs or smoke grenades would move them."

"The smoke might be less effective, but the flash-bangs would do it," Dennis agreed.

"We have an M79 grenade launcher and a small supply of stun-grenades in the armory at headquarters," Hewitt confirmed.

"Do you want me to get them, captain?" Dennis offered.

"No, I know the codes for the keypad that secures the locker," Hewitt grumbled.

"Captain, you can't go alone," Lil stated. "I'll go with you."

Hewitt eyed her with suspicion for a moment.

"She has a point, captain," Dennis concurred.

"All right," Hewitt sighed.

Lil turned to Albert. "Do you know any way we can end the convergence before it takes over completely, and we all end up in *Nkantahkink?*"

"I am not aware of one. According to the legends of the tribe passed down over many years, the convergence occurs on one night when the moon is at its closest. But, it shall all end by the morning."

"If we can stay alive until then," Dennis observed.

Lil looked around. "There must be another way."

Dennis nodded. "I'm open to suggestions."

"Are you coming, Ms. Slavik?" Hewitt barked.

"Yes, captain," Lil said, and crouched as they moved out of the barricade. She scanned the sky with the semi-automatic as Hewitt got into the SUV and unlocked her door.

She got in and Hewitt turned to her. "They're not attacking."

Lil closed the door. "Not at this moment, sir, I think they're regrouping. They've never met resistance like this at any previous attacks."

Without another word Hewitt started the car and headed up a side road to police headquarters.

Lil watched the streets, looking at the destruction. Hewitt had to slow the vehicle and go around several huge bodies of their fallen attackers.

They arrived at the one-story building in a few short minutes, and Lil thought she saw a *Piasa* lurking on the roof. The captain couldn't pull near the door as a number of cars filled the small lot.

"Where did all the cars come from?" Lil said.

"People panicked and came here," Hewitt told her, his jaw tight. "It started before I headed over to the center of town."

"There's one of the creatures on the roof."

"Then cover me, this is as close as we can get."

"Let me go first."

Lil opened the door and came out low, then raised herself and let fly several shots at the creature hidden on the roof. This made it shriek its terrible cry and it rose in the air, the huge bat wings open and flapping.

Lil gritted her teeth and let loose with another pair of shots, one to the head and one to the chest, which made the monster collapse back to the roof. Its damaged head hung off the edge of the building and dripped green slime.

Hewitt got out, and with his own shotgun in hand, made his way to the front door, just as another *Piasa* shrieked and dove from a nearby rooftop.

Hewitt went to one knee, lifted the shotgun and discharged a blast at the creature, which screamed again, fell to the pavement, and rose up, wounded but still attacking.

Lil's weapon barked again, the gunshots took the creature down. She ran to Hewitt, pulling him to his feet. They both stared at the monster, the bat-like wings still moving from involuntary muscle contractions.

"That is the damndest thing," Hewitt gasped as they headed to the door of the station. "It's like a fucking nightmare."

"Agreed, sir," Lil said, and pulled the outer door open.

People moved back from the door, men, women and children were all huddled in the unlit narrow halls of the police station. Several of the children were crying, and the women looked grim.

"Captain Hewitt, what's going on?" a brown-haired man demanded, stepping forward to block the chief. The red light coming through the door's windows cast weird shadows on his face that made him look satanic.

"Things are trying to kill us," Hewitt barked, then he looked around and yelled, "Huey!"

"Yes, Captain," a man called back from the side room.

"Any luck with the radio or the phones?"

A tall man with a shaved head and a thick mustache poked his head out of a doorway. "No luck, sir."

"Captain Hewitt," the brown-haired man repeated. "I insist you talk to me."

Hewitt turned and faced the man. "Mayor Tobin, I'm afraid I'm busy right now."

"These families have all come here for you to protect them—"

"Which is what I'm *trying* to do," Hewitt said and surveyed the room. "Now look, those creatures might come here, and they're smart enough to open doors. Anyone know how to use a gun?"

A gray-haired man raised his hand.

"Great, I want you in front of the others with a shotgun that I will give you. If any of those creatures get through this door, you shoot it, okay?"

The older man nodded.

"What are these things?" one woman asked, her eyes wide and haunted. She stood next to a girl about ten years old.

Hewitt shook his head. "Best as I can tell you, these things look like the Jersey Devil. There are hundreds of them, and they are attacking us. If you can just hunker down here and let us do our job, you'll be okay. Now folks you have to let me by. I need to get to a weapons locker."

Hewitt began to move down the hall, and people moved to the right and left to let him pass. The light of the red moon illuminated the dark hall from the windows, making it bright enough to see, but not much else.

Mayor Tobin followed the captain and Lil.

"Where did these things come from?" Tobin questioned. "Why weren't we prepared for this?"

Hewitt turned into a room and walked up to a tall safe made of heavy metal with a keypad on the front.

"Will it work without electricity?" Lil asked.

"It's manual, don't worry," Hewitt told her.

Lil pulled out her smart phone and used the flashlight to light the keypad.

"Aren't you going to answer me, captain?"

"Mayor Tobin," Hewitt said as he hit the numbers. "We are being attacked by things that, until a little while ago, I didn't think existed. There is some kind of electrical disruption, like an EMP, I guess. It is knocking out communications and power. Right now, I have to get a grenade launcher and take it back to fight them. We have to keep them focused on attacking us, so that they don't go after citizens."

Tobin was undaunted. "But you said the Jersey Devil. That's a fable, something used to scare children."

Lil spoke up. "They are known as the *Piasa*, and it isn't one creature, it's hundreds, maybe thousands. It's the reason Pines Edge vanished. The people were carried off by these things."

"Look, Your Honor," Hewitt told him as he pulled the door open and exposed the cache of weapons. "We have them in the center of town, and I want to keep them there. You keep everyone here, and safe."

Hewitt handed Lil the M79. It was about the size of a shotgun with a heavy wood stock and a thick tubular barrel to hold the large projectiles it fired. He also pulled out a heavy cloth backpack and began to put the large cylinders for the weapon into it.

He pulled out a shotgun, grabbed some shells, and gave them to Tobin. "This is for the guy up front to guard the door. Make sure there is someone on it all night. Take shifts if you have to. I'll leave the locker open in case you need more weapons."

"But there are children here," Tobin whined.

"Then don't let them play with the guns," Hewitt advised.

"If those things get in here, you'll need weapons," Lil added. "The monsters don't."

Tobin glared at Lil. "And who are you?"

"This is Lil Slavik, she grew up here, which is more than I can say for you, Mayor," Hewitt snapped. "She has been deputized and is one hell of a shooter."

"I see," Tobin said, apparently mollified by this.

"Now, if you don't mind, Your Honor," Hewitt said. "We have to go kick some ass."

TWENTY-FIVE

Reinforcements

W hen they arrived at the barricade, Dennis was on the radio as Lil and Hewitt got out of the vehicle. Lil carried the backpack of shells and could see the strained look on Dennis' face.

"Things aren't going well on the other end of town." He clipped the radio to his belt and helped her with the heavy pack. "Max says they've lost three people to the creatures. Take a look what's happened since you left."

Dennis pointed down the wide Main Street where several blocks away another rectangular portal had appeared. The opening was rising up into the sky and expanding across the width of the street.

"Are we getting shut off from the other end of town?" Hewitt asked.

"Looks like it, captain," Dennis fretted. "I'm worried it could affect the radios and give the *Piasa* another way to ambush us."

The captain looked at the rectangle of red light, then the rooftops. He growled, "Let me have the cartridges."

Dennis placed the bag next to his feet, as the captain pulled on a pair of gloves. He raised his voice so all could hear. "Listen close everyone. We are going to send some stun grenades at the rooftops. I will announce which one. You will all focus your fire on anything that comes off that rooftop. Got it?"

The crowd murmured in assent.

"What if they attack all at once, Captain Hewitt?" Molly asked. A long piece of gray hair had come loose from her ponytail and hung over her right eye.

"If they attack at random, then fire at will," Hewitt said as he slipped a large cylinder into the oversized barrel and shut the weapon with a click. "Focus your fire to the roof of the liquor store!"

He shouldered the weapon, adjusted the rectangular sight for the height of the building, and fired. It made a loud "whomp" and in a moment there was an explosion and a very bright light on the roof of the targeted building.

Four of the *Piasa* flew off, and Lil and Dennis, along with the others, fired upon them, dropping all four out of the air, where they crashed to the paved road below.

A cheer went up from the shooters, as Hewitt pulled the spent shell and shoved in a second.

The cheers were silenced as a series of shrieks rose from the buildings up and down Main Street, so loud that it made everyone flinch from the cacophony.

Piasa were leaping off the different buildings and heading toward them *en masse*.

Without hesitation, Hewitt fired the launcher directly in the middle of the attackers. The grenade struck one of the flying monsters and went off with a loud explosion and an incredibly bright light.

People turned away, but their eyes were dazzled.

"Damn, I can't see," Lil yelled.

"We have to shoot!" Dennis shouted.

Lil recognized Molly's screams. She glanced over to see one of the monsters had grabbed her. It roared, spread its hideous wings, and lifted off into the air.

Lil aimed, although the creature's head only looked like a large pink dot. She pulled the trigger and the creature fell, dropping Molly. They were only about eight feet in the air but Molly crumpled to the ground.

"Molly!" Tim yelled, and pulled away from the blockade to rush to her crumpled form.

Lil jumped down and moved to Tim, who cradled Molly in his lap. "We have to get her to cover—"

"Okay," Tim agreed, as Lil helped him to stand with the fallen Molly in his arms. Lil fired up into the air as they made their way back to the truck barricade.

Lil could see enough to be aware that the monsters were flying into each other, their vision equally affected by the brilliant light. Several crashed and fell to the ground, where the armed citizens were able to take them down.

"Do another one of those," Lil yelled to Hewitt.

"But warn us this time," Dennis added.

Lil and Dennis fired up into the air again, as Hewitt pushed another green canister into the launcher.

"Cover your eyes," Hewitt shouted, and fired into the air.

There was another "whomp" as the grenade flew, and again, it hit one of the flying creatures, with a resounding concussion and a brilliant flash.

The shooters had all turned away from the light, and this time when they faced their adversaries, they could see, though the creatures were blinded.

Lil grabbed the first-aid kit from where it lay in Dennis' truck bed, and moved to Tim, opening the kit as she went.

She crouched down next to Tim, who looked up at her with tears streaming down his face.

"She's dead," he muttered.

Lil froze unable to feel her arms or legs. "What?"

"She hit her head when she fell," Tim said. "She stopped breathing…"

Lil looked at the fallen woman, numb. "It was my fault—"

"That thing would have carried her off," Tim said, and wiped a hand across his eyes. "For Christ's sake that damn thing would've *eaten* her. You didn't have a choice."

Lil couldn't meet his eyes. Once again, she had used her weapon, reacting without thinking, and it had gotten someone killed. She liked Molly, she seemed like a feisty woman who pulled no punches. And now, her body was an empty shell that would never move again.

She rose, the feeling of numbness spread over her.

"Lil, get down," Dennis yelled, as he pulled her against the truck.

She looked up at him, her eyes wide. "Molly's dead."

"I heard. Are you okay?"

She looked into his eyes. What a stupid question. How could she be 'okay,' when death seemed to follow her at every turn? She wasn't a brave heroine, she was a stupid woman with a stupid gun who kept making the wrong choices.

Dennis grabbed both her arms. "Lil, it wasn't your fault."

"Wasn't it?" Lil said as flashes of light appeared in her view.

Dennis gave her a shake and it wasn't gentle. "Lil, you have to keep fighting, or everyone will die."

Her vision cleared, and she blinked several times and took a deep breath, feeling as if she'd forgotten to breathe for several minutes.

She gritted her teeth and looked into the air, where the creatures were flying and gunfire was forcing them back. "Yes."

Dennis released her and lifted his own rifle to fire up at the sky. Lil worked her way between trucks just as Max's car pulled up.

One of the flying monstrosities flew over her, its claws reaching for her. She turned to fire, but missed.

The huge monster landed on the back of the crumpled car, just as Max came out of the vehicle.

Lil held her gun in front of her, but the creature was too near the gas tank.

Max stepped out with his gun, and as the monster moved to grab him, he lifted the shotgun and fired right into the face of his attacker.

The gun made a huge sound, and the creature was knocked down and off its feet, half of its face gone. Lil moved to Max to pull him into the safety of the barricade.

Max was wild-eyed and gasping as Lil held him. "You're all right, you're all right."

She dragged him to Dennis' truck and the pair of them fell to the ground next to the front tires.

Tim ran screaming toward the flying creatures, firing his own shotgun again and again. "Damn you!"

"Tim!" Dennis yelled, just as a *Piasa* dived and hooked its ghastly talons into Tim's thin shoulders. Tim was carried off into the air, the huge creature hadn't even slowed as it picked the man up. Tim screamed as several shots were fired at it.

"Damn!" Dennis cursed. "I can't get a clear shot!"

The creature held the dangling man and disappeared into the growing red rectangle in the middle of the street.

"Everyone down," Hewitt yelled as he fired another stun grenade into the mass of attacking monsters. This time, aware of the grenade's power, they all avoided the projectile and it exploded inches from the ground with a loud *bang*.

"We need help," Dennis yelled, his hearing affected by the nearby concussion.

Lil checked Max. "You all right?"

"I think so," Max said, licking his lips.

She raised her weapon and stood to look out over the Main Street. Figures poured out of the huge red portal that blocked the middle of the town, and she was worried that more of the *Mehuwe*, the cannibalistic giants, were stepping through.

She grinned when she saw feathers and war bonnets, as a group of very tall men and women stepped from the red radiance with spears and other weapons.

Arrows flew into the air, striking the monsters and penetrating their bodies, as effective as the bullets.

Lil grabbed Dennis. "Look, it's help!"

Dennis yelled to the others. "Don't shoot the people coming through the portal. They're on our side."

Lil lowered herself and put her back to the truck fender as Max sat on the ground, panting.

Directly in front of her was her grandmother, Natalia.

The world faded to a soft focus, as Natalia spoke. "It is time, my precious one."

"What do I do, *Mami*?" Lil asked.

Natalia nodded slowly. "You have the key. You must close the door from the other side."

"The other side?" Lil repeated, unsure.

"Yes, from a holy place," her grandmother assured her.

"Lil," Dennis shouted to her, "we have to focus our firepower on the flying ones."

She glanced up at Dennis and when she looked back, Natalia was gone. Max was getting to his feet, in control of himself once again.

Max lifted his gun to fire at a flying monster, as it passed far overhead. "What are they doing?"

"They're flying high to get out of range," Lil said. "They'll regroup on top of the buildings and hit us with another wave."

Lil looked around and saw Albert on his knees, treating Officer Julie Hogan's wounds. She ducked between the vehicles and moved to him. Molly lay nearby, unmoving, and Lil glanced over to see that Tim had closed her eyes before he was taken. Regrets aside, Lil had to keep going, because if Natalia had been right, she might have the ability to end this.

"Albert," Lil hissed.

The older man looked up. "Yes, Lil."

"I think I can use the rock I have to close the portals between worlds."

"Are you sure?"

She looked over the destruction. "No, but I believe I can only do it from your side. And I need your help."

"What can I do?" he said as he finished binding the last of Julie's shoulder wounds.

"You have to come with me and help me find the right place."

Albert considered this. "I have no idea where that would be."

"Someplace important. Some place the *Clova* consider holy," Lil explained. "I can't talk to them, and even if I could I don't have the trust that you do."

"Very well. How would we get there?"

"Through that portal." Lil pointed.

Albert looked at where Lil indicated. "That must be a hundred yards away."

"Can you walk with me? The Clova will recognize you."

"Very well. I have bandaged this woman as best I can."

Lil looked at Julie. She was pale and obviously in a lot of pain. "Will you be okay, officer?"

"I'll get by," she said bravely. "If y'all can stop this, you'd better git."

Lil crouched and moved back to where Max stood. "Max you need to go with me."

"Where?"

"To the Hidden Land."

Dennis spoke up from behind her. "I'm going as well."

She turned to Dennis. "You need to be here, for these people."

"Why do you need to go, Lil?" Dennis asked.

"Because my stone can shut all the portals, but I have to do it from their side."

Dennis considered this. "But your friend Albert said that the portals closed for years after this event."

"That's what he said."

"Lil, if there is a way to stop this, I have to go with you. You need as much backup as possible," Dennis told her.

Lil looked at him for a long moment. "All right, then let's move out."

"Listen up," Dennis yelled. "We're going to go through the portal and try to close it. We need all of you to keep the firepower on anything that tries to stop us."

Hewitt spoke up, directing his words to Lil. "I thought you said this lasts all night."

Lil nodded. "Just help us get to the portal."

Albert joined the group, looking up at the sky. "The *Piasa* have pulled back. This would be the most advantageous time."

Hewitt shouted. "You heard them, folks," he yelled to the crowd. He looked at the four people. "You guys move out."

Dennis handed his truck keys and the radio to Hewitt. He looked at Max, Albert, and Lil, and they began to move.

They crouched low and advanced as a group. The huge flying creatures had retreated from the added onslaught of spears and arrows from the newcomers.

As they moved closer, Albert yelled to the gathered Clova, speaking in their language.

Lil assumed he was telling them of her plan.

"Are you able to follow what he's saying?" she asked Max.

"Some of it. Their pronunciation is very different from what I learned," Max replied as they proceeded quickly towards the large red rectangle. "Something about escorting us to a holy place, but that's all I'm getting."

A screech came from the sky and Dennis turned and fired off multiple shots from his semi-automatic rifle. "Come on, keep moving," he bellowed.

The *Clova* warriors had come forward to meet them, retrieving arrows and spears from fallen *Piasa*. The towering natives from the Hidden Land soon surrounded them, shouting and firing arrows at any adversaries.

They reached the opening and Lil stepped through first, feeling that strange 'pins and needles' sensation once again. The three others followed, and also one *Clova* warrior woman, who carried her bow with the arrow notched.

They were surrounded by the strange red trees and appeared to be in a grove, with the red clay on the ground and small patches of the scarlet grass. The entire area was brightly illuminated by the light from the huge moon, so large that it appeared to hover just beyond the trees.

Albert spoke to the tall woman easily and quickly, as the woman nodded and spoke a rapid reply, pointing to a place in the distance.

"So, *this* is it," Max said looking around, the shotgun against his chest. "It smells of sulphur."

"I noticed that the last time I was here," Lil told him. "Albert, what did she say?"

Albert faced the group. "This good lady, Cholena, suggests that we must go to the 'sharp rock place' on the next hill. But she warns that this is a place often guarded by the *Piasa.*"

Dennis moved to the head of the group. "Then we'd better move, any time we spend here will leave us open for an attack."

"Friends," Albert said. "Please be aware, the trees have thorns that can injure you quite easily, and there are creatures that hide in the treetops and attack once you step into the open."

They began the trek and Max spoke haltingly with the warrior woman. She smiled and spoke back to him as the group made their way to the edge of the grove.

Lil could see a large butte nearby. On its top, silhouetted in the red light of the full moon, were thin cones rising from the flat top of the hill.

"That would be our goal," Albert whispered. "It is a sacred site."

"What's it like?" murmured Dennis.

"I cannot tell you. I have never been allowed to observe any of the rituals held there."

Lil looked back to see Max talking in low tones with Cholena and the woman was smiling. She shook her head, observing that Max certainly could charm the *Clova* women.

Cholena spoke several words to Max then she reached down and ruffled his hair, as you would a small child and the pair chuckled in amusement.

"Max!" Lil hissed.

Max waved to Cholena and moved up to the front of the group then glanced back over his shoulder and whispered to Lil. "I think I am in love."

"What was that thing she did to your hair?" Lil wondered.

"She told me that she likes it, that my hair is different from any man she had ever seen."

"She could snap you like a toothpick," Lil muttered.

"It would be worth it," Max sighed.

Dennis spoke up. "Okay everyone. Stay low, keep your eyes on the treetops. Let's move out."

Dennis went first and aimed his sharpshooter rifle up and around. The others followed: Cholena with an arrow notched in her bow; Max with a tight grip on the shotgun; Albert who had taken out the pistol that Lil had given him, which he held in his right hand. Lil brought up the rear, vigilantly checking their surroundings.

They moved slowly down through the small valley and started up again toward the hill. Lil slipped her hand into the pocket of her waist pack and touched the cloth that held the stone, feeling the reassuring weight of it.

They began to climb when a cry came out of the sky, and a large *Piasa* streaked out from the top of the hill, talons exposed, teeth bared.

Dennis and Lil hit the ground as an arrow struck the chest of the monster, followed by two rounds from Dennis' semi-automatic. The creature fell and rolled toward them. Cholena grabbed Max and lifted him bodily out of the way, as Lil sent two more rounds into the fallen creature.

It slid down the red earth to the bottom of the hill and lay motionless.

Cholena gently put Max on the ground, and he looked up at her and said, "*Wanishi*," which Lil figured meant, "Thank you."

They all crept up the hill on high alert, but there was not another battle cry from above. Dennis held up his hand at the crest of the hill and everyone stopped. He peeked over and signaled the others onward.

As Lil came over the rise of the hill, the sight took her breath away. It was an open space, a circle of flat stones sunken several feet into the ground. This formed an earthen wall around the circle. On the outer edge, like a protective barrier, were a collection of pointed stones, similar to stalagmites. She was surprised to see them outdoors, instead of within the confines of a cave. They rose up in uniform spacing against each other, holding the sod wall in place. The odd thing was that these pointed rocks were white, in contrast to the dark soil.

She could sense that this place was special, even holy, as she carefully reached the top and stepped into the circle.

Albert and Max followed, both being careful of the sharp rocks that extended above the dirt and stone wall. Cholena had to move very carefully, as her tall and thin frame made it more difficult to avoid the protective layer of cylindrical stones.

They moved into the center of the circle, and Cholena got down on one knee to lower herself to the height of everyone else standing. All of them studied the sky, but nothing moved and there was no breeze in this place. Only the huge red moon hung in the distance.

Dennis looked at Lil. "What are you waiting for? We've got your back."

"I don't know. I guess I expected a vision or something," Lil said.

"What do we do if it works?" Max asked. "I mean, how do we get home?"

Dennis put his hand on the man's shoulder. "Sorry, Max, this may have been a one-way trip. But our town will still be in one piece."

Max tightened his jaw and nodded.

Cholena spoke several words with a serious tone to her voice.

Albert interpreted. "She says if it works, many bad things will come."

"Bad things?" Dennis worried. "I don't see how they can get worse."

"If that rock can do it, you'd best get started, Lil," Max suggested.

Lil let her weapon hang from its strap and pulled the cloth from her waist pack to unfold it in the palm of her hand. The polished stone began to catch the light of the huge moon and appeared to glow with a red hue of its own.

She slid the stone into her palm, flesh against stone. She lightly stroked its polished surface.

She closed her eyes, and suddenly the image of her grandmother Natalia was in her mind's eye. She looked as she had when Lil was young, vibrant and full of life.

Her grandmother spoke. "You are the key, precious one, the stone merely helps you focus."

"I don't know what I'm doing, *Mami*," Lil whispered.

"Don't make it happen, precious one, *allow* it to happen," the older woman told her.

The sound of thunder made her open her eyes and Lil looked up. The calm space atop the hill was suddenly filled with wind and dust.

Dark thunderheads began to cover the moon at a speed that defied physics.

"What the Hell?" Dennis blurted, looking up at the canopy that quickly covered them. "That's not possible."

"Time is different here," Albert said, his eyes wide.

"Well, if those clouds completely cover the moon, we won't be able to see," Max worried.

"Then again, it shall be harder for the monsters to see us," Albert offered.

There was a flash of lightning, bright and frightening.

"If you're going to do it, Lil, do it now," Dennis worried. "We're not alone."

Coming through the large portal on the next hill, hundreds of the *Piasa* broke through, screaming as they arrived.

TWENTY-SIX

Turning The Tide

I n the circle of flat stones, Lil could hear the cry of the *Piasa* as they returned to their own world. They sounded angry and desperate.

Cholena stood, looked over at the other hill from which they'd come, then crouched again. She followed this action with a string of rapid words aimed at Albert.

"What is it?" Max hissed.

Albert spoke up. "Many of the *Piasa* have returned, as well as Cholena's tribesmen. The warriors cannot stop them all."

"Okay. We're basically in a fort here," Dennis observed. "Max, get over against the stone wall and shoot anything you can."

"Got it," Max said, moving quickly.

Max and Dennis parted from the group and made their way to the earthen wall, just beyond the pointed spires. They peered over the top and began to fire their weapons.

Lil focused on the stone, which appeared to glow brighter as black clouds hung over them like malevolent angels, darkening the light of the moon.

Close the portals, shut them all down.

She repeated this mantra over and over in her mind, her lips moving as she thought the words.

The stone made a hissing noise, and Lil dropped it with a cry.

"What's wrong?" Albert asked, speaking loudly over the gunfire.

"The stone, it burnt my hand," Lil moaned, clutching her right hand against her chest.

"Let me see," Albert said, and gently took her hand. Blisters were already forming on her flesh. "That is quite a burn."

The stone was glowing like a forge where it lay in the center of the circle.

Cholena spoke a few words in her unusual tongue and pulled a strip of woven cloth from a small leather bag at her waist.

Albert carefully bound the hand with the cloth. "Whatever you were doing, keep doing it."

"I was holding it," Lil said. "I can't do that now."

"Keep your attention upon it," Albert suggested.

There was another bolt of lightning that flashed white and dazzling, making the flying *Piasa* squeal and soar away. The bright light was far too much for their dark-adapted eyes to handle.

Clova were arriving on the far hill by the dozens, shouting and yelling warrior cries while firing upon the monsters with their arrows and spears.

Dennis lined up shots and took out the *Piasa* one at a time. His ammunition was running low, and he had to make each shot count, so he was focused on the beasts that were more stationary instead of the ones flying about.

Max rose to his feet and fired another blast from the shotgun.

Cholena cried out and pointed. A large *Piasa* had landed unseen behind Max and Dennis in the circle of stones. It had to be eight feet tall. It lunged forward and latched onto Max's shoulders, lifting him like a rag doll into the air.

Exactly what happened in Lil's dream before they had met.

"Max!" Lil screamed.

Dennis leapt to his feet. Using his rifle as a club, he struck the monster again and again right in the face. The huge monster released Max, and went for Dennis, lifting its claws and striking at Dennis' head.

Dennis fell to the ground, blood poured from wounds across his face as the creature jumped on top of him.

"Dennis!" Lil screamed, and the glowing stone flashed and faded a bit.

Albert was already on his feet, moving fast for a man his age. In one quick move, he placed the pistol against the back of the creature's head before it could react and pulled the trigger.

The monster shrieked and swung its huge tail, knocking Albert to the ground. It turned from Dennis and jumped onto Albert who raised the weapon and fired directly into the monster's face.

The huge Devil fell, landing its full weight onto Albert.

Cholena and Max yelled out as it covered the older man's form with its huge body and thrashed wildly in its death throes.

Lil rose to her feet and fired one shot into the creature. Finally, it lay still.

"Max, help me," she shouted.

"My shoulder," Max gasped.

"Please!"

Dennis' face was streaming with blood and he was not moving.

Cholena and Max helped Lil pull the enormous creature off Albert.

Albert lay on the ground, a trickle of blood coming out of his mouth, and Lil could see that one of the monster's taloned claws was sunk deep into the older man's chest.

"Oh, Albert," Lil moaned. "No, no."

Cholena said something in her language.

The old man's eyes opened to look up at Lil, and he took a rasping breath. "Close the portals, Lil."

"I can't, I don't have the power, Albert," Lil lamented.

"You *do*. Close the portals and save your town," Albert grimaced. He exhaled in one painful gasp and didn't draw a new breath.

Cholena gently closed his eyes, then both she and Max moved to Dennis.

Tears poured down Lil's face, and she turned from their fallen comrade to face the center of the circle and the stone that was not glowing as brightly as it had before.

I am the key.

She focused her attention on the luminescent rock. She thought about her grandmother Natalia giving her the shiny stone. She saw her parents, smiling at her, and the alpacas with their serene air. She saw herself naked with Dennis in the back of his station wagon as they gave themselves to each other freely. Images of Chad passed through her mind, his smile, the last time they had made love, his head ripping open from the bullets.

Then her mind reeled from the awareness that all of the parts of her life had pushed her to this moment, to this place. The totality of her existence, each step along this path, seemed to be revealed to her, and she was here to do only one thing, and she *could* do it.

As Max moved away to fire his shotgun at new attackers, she looked at Dennis. His face was covered in blood, but he raised one hand, his eyes opened, and gave her a thumbs up.

Overhead were the indignant screams of the monsters as they had their hunt taken from them. She doubted she would survive, as once the portal was closed, the flying monsters would let loose their fury on the people that had invaded their space.

She reached out and felt the power of the stone, as well as her own personal power. The round obsidian stone began to glow again, brighter and brighter.

With everything she was, and all she could be, she willed the portals to close.

The stone glowed like a supernova, sending dazzling light in all directions. The *Piasa* cried out in agony from the pureness of this light as it cut through the darkness of their shadowy home.

Lightning flashed again and again, and then she heard a cry from the other hill, a joyous shout from the assembled *Clova,* and knew that she had done it.

She looked over to the other hill and the portal was gone.

All of them were gone.

PART IV: AFTERMATH

TWENTY-SEVEN

Four Years Later

V ano Slavik went to town in his old truck. It was his traditional yearly visit to see Captain Hewitt and ask of any knowledge regarding the search for his daughter.

Hewitt, whose hair had gone white ever since the incidents of that awful night, greeted him warmly. This time however, the captain took him to the Dine Rite so they could talk and share a cup of coffee.

"I never asked you about that night," Hewitt said. "You were attacked as well, weren't you?"

Vano shrugged. "A few stragglers landed at my farm, went for the alpacas, but we shot them. When the sky became normal again, the creatures…they disappeared."

Hewitt nodded. "That's what happened in town. First there was, I don't know, lightning or something. Then all those monsters flew away into those red glowing things. Then those disappeared, and with them every one of the corpses of those monsters, leaving me with a street full of damage and dead and wounded people."

"Many people died that night," Vano agreed.

"Have you seen the memorial?" Hewitt asked.

"I am planning to visit it today."

"It's nice, tasteful."

Vano frowned. "It says they all died in a forest fire?"

"The town fathers decided this was the best course of action, for the sake of posterity."

"But everyone in town knows the truth," Vano said with lifted eyebrows.

"As time passes, everybody who knows the truth will be gone." Hewitt sipped his coffee. "Then, only the tale of a great fire that turned the sky red will be what anyone knows."

"That does not seem fair to the brave people who died," Vano responded.

"Life ain't fair, Mister Slavik," the captain sadly confessed. "If it was up to me, your daughter would have a medal, instead of one line on a damn memorial."

After paying for his coffee and bidding the police chief goodbye, Vano drove over to the baseball field that faced the municipal hall. A memorial marker had been put up, a creation of stone that was about three feet high and unobtrusive. It listed the name of every person who had perished that night.

For the lives lost
the night of the
great forest fire
March 20, 2019

The stone had the date carved just below the dedication. Vano brushed the monument with his fingers, gaining some comfort as he felt the letters of his daughter's name: Liliana Slavik.

He wanted to cry, but he had no more tears to give. His only daughter, the one who would take over his little farm and give him grandchildren, was gone and there was no emotion that could express the emptiness he felt within his heart.

A part of him wanted to curse his wife's mother, Natalia. She had no right to bequeath such a terrible burden on his daughter.

He got back in his old truck and drove home, not looking forward to repeating to Selina the empty promises Hewitt had given him that they would never stop looking into it.

At least they had each other, and Selina had finally agreed to hire a new man to oversee the alpacas and the blueberry bushes. It's not that Vano couldn't handle it anymore, he just needed some help.

The gravel crackled under his tires as he pulled into their driveway, and he got out of the truck to find his wife standing outside the back door. She was wearing jeans, a jacket, and heavy shoes.

"What is all this?" he asked. "Did you visit the alpacas?"

"No, we're going for a walk," she told him simply.

Vano frowned. "A walk? Since when do you take walks?"

"Since my momma came to my dreams and told me to," Selina confessed.

Vano exhaled with disgust. "I thought we were finally free of the old witch."

Selina's hands went to her hips, and she glared at her husband. "She was a great seer!"

"Yes, but I thought after she died, maybe she wouldn't visit so much."

Selina's jaw tightened. "I am going for a walk. Are you coming or not?"

Vano stood there and faced her. There were always many things to do, but today was a hard day, and he knew it. If this was his wife's way of expressing her pain and loss, it was a little thing to ask.

"I'll go with you, so you don't scare the animals."

"What is that supposed to mean?"

"Nothing. I just know your temper, they do not. You will frighten the creatures of the forest if I am not there."

She trudged off towards the blueberry fields and the woods beyond, and Vano followed, walking quickly to keep up.

Since it was only the middle of March, the blueberry bushes had not yet begun to bud, and Vano knew that in the afternoon he would have to fertilize them.

"A proper man would take my arm and escort me," Selina complained.

"I'm your husband, and not a proper man," Vano gibed. But he moved to his wife and took her arm as they walked down the path into the woods.

"Is this where Lil jogged?"

"Yes," he said and pointed to a small clearing. "Over there was her shooting range, where I taught her to shoot."

"She used to go shooting with Dennis."

"Yes, when they were in high school," Vano remembered.

Selina sighed as they walked. "I miss her so much."

They continued in silence until Vano finally admitted. "I miss her, too."

They reached the end of this path, with a sugar sand road that ran to the left and right. Directly ahead was a copse of trees shaded in darkness on the sunlit day.

"We have to go in there," Selina announced.

"Why?"

"Because I say so," she said as she moved into the covered area.

Vano muttered under his breath, but followed.

It was a little chilly in the darkened area under the canopy of evergreen trees and Vano looked up and around. The place seemed odd, alien, and being there made him nervous. It was too quiet and he stepped lightly to avoid making a sound.

Selina stopped walking and looked at a shadowy space between two trees.

Vano glanced around. "What is it?"

"This is the place," Selina whispered.

"What place?"

"The place we are supposed to be."

Vano looked at the clearing and shrugged. "Is something going to happen?"

"Yes."

"When? Woman, I have work to do," Vano complained, but Selina held his hand tightly.

"Stay with me, a few minutes more," she said without looking at him.

He sighed dramatically and waited, thinking of how he needed to organize tools for that afternoon. Then he stopped thinking and listened.

There was a hum in the air.

"What is that?" he asked.

"Shh."

The hum grew louder and an unexpected beam of sunlight burst through the cover hitting the shadowy place between the trees and making it appear brighter.

As Vano stood in rapt attention, a ball of light appeared in the center of it, and it began to grow.

"Just as my mother told me it would," Selina mumbled in awe.

The ball began to flatten and stretch outward until it formed an oval that touched the ground and rose up to almost eight feet high. Its shimmering surface moved and wavered before them.

An arm appeared, a man's arm, followed by a leg stepping through the oval. Then all at once, Dennis Decatur stepped through.

This happened so quickly and unexpectedly that both Selina and Vano stepped back and gave a small cry.

The tall man was wearing heavy clothes that bore several patches. His eyes were bright and clear, but three faded lines of scars now crossed his face.

In his arms, he protectively carried a child.

It was a newborn and small, but it looked around with amazed eyes.

"This looks like the right place," Dennis said, and stepped to the side. He held his arm out to the Slaviks. "Can you move back a bit, please?"

Vano and Selina were both in a state of shock, but stepped back obediently.

An extremely tall woman stepped through the oval, ducking her head as she went. She carried a child as well, though her child had darker skin and was much bigger than the infant Dennis carried.

"Is that his wife?" Selina asked her husband, who just shrugged in stunned amazement.

Next through the glowing light came another man, shorter than Dennis with dark skin and straight hair. He wore what appeared to be red buckskin pants and a fringed vest with his hairless chest exposed. He wore a pair of glasses that appeared to have been repaired numerous times.

He guided the tall Native American woman out of the way of the portal, and all of them looked at the glowing circle.

Lil stepped through the glowing window.

Selina gave a cry and ran to her daughter to hug her, as Lil covered the glowing stone in her hand with a dark cloth and slipped it away into the worn leather bag she wore.

Vano walked over and hugged his wife and daughter as the glowing portal behind them shrunk to a ball of light and faded away.

"We thought you were dead," Selina sobbed.

"I know, it's been over a year."

"Four years," her father corrected, tears in his own eyes as well.

"Four?" Lil questioned.

"It makes sense," Max said, standing next to Cholena. "The time difference and all."

Lil pulled herself free. "Come, meet your grandson."

She turned her parents to face the child in Dennis' arms. He was healthy and looked well-fed, and had a head full of black curly hair. The child was wrapped in a hand woven swaddling cloth, and he stared at them with the most remarkable blue eyes Vano had ever seen.

"My *grandson?*" Vano repeated in a solemn tone as tears stung his eyes.

"This is Albert," Lil said. "He was named after a dear friend."

Selina held out her arms for the tyke, and Dennis carefully handed the child to her. "How old is he?" she questioned.

"About a month, I guess," Dennis said with a shrug.

Selina held the baby and stared into its bright blue eyes.

"*Four* years?" Lil said. "Has the cottage got someone living in it?"

"Yes," Vano said as he touched the baby's hair. "We got a new workman."

Dennis sighed and moved close to Lil, putting his arm around her protectively. "Pity, we would all love a shower."

"Yes, of course," Selina said joyously, and handed the small child to Lil. "And I must cook for you, all of you!"

"Come, we go," Vano said and gestured towards the path.

The group began to walk, the tall Native American woman glanced around and spoke in odd words to the short dark man, who answered her.

"What are they saying?" Vano asked as they walked.

Lil translated. "She asked if this was her new home, and Max told her it was and that she will like many things."

"How did you get back?" Vano said to Dennis.

"That stone Lil was given by her grandmother. Every day we went to the portal that was closest to the caves where we lived and held it out. Nothing happened until today."

"Amazing," Vano marveled.

"And I want you to know, sir, that Lil and I were married by the chief of the *Clova* tribe himself," Dennis explained.

"We'll probably need to do paperwork," Lil pointed out.

Dennis considered it as they walked. "Oh yeah, not to mention the IRS."

Lil moved to him and offered the baby, which he took. "That's for tomorrow. Today is for celebration."

That night, the small farm was made into a place for a great party. Dennis, Lil, and Max spent much of that day contacting friends to let them know they were alive and had returned.

There would be challenges in the days ahead. Dennis, Max, and Lil needed to find a story for where they had been, as well as an explanation for Max's abnormally tall wife.

The difficulty would be that there *was* no logical explanation.

But for that one night, there was joy and laughter, and that little farm deep within the Pine Barrens of New Jersey never shone so bright.

Author's Note

T his book was not merely a flight of the imagination, but a combination of information and inspiration. I think you would be surprised by just how many of the legends I included verbatim, rewritten to use the language of the characters and the situation.

The Jersey Devil is a legend that has long inspired tales, as well as real fear, in the citizens of South Jersey for over 200 years. *The Piasa Bird* is a famed story in the Midwest, where there was once a drawing carved into the stone of a mountain. There is a modern version that is still in display on a bluff in Alton, Illinois.

The disappearance of two Native-American Tribes in the late 1600s did occur, though it is believed they were conquered by a third tribe. The story of seven-foot Native-American people is based on skeletons of such tall warriors found by Arthur Jillson in the 1870s in Tuckerton, New Jersey.

I also drew inspiration from the book by James F. McCloy and Ray Miller, Jr. titled simply: *THE JERSEY DEVIL*. This little book charted out the legends as well as the multiple sightings of the creature (or creatures) in 1909.

As far as Pines Edge and Apple Hill, I created Pines Edge for my own purposes, but the town of Apple Hill was a genuine place that simply faded away, as many small towns do within the Barrens.

In my research, I drove through the area, visited several of the places mentioned in the book, but only during daylight hours. I can only imagine trying to travel those desolate sugar sand roads at night, and the idea gives me a true sense of terror.

I do want to say that everyone I met doing research around that part of my home state was always polite and helpful in my quest for information.

My editor, Libby Broadbent, made multiple suggestions with the first draft, and all of these recommendations improved the story enormously. My first and most important beta-reader, my wife, author Debra Snow, fixed my multiple misspellings and corrected my misuse of commas, as well as proposing needed changes as well. I also had several intrepid beta-readers who found wrong words and incorrect possessives. I am indebted to them for their voluntary assistance.

And most of all, I want to thank you, my readers, for allowing me to take you on another journey into the macabre. I hope you enjoyed reading it, as much as I did writing it.

Arjay Lewis
September 2020

About the Author

Known as the "Wizard Of Odd", Arjay Lewis is an actor, magician, and multi-award-winning author.

I write tales of the strange and the horrifying.

I have spent my life as an entertainer, amusing people as a street-performer in the 1970s; a Broadway and casino artist in the 1980s; a party performer in the 1990s and 2000s; a cruise ship performer in the 2010s.

Stories have always been in my mind, and I have been writing since the 1990s. My reason to write is simple: to entertain. I write the type of books that I like to read: murder mysteries, strange tales of unnatural gifts, odd happenings and horror.

Please visit my web site and sign up for my mailing list to be "in the know" for upcoming books. Visit me on Facebook, Twitter, or my Amazon Author page.

And thank you for reading. You are the reason I write.

www.arjaylewis.com
www.facebook.com/arjaylewis
www.twitter.com/arjaylewiswrite
www.amazon.com/Arjay-Lewis

Also by Arjay Lewis

Doctor Wise Series
Fire In The Mind
Seduction In The Mind
Reunion In The Mind
Haunted In The Mind
Devotion In The Mind
Asylum In The Mind
Specter In The Mind
Vengeance In The Mind
Echoes In The Mind
Infection In The Mind
Justice In The Mind
Ritual In The Mind
Vanished In The Mind

Horror
The Muse
Kept In The Dark
The Vanishing
Digger

Romantic Suspense
(with Debra Snow)
A Study In Murder

NYPD Wizard Detective
The Wizards Of Central Park West
The Vampires Of Greenwich Village
The Werewolves of Washington Square

FREE NOVELLA

VOWS

AND OTHER TALES OF THE MACABRE

For those who enjoy a good scare, here is a collection of stories designed to give you nightmares. These stories that have been published in *Weird Tales, H.P. Lovecraft Magazine Of Horror, The Ultimate Halloween,* and *Sherlock Holmes Mystery Magazine.* If you tried to get them from their original source they would cost over $20.00. But you get them for FREE by signing up for Arjay's Newsletter

VOWS: A story of devotion that extends beyond death itself.
SIREN: A Sci-Fi fantasy of a condemned prisoner lost in space.
THE DARK: A guard sees creatures in the night...are they really there?
DREAMCATCHER: A walk in the woods...but you are not alone.
THE TRAVELER: What do you do if your flight is delayed...forever?
INTO THE ABYSS: A makeup artist gets the dream job...at a price.

www.arjaylewis.com/free-stuff.html